JACKIE & ME

JACKIE & ME

a novel by

Louis Bayard

ALGONQUIN BOOKS OF CHAPEL HILL   2022

Published by
ALGONQUIN BOOKS OF CHAPEL HILL
Post Office Box 2225
Chapel Hill, North Carolina 27515-2225

a division of
WORKMAN PUBLISHING
225 Varick Street
New York, New York 10014

Jackie & Me is a work of historical fiction, which means that, where necessary, I have reshuffled chronology, speculated, and invented. And while I have hewed as closely as possible to the documented psychology of the people in question, nothing in these pages should be taken as definitive history.

LIBRARY OF CONGRESS CATALOGING-IN-PUBLICATION DATA
Names: Bayard, Louis, author.
Title: Jackie & me / a novel by Louis Bayard.
Other titles: Jackie and me
Description: First edition. | Chapel Hill, North Carolina :
Algonquin Books of Chapel Hill, 2022. | Summary:
"A historical novel depicting a naïve, career-girl version of Jackie Kennedy and her iconic marriage-in-the-making to an elusive John F. Kennedy, narrated by Jack's best friend and fixer, Lem Billings"—Provided by publisher.
Identifiers: LCCN 2022000412 | ISBN 9781643750354 (hardcover) |
ISBN 9781643752952 (ebook)
Subjects: LCSH: Onassis, Jacqueline Kennedy, 1929–1994—Fiction. |
Kennedy, John F. (John Fitzgerald), 1917–1963—Fiction. |
Billings, K. Lemoyne (Kirk Lemoyne), 1917–1981—Fiction. |
Courtship—Fiction. | LCGFT: Biographical fiction. | Novels.
Classification: LCC PS3552.A85864 J33 2022 |
DDC 813/.54—dc23/eng/20220106
LC record available at https://lccn.loc.gov/2022000412

10 9 8 7 6 5 4 3 2 1
First Edition

In memory of my mother

∾

Young men want to be faithful, and are not; old men want to be faithless, and cannot: that is all one can say.

—OSCAR WILDE, *The Picture of Dorian Gray*

JACKIE & ME

ONE

*O*f all places, the East Village. *Miles* from the Upper East Side, and there she was, sauntering down Avenue A in a linen skirt and black blouse. The Nina Ricci sunglasses clamped on like aviator's goggles, the carriage nowhere more equestrian than when she stepped over the snoring, splayed drag queen. Was she coming or going? Catching a flick at the Hollywood Theatre or meeting a friend at Old Buenos Aires? There was no way of asking, with the gentleman-thug from the Secret Service following ten feet behind. I could have damned the torpedoes, I suppose, but I'm embarrassed to say that at the sight of her I did what every other New Yorker does. Stopped and gawked. As if she were some golden hind, yes, trotting out of a glade.

Imagine my frustration. Some six years have passed since I last gazed on her—*her*, I mean, and not her immaculate Christmas cards—so it was startling to have the universe, after all this time, grant me such a clear angle on her—and, in the next breath, withdraw it. One second, I mean, she was coming straight at me. The next, she was turning the corner at East Sixth, her shoulder bag swinging after her.

Now it's certainly possible that, before she made the turn, she caught sight of me. It's also possible that, even if she saw me—and this is the scenario that haunts me a little, a few hours after our crossing—she didn't know me.

I bring that up because I don't cut the same figure I used to. Since we last laid eyes on each other, I've become a stouter specimen, slower. The lungs whistle, the hair's longer. I've watched friends of long standing pass me in the street without a second glance, and in my mind now, I imagine myself somehow slipping past the Secret Service goon and stealing up to that sunglassed figure and murmuring in her ear. "It's Lem," I would say.

And Jackie, having failed until now to connect the spectacle before her with the man she used to know, would hear my *voice*, climbing always higher than I mean it to, and would call up every inch of her breeding and say something like, "How perfectly lovely to see you."

The thing is it *would* have been lovely. No bean counting about all the times she *could* have seen me. Just the two of us, leaning in like old conspirators, the years laughed away. "Do you remember," I'd say, "listening to Margaret Truman? And getting stuck on the Ferris wheel? Watching J. Edgar Hoover eat?" Such a pure back-and-forth that the bodyguard would instantly relax his grip on the hip holster and let us carry on untroubled down East Sixth—hell, all the way back uptown, that's how much catching up we'd have had to do, Jackie and me.

And really, if I *had* gone to all the trouble of approaching her, if I *had* risked the full hail of Secret Service bullets, I wouldn't have squandered the moment by asking her something as banal as *How are you?* I mean, there are whole news organizations dedicated to exploring that question. Photographers have been legally enjoined from pressing it too hard. Maybe all I would have said was "I'm sorry."

NOW THAT'S ODD. In conjuring this scenario, I wouldn't necessarily have guessed the words that would come tumbling from my mouth.

Also unexpected: that I should have had to go all the way down to the East Village to catch sight of the great Jackie Ohhh. I mean, she lives no more than three minutes away from me by foot. Several friends have reported seeing her jogging, escorted, around the Central Park Reservoir. More times than I can recall, I've walked Ptolly past 1040 Fifth and silently counted up to the fifteenth floor. If it's morning—say, seven-thirty or eight—I might imagine her greeting the day. (For, of course, she's back to paid employment.) The ablutions. The hair piled in its Amazonian helmet. Shoulder pads, belted dress, and then, perhaps in the very moment of sallying through the lobby, the Nina Riccis clapped on. The whole Onassis carapace that the world is already expecting, the one it thinks it *knows*.

Only it doesn't know how she got there.

But I do. I was along for the ride.

And maybe the reason I couldn't go up to that armatured creature on Avenue A was because she bears only a passing relation to the Jackie I once knew. The scrapping career girl, I mean, with the homemade clothes and the ladders in her stockings and the childlike sense of the ridiculous. The girl whose skin broke out every so often, who doubted herself at every turn, who wasn't even sure she wanted to marry at all—certainly not the kind of man she was supposed to marry. The Jackie nobody else knew but me, really, and the Jackie who can no longer *be*.

It shouldn't be too hard to recollect her. I am by nature an archivist and have assembled comprehensive scrapbooks of all my friends' lives. News clippings, magazines articles, letters, telegrams, menus, leaflets, ticker tape, parking tickets, they're all here, ready to jar loose every associated memory. It shouldn't be too hard at all. The only hard part will be finding myself in the mix.

FOR, OF COURSE, I was there too. Some version. Which, in this moment, feels like it wants to be known, too, no matter the reckoning. Words were said, deeds were done, and they can't be called back, but they can be heard again in a new light.

AND I ASK myself: Do I really have any better use for my remaining hours? There are only so many books to read, episodes of *Magnum, P.I.* to watch. Only so many Kennedy relations requiring a guest room or a vomitorium. Only so many times you can read your own will and wonder if you've got it right.

Times Square is a terror, Central Park a savanna. The buses and subways are in the crapper. Our current president is a former Warner Brothers actor, and everyone in America is waiting for a giant panda in the National Zoo to get knocked up. All in all, it might be just the time to leave 1981 behind—a lark, even, to travel back to the passenger seat of Jack's Ford Crestline, and reintroduce myself to the fellow who's sitting there.

It's the weekend before St. Patrick's Day, 1952, and there's still a late-winter nip in the Virginia air, but Jack always keeps the top down because, by age thirty-four, he knows how dashing his hair looks in high wind. We're due at Bobby and Ethel's that night, but Jack instead cuts across Chain Bridge. I shoot him a look, and he says—imagine the offhandedness—that we have an additional passenger.

"Oh, yes?" I say. "And who should that be?"

"A Miss Bouvier."

Mind you, there's nothing in that honorific *Miss* to signify a lady of distinction. He refers to virtually all his girls that way. She might be a cashier at the Montelle Pharmacy or Finland's deputy chief of mission, and you won't know until you've pulled up in front of her apartment building and seen her tottering through the front gate, a blonde in a crewneck cardigan or a brunette in a bullet bra, and it's always the latter who raises her hand for you to kiss and the former who comes at you straight on like an encyclopedia salesman, and whoever it is remains "Miss" in our conversation until such time as the business is consummated, at which point she devolves into her component parts.

There is nothing, in short, about a "Miss Bouvier" to separate her from her predecessors. Were I to search his face—his soul—down to the most granular level, I would find no clue, for there is perhaps none to find. Miss Bouvier is a destination. And now that we've crossed into Virginia, the only thing left to figure out is where she might live. Clarendon? Cherrydale? A group home in Fort Myer, maybe. But we speed past all those destinations before steering up Old Dominion Drive. Nature rushes forth, and the car dealers and the Hot Shoppes fall away before dogwoods and tulip trees, tatters of forsythia.

"Have you known her long?" I ask.

"Not so very."

"Define *not so*."

"A year. Off and on."

"More off or more on?"

"More off."

"Young or old?"

"Young."

"Dewy?"

"Engaged," he says. "Or was."

I glance at him. "To you?"

"Don't be disgusting."

"Will we be chauffeuring her fiancé, too?"

"We'd have to drive clear to New York for that. I understand he's not worth it."

By now, my glasses are fairly crusted over with pollen, so

I'm making windshield wipers of my index fingers as I ask what it is that Miss Bouvier does with her days.

"Journalism," he says.

"Is that how you met?"

"Oh," he says. "I'm not on her beat."

There's something half buried in that remark, and I don't know how to disinter it. Forests of redbud and magnolia are thickening around us, and somehow they're all in on the secret, and Kay Starr sings "Wheel of Fortune" on the radio, and, during the second chorus, I sneeze, and Jack says, "Perfectly in tune, Lem," and then the song is over, and we're pulling up in front of . . .

Well, where? I can't even tell. All I can make out through my encrusted specs are a row of white pilasters and a front portico. Where sits a girl.

Doesn't she hear the car's tires on the gravel? Or see our headlights slicing through the trees? When we first happen upon her, her face is angled away, as though she's cocking her ear for a nightingale. Her knees are drawn protectively to her chest, and there's something quite exposed about her. I mean, she doesn't look like she belongs there any more than I do, and I briefly wonder if she's a housemaid or a nanny, taking her one allotted evening out. Abruptly, she stands and gives us two quick waves and then, as she jogs to the passenger side, comes briefly ablaze in the headlights.

By now, of course, I'm extricating myself from the front of the car and inserting myself with no great grace into the back, and the operation is so consuming that, for a second or two, I lose all consciousness of her, and then I hear her say—in that *voice*, like a ghost whispering through the pipes—"You must be Lem."

I mutter something on the order of yes, I must be, and she smiles. A wider smile than I would have guessed possible. The eyes even wider. *Goat's eyes*, that's my first churlish thought, *or a madwoman's*, but maybe that's to forestall the sense that I'm being seen through a wider lens. All in all, there's a certain relief in being able to retreat into the Crestline's back seat. A planetarium-like darkness, with the two of them swimming like moons. She has dabbed herself with Chateau Krigler 12 (I consider telling her it's my mother's favorite), and there is the complicating counter-aroma of Pall Malls, and somewhere at the back, simple bovine perspiration. For the first time, I begin to wonder if Miss Bouvier is nervous—though it's difficult to confirm because she has a small voice and the wind seems to slap every word back down her gullet. Her general lilt, as best I can tell, is interrogative, but why should that be a surprise? Girls in these days are instructed to shoot out a clean, firm thread of inquiry at all times. The more interested they appear to be, the more the boys will understand they don't have to be, in themselves, interesting, which is a relief to both parties. Jackie, I imagine, is now asking the name of Bobby's daughter or wondering if Eunice will be there and which one is Pat? For all I know, she's speculating about the Washington Senators' pennant chances. If pressed, she'll fall back on the weather. How chilly it is for March.

The point is there's no way of knowing what they're saying, and Jack sometimes gets cross if I talk too much with his dates (unless I'm doing something useful like showing them the door). Nothing for it, then, but to watch Miss Bouvier's head—under the weight of her impending introduction to the Kennedy clan—loll ever so gradually to the right.

It's when we're crossing back over Chain Bridge that she rouses herself to ask: "Jack, what color is your car?"

Queer question. But then I realize she's never seen Jack's car (or Jack himself, maybe) in the naked light of day.

"I don't know," he mumbles. "Red."

"Pomegranate," I say.

Something quickens in the column of her neck. By easy degrees, she turns around and bestows on me a fuller version of that first smile. Then she leans toward Jack and, in a whisper stagy enough for me to hear, says, "I like your friend."

TWO

*O*ne of the things about being retired is you either give up on reading all those books you said you would or you finally get around to them. Lately, believe it or not, I've been boning up on quantum mechanics—in part, I suppose, because the subject aligns with the trend of my own thoughts. Now, we tend to think of our destiny as a sealed deal, but you take old Heisenberg. He said you can know where a particle is or you can know how fast it's moving, but you can't know both things at the same time, and the more you know about one, the less you know about the other. Schrödinger's poor cat, cooped up in its meager little box, is neither dead nor alive or, you might say, is *both* dead and alive, until a single observer peeks into the box and settles the question—but only to the observer's satisfaction.

So imagine that, embedded in every human life, there are traffic crossings, where—if we were but to peek into the box—we would see the contingencies of our fate coming together and commingling, before charging off in opposed directions. From the vantage point of 1981, for example, I look back at my own life and force events into a certain sequence. That point in my childhood, for instance, early in the thirties, when my father up and died. Looking back, I can say that, in one iteration, the dons of Choate respond to that calamity by graciously offering me a scholarship, which is how I am still around to meet Jack, which is how I come to be invited to Hyannisport, which is how I come to meet the Kennedys. In another iteration, Choate responds by casting me fatherless to the winds, and I scramble for a spot at Sewickley Academy, and I never meet Jack, never go to Hyannisport. Never meet Jackie. What does that Lem look like? And is he even now living that life while I'm marching through mine?

Whoever he is, he can't escape the basic infirmities of his genotype—asthma, nearsightedness, the voice that climbs always higher than he likes. Everything else is up for grabs. Depending on where he's being observed, he might at this moment be an insurance salesman in Fox Chapel or a building contractor in Ligonier. He might be painting boardwalk portraits in Atlantic City. But why aim so low? He might be a personage—an entry in *Who's Who*, though for what I can't say. He might have inveigled some wretched woman to the altar, acquired a child or two, a grandchild. Nothing, as I've said, is off the table. My friend Raul has said more than once that, in another life, I should have been an interior decorator, a job title I don't necessarily care for, but I acknowledge that, with all the flipping I've done of Baltimore row houses, it amounts to nearly the same thing.

Turning now to me and Jackie, I can stipulate that, right from the beginning, we shared a spark of fellow feeling, and yet it might have gone nowhere, nowhere at all, if circumstances hadn't played out the way they had. There was no guarantee that I would ever see Miss Bouvier again after that night or have cause to remember her as clearly as I do. As for Jackie herself—well, at that time in her life, any number of opposed destinies were possible—she was just out of college, for Pete's sake—and she tried them all on, didn't she, like gowns. So if I'm to peer into the box and catch the quantum moment when her destiny collides with Jack's, I have to do it through the eyes of Charlie Bartlett.

Back in '51, he was the quickly rising, well-liked D.C. correspondent for the *Chattanooga Times*. He had recently joined his Lake Shore fortune to the dowry of a U.S. Steel heiress, but he'd always nurtured a bit of a flame for Jackie, for which he assuaged his Catholic conscience by seeking potential husbands for her. Wildly unsuitable, many of them: a chemist with the Atomic Energy Commission, a lobbyist for sorghum farmers, an entertainer at children's parties. Was it Charlie's idea of a joke? So when he rang her up in May to invite her to yet another Sunday supper, the lie rose to her lips.

"Gee, Charlie, I've already got a date that night."

"When's he picking you up?"

"Oh, I think—eight or eight-thirty or some such . . ."

"Perfect. You can come by at six and get some drinks and nibbles, and your beau can pick you up at our place."

"He's not my beau, really . . ."

"Of course he isn't, I haven't approved him yet. Now don't be too late about it because somebody interesting will be there."

Dear God, she thought. *Somebody interesting.*

She might still have demurred, but she realized suddenly that Sunday was also Mother's Day, and the thought of spending the whole stretch of it with *her* mother overrode her misgivings.

"All right," she conceded. "But I can't stay long."

Now, of course, having pretended to have a date, she would have to procure one. This was perilous for a girl of that era. She could not actually ask a boy out, she could merely propose that he join her for an activity in some region proximate to his with the possibility of there being fun. Jackie phoned this vagueness around to five men before landing on Michael O'Sullivan, a Comp Lit major from George Washington who had never, to her knowledge, made advances on a girl living or dead. Sensing interest, she at once dispelled the vagueness and instructed him to meet her at 3419 Q Street, Northwest, eight-thirty sharp. A little after six, she was stepping gingerly through the Bartletts' doorway, scanning the room with dread. The guests, she noticed, were almost entirely female—perhaps the somebody interesting had found somewhere more interesting. A half hour later, there came a rapping of the Bartletts' knocker. A grin broke out on Charlie's face. "You took your sweet time," he called, and with that, the evening's final guest stepped in.

By this point in American history, he was known to everybody in the room and would have been known to everybody in the house next door and the one next to that, but the sight of so many eyes bent his way seemed to affect him as an invasion, and his response was to take a half-step back and to yank at the knot of his regimental tie, a gesture that might have registered as man-of-the-people to anyone but Jackie, who saw only the compulsiveness of the tic. Who noticed moreover the gap between his shirt collar and his neck, the baggy folds that his jacket formed around his shoulders. Her first impulse was not to fawn but to fold her arms around him. *There, there.*

He paused, retraced the half step he had just retreated and bestowed on this crowd of friends and strangers the democratizing smile that was still two years away from the cover of *Life* magazine. "Good evening," he said. "Good evening, friends."

The room had been conquered in advance. Hands had extended, lips had parted. Bars of pink sprouted on Martha Bartlett's cheeks. A wave of almost nauseous delight climbed through Pat Murray Roche (who had forgotten perhaps that her parents back in Bronxville used to snub the Kennedys at every turn). As for the party's *other* single girl . . . well, Hickey Sumers ditched her cigarette holder and got herself a highball, which she didn't drink so much as *apply*, in strict allotments, to her mouth for the purpose of making it shine. Sidling now toward her quarry, she kept her glass very close to her chin, as though it were a folded fan ready to spring open.

"Oh, Congressman, you're so good to make time for us. I mean, all the demands on you. I mean, what an honor."

The only one who didn't make a move in his direction was Jackie, and as she later recalled, that had less to do with her dismay at the general spectacle than with the implied assumption that she was to join it. One more of the bob-by-soxers. She remembered then her mother's advice. When set down in a room with two men, always bestow your smiles on the *less* attractive—it will please him and pique the other. In this case, Charlie being such an old pal, it wasn't hard to bend some rays in his direction. Twice, the Congressman asked her something benign; twice, she answered coolly and briefly. She allowed Hickey to sit beside him during cocktails, and whenever his gaze swerved her way, she sent her glance toward Q Street, where even now her knight in armor, Michael O'Sullivan, might be palely loitering. (Though she realized she no longer remembered what he looked like.)

Dinner was put off in favor of old-fashioneds and Charades, and when the Congressman specifically asked that she be put on the opposite team, she took it as a sign of the antagonism that had quietly risen between them. It was during the second round that he reached for one of the torn-off memo-pad sheets on the conch-shell coffee table, penciled something across it, folded it in half and, like a Western Union messenger, handed it to her.

Sam Houston.

"Very well," she said.

She began by making the shape of an hourglass, then she waited until her team winnowed it down to *sand* and then *Sam*. At her periphery, she could see Martha the time-keeper squinting down at the old Buck family watch. With a ferocity that surprised her, she made now as if to strike the antique Sheraton armchair on which she'd been sitting. *Strike* became *cleave* and then, like an annunciating angel, Pat Murray Roche sang out:

"Hew."

Nothing more was needed. The whole exchange lasted less than a minute.

Afterward, the Congressman raised himself with care from the other Sheraton armchair and confided to her in low tones that he'd had Sam Houston on the brain lately. "If the subject interests you, Miss Bouvier, I know of a biography you might—"

"Marquis James."

"You've read it."

In truth, she'd only ever known it as a spine in her step-father's library.

"Next time," he said, carefully preserving the distance between them, "I want you on my team."

"Jackie!"

She spun around to find Martha Bartlett tapping the Buck family watch. "You said you had to leave by eight-thirty, darling."

"Gee, that's too bad," said the Congressman.

"Yes, isn't it?" said Martha, reaching for her guest's cloak. "Oh, darling, it's been grand having you. And now that we know what a talented clue-giver you are, we'll have to make you a permanent charades fixture. Won't we, Charlie? But next time, please do bring your date!"

Martha must have been more invested in her friend Hickey's success than she'd let on because the shelf of her pregnant belly was acting now as a prod, edging Jackie closer to the door. The Bartletts' terrier was herding her in the same direction, and she had just enough time to send out a half wave to the other guests before the door closed after her.

She stood there for some seconds on the Bartletts' stoop, wondering if she hadn't perhaps overplotted the whole evening. Wouldn't she rather be handing the Congressman a clue of her own and watching him squirm? Feeling the rivalry mount around them? Or was this the happier outcome? A free woman in a free land.

She took a few paces down the street, then heard at her back the scatter of claws on brick. It was the Bartletts' terrier, who, having caught up to Jackie, subsided to an easy trot that seemed to convey they'd been plotting their escape together. Then, at their back, another sound.

"Miss Bouvier! Do you need a lift?"

It was the Congressman, standing coatless on the stoop. And again, what surprised her was her own maternal impulse. *He'll catch his death.*

"Oh, gee!" she called back. "That's awfully sweet. I brought my car, you see!"

With a cringing smile, she cracked open the Mercury's front door, which was the only invitation the Bartletts' terrier needed to leap inside. A second later, a growl, then a man's strangled cry. The passenger door of the car burst open, and out jumped Michael O'Sullivan.

The surprise lay in how presentable he looked under the circumstances. *Yes*, she thought, taking in the gloss of black hair, the mouth crooked into a half smile. *He'll do.* How important it was in this exact moment that he should.

"Good night," she called to the Congressman.

"Some other time," he said.

THREE

As she drifted to sleep that night, the image of him kept cycling before her, and with each turn, the maternal feeling ebbed and something more appetitive crept in. She recalled the unaffected ease with which he'd stood on the Bartletts' porch. She imagined that, had she given him a word of encouragement, he would have crossed the stretch of ground that stood between them, claimed it step by step and, for all she knew, claimed her, too, if Michael O'Sullivan hadn't popped up, vaulted into the driver's seat and driven her and the Bartletts' dog to—well, where? That was the question that awaited her the next morning.

Some other time, he'd suggested. Yet Monday morning came and went with no word from him, and as the hours passed, she found herself toggling between stoicism and disappointment before resolving into self-reproach. All the pride she had taken in holding herself apart from those other girls, where was it now? Gone with a May wind. The only consolation was that she hadn't (as she was briefly tempted to do) telephoned Charlie Bartlett and peppered him with questions. *Did he find me amusing? Did he ask for my number?* She and her mother disagreed on many things, but on this point they were united. A note of desperation, once uttered, could never be unheard.

Her mother, as was her wont, took it a step further. "Desperate girls," said Janet Auchincloss, "lead desperate lives." Though it was hard to see how she squared that with her own desperate hours. A creature of *her* time, Janet had graduated into adulthood with a slim but rigorously managed suite of skills. These included French, horse riding and the echolocation of husbands. In that last department, she had staggered quite badly out of the gate. Husband number one, Black Jack Bouvier, as his nickname suggested, was a set of cards upon which no girl should stake all her chips. He was nearing forty, his sexual exploits had passed from gossip into legend, he drank the way monks meditate, and he was hard at work squandering a $750,000 inheritance (for it takes effort to lose money as fast as he did). As for his softly bruited claims of French nobility, he never troubled to document them or even, after a couple of martinis, sustain them.

On the asset side, he was in the Social Register and was considered one of New York's top four hundred citizens. Better still, he looked nothing like the other three hundred

ninety-nine. Photographs from his youth show a disquiet-
ing cross between Clark Gable and Hollywood-style bandit,
with eyes of Lake Louise blue and a look of disreputable
masculinity that offsets the dandyish accents of silk handkerchief (blossoming just so from the pocket of his hunting
jacket) and brilliantined black hair (parted down the middle
with Euclidean precision).

Well, Janet was in those days a creature of the senses. She
fell hard, and kept falling—for there was no one to catch
her. And when she landed, there was nothing but wreckage.
Money gone, home gone. Pride gone more than anything,
for although marriage may have given Black Jack a pair
of daughters on whom he doted, it caused not the slightest
hiccup in his quest for pussy. Say this about our Janet. She
extracted herself from the rubble and, rather than retreat
into the divorcée's genteel exile (in a back bedroom with
a hairpin to keep the bun in place), she made the strategic
decision not just to marry again but to set her cap for a
Standard Oil heir.

To her exacting eye, Hugh Auchincloss was everything
Black Jack was not: benign and pliable and half-deaf and
functionally impotent, with two lightly crumbling mansions
to his name. This time Janet fell *up* and, so doing, acquired
a passel of stepchildren, who regarded her alternately with
banked resentment and naked fear. But even her bitterest
rivals would have to confess that she had triumphed against
the odds and had done it by keeping her spirits buoyant and
her mouth slightly ajar (which, she had learned from practice, men found suggestive) and her eyes on the prize.

In her world, of course, matrimony was the only prize. There could be no other. So it troubled her single-furrow mind that her oldest daughter should let her eyes wander and should even, at troubling intervals, fix on some other life track, not yet clearly visible to anyone. Janet had resigned herself to a certain amount of rebellion, but her daughter's waywardness had been easier to confine within the parameters of equestrian events or Miss Porter's School, which granted girls a certain amount of rein before snapping it back. Jackie, though, had insisted on college and, after two years at Vassar, a year at the Sorbonne, a gesture that went beyond rebellion to affectation. How much French did a girl need? What kind of bridal dowry was Malraux or Camus? "My daughter *l'existentialiste*," grumbled Mrs. Auchincloss. It was Hughdie, finally, who suggested that Jackie might need to "get it out of her system," though he himself had never felt the need and had only a wary acquaintance with systems. More crucially, he offered to pay.

The year in Paris went by with no great incident; no disastrous attachments were formed, at least not to Mrs. Auchincloss's knowledge; and each week, Jackie, in a semblance of gratitude, mailed back a postcard ("Camus asked me out for tea") or a whimsically illustrated letter. In sharp contrast were the blocks of Vieux Lille cheese that a Parisian *fromagerie* delivered to Merrywood every month and that emerged from their Air France cartons smelling like vengeance itself. The cheese could neither be eaten nor decoded, but if this was the worst Mrs. Auchincloss had to put up with, she would call herself fortunate; and when Jackie, upon her return, declared she would finish out her final year at George Washington University—the very opposite of the Sorbonne, a reluctantly desegregating commuter college that would cause no suitor discomfort—Mrs. Auchincloss chose to see that as accommodation and waited out the final months of Jackie's senior year the way one waits for a balloon to give up its last reserves of air. When her daughter was ready to do business, she would be there.

But what business did Jackie have in mind? She was a creature bending both toward and away from matrimony. Her high school yearbook photo, for instance, was a study in maidenly abstraction with rills of brunette tresses designed to make some poor fool lose his head. (By then, one or two had.) But if you let your eyes travel to the accompanying text, you find that her devoutest ambition was "not to be a housewife." It was this innate instability that made her maddening to somebody like Mrs. Auchincloss, for whom matrimony was an institution so sacred she'd gone at it twice to get it right. She knew that, in the vast majority of cases, life granted to each girl a remorselessly shrinking interval in which to close the deal, and as she looked about, she couldn't help seeing how many girls, Jackie's age or younger, had grabbed in a single nervy jump the summer place at Watch Hill, the life membership at Indian Harbor, the ski chalet at Canandaigua, the charge accounts at Tripler's, Brooks's and Abercrombie's. To be sure, their husbands drank too much and, over time, acquired "directorships" that kept them very late in the city, but it was assumed that any wife would happily go to bed alone if it was on D. Porthault sheets and that the very softness of the sheets came from the hard terms that had secured them and from the knowledge they could never be taken away. What girl could wish for anything else?

In reply, Jackie might have told her about Cressida.

She was a girl Jackie first encountered during a subscription ball at the Biltmore. Slight, bony, grotto-pale, edging dangerously past twenty-one, with straight black hair and a quality of barely sheathed rage. She sat alone on a couch in the ladies' room, smoking Raleighs, while the other girls clipped and curled themselves like terriers. When the time for dancing came, she took one turn with her brother, another with a step-cousin, then vanished down a circular stairway. It was only when the evening was winding down that Jackie stumbled across her in the Biltmore bar, reading by the light of a revolving pyramid of vodka bottles.

"Are you going to sit here all night?" Jackie asked.

"Why shouldn't I?"

When the other girls spoke of Cressida, it was in tones of reflexive pity. Poor thing. No money of her own. Couldn't afford a coming out. Sits in her grandfather's library all day. Won't go to college or even secretarial school. The most consistent critique was that she didn't *care*. About her plain face (anyway, she wore no lipstick) or her blighted financial hopes or her borrowed evening dress, or the incontestable fact of her unpopularity. But the boredom that so enveloped her in social settings suggested she was beyond judgment's reach. It was as if, having anatomized the limits of her world, she was now, with every silent passing second, plotting her escape, like a convict taking a gnawed spoon to the cell wall.

Jackie made a point of saying hello whenever their paths crossed, and if the greeting was returned, she might venture a conversation on some book she'd read or a news item in the *Herald Tribune*. Cressida neither resisted nor joined in; she simply waited for the overture to die a natural death. *You don't understand*, Jackie wanted to say. *I'm not like the others*. Only she knew that, in all essentials, she was, and that, on that day when America's proletariat had finally shaken off its chains and come swarming over the Madison Avenue barricades, it would be Cressida, still smoking her Raleighs, who would mark Jackie out for the long knives. "You'll want *that* one. Debutante of the Year, 1947."

The wonder was that Jackie couldn't just dismiss her as all her friends had. Quite to the contrary, she carried a little bit of Cressida into the world with her. Whenever she felt herself working a little too hard for a man's approval—batting her eyelashes at some soused lacrosse player or pretending to a trust lawyer in a serge suit that she had no idea who Albert Schweitzer was—she felt the fork-prick of that old reproach. And when, seemingly on impulse, she left the lacrosse player or trust lawyer standing by the punch bowl, she imagined Cressida grudgingly dispensing a line of approval.

It could be I was wrong about you.

Well, Janet Auchincloss wouldn't have known Cressida if she'd tripped over her on the way to the open bar. She knew only that Jackie, at the age when she was supposed to be growing pliable, was stiffening. The harder the push, the less the give. Tell her that Mrs. Palmer of Greenwich had the most charming son, practically coining money at Morgan

Stanley, and Jackie would twitch like one of Galvani's frogs. Tell her she should dance with every man as if he were Gary Cooper because Gary Cooper might actually be watching, she would transform herself into a Rand McNally atlas and sketch for her mother the exact geographical route that Gary Cooper would have to take to bridge the distance between the Hollywood hills and Darien. God forbid you told her that her left stocking seam was crooked or her right-hand top coat button about to fall off. She'd turn on you and, in a Frigidaire voice, say: "If I had a job, you wouldn't have to look at me all day."

Job. No other word could so resemble a Molotov cocktail when tossed in Mrs. Auchincloss's direction. Her first thought was that Jackie was bluffing. No girl could get a job without a Social Security number, could she? And what well-raised girl had one? Yet, in the months that followed Jackie's graduation, *job* was the idea she increasingly fell back on—whether or not she was peeved, whether or not they'd argued.

I should probably say that Mrs. Auchincloss's aversion stemmed from not just class prejudice but bitter experience. As a still-young divorcée, she'd been forced to work as a Macy's department-store model in order to pay for Jackie's riding lessons. Having to seek employment was bad enough, but to be forced to wear Macy's clothes in full view of the public—that, for Janet, was a shame as great as Dickens's blacking factory, and the idea that her daughter, after all the sacrifices made on her behalf, should so blithely steer for that deadly shoal was more than Mrs. Auchincloss could bear. Night after night, she raged at Jackie's ingratitude, her malice, until Hughdie, with a suppressed yawn, said:

"Why don't we just *get* her a job? Then she'll see what a bore it is."

Janet let the idea marinate for twenty-four hours, then gave her cautious assent. Hughdie put in a private call to Allen Dulles at the CIA; the old-boy network drew in upon itself; the very next Sunday, over lunch, Mrs. Auchincloss announced to the whole uneasily gathered family that Mr. Dulles had found Jackie a position at the State Department.

"Doing what?" asked Jackie.

"Well, gee," said Hughdie. "I guess they need clerks and secretaries just as much as the next fellow. Even more so, I'd guess."

"I mean, you have to start somewhere," said Janet.

"But I can't type," said Jackie. "Or take shorthand."

"I'm sure they need interpreters, too, darling. It's just a matter of getting one's foot in the door."

"You'll meet perfectly fine people," offered Hughdie. "Dulles says there's a polyglot in every room."

"And it's just a twenty-minute drive to Foggy Bottom. Why, it would be like going back to school, wouldn't it? Only with a little paycheck at the end of the week. You could burn it up at Garfinckel's in two hours."

"Why, the Reds will never know what hit 'em! Not that anybody expects you to bring down Stalin."

"Of course not. It's just *until*, darling."

Jackie needed a few moments to register the preposition.

"Until what?"

"Un*til*," said her mother, with a touch more vehemence.

"I'm still not following."

Janet stabbed lightly at her crown roast. "Really, must you be infuriating on Sundays, too? I should have thought you'd like a day off."

"That's all I have, Mummy, are days off."

"Then why can't I get one, too?"

Jackie sat silent for a time, frowning at a vase of hyacinths. Then, as if speaking to nobody in particular:

"Please tell Mr. Dulles that I greatly appreciate the offer, but I already have a job."

FOUR

The news produced the tiniest spasm in her mother's face, just below the left eye. Like the pennant that starts flapping just before the monsoon.

Don't look at me, Jackie wanted to say. *It's your fault.*

Some months earlier, while sitting under a hair dryer and thumbing through the pages of *Vogue,* Janet Auchincloss had come across a notice for the magazine's annual Prix de Paris contest. The winner would work as a junior editor for six months in New York, then spend the next six months covering the Paris shows. If she proved her mettle, she would then win a permanent spot on the masthead. There was no more prestigious entry point into American fashion journalism, but when Janet tore out the notice and handed it her daughter, it was probably in the spirit of larkishness, for she forgot all about it. Jackie nearly did herself. She grasped how many thousands of college seniors would be applying— many, if not most, of them more qualified.

But a curious thing happened. As soon as she convinced herself she had no chance, the application process became not an ordeal but a game. She fairly sprinted through the application, free to follow her whims because who would read it anyway? Why not slip in an autobiographical short story about her grandfather's funeral? And under the heading of "People I Wish I Had Known," why not park the names of Baudelaire, Wilde and Diaghilev? In a rush of exuberance that almost made her giggle, she declared herself ready to be "Overall Art Director of the Twentieth Century." Then she mailed it off and forgot all about it.

Months went by. Then, on the cusp of spring, came a letter from Mary Jessica Davis, editor in chief at *Vogue*. Jackie was one of the twelve Prix de Paris finalists. Would she be so good as to come up for the final round of interviews?

The effect, she later told me, was of sitting in a séance, perfectly agnostic about the whole enterprise, only to have a ghost whisper in your ear. The only question was how to get to New York. She spent two days furiously sifting through stratagems, only to fall back on the simplest one.

"I think I'll go see Daddy," she announced over breakfast.

Without dropping a stitch, her mother said, "Is he still alive?"

The two days in Manhattan were blurred by her own terror. She remembered her hands actually shaking as she applied her nail polish. She remembered the official *Vogue* photographer pausing before he snapped her to ask if she really wanted to part her hair down the middle. She remembered sitting for the final interview in Schrafft's, sweating through her silk blouse and tweed skirt, barely able to eat her chicken salad and then being told to make room—room!—for a hot fudge sundae with almonds and ladyfingers. She prattled, there was no other word, and it was here, surrounded by lady editors in boxy suit jackets, that she had the first intuition of herself as a man's woman. All her innate (or perhaps learned) responses to stress—the grab-bag of murmurs and demurrals and sudden feinting smiles she had been building up from childhood—the bag of *tricks*, a cynic might have said, only to her they were just helpless confessions of herself—all seemed calculated to enrage the females of Condé Nast, who had risen on much more than cow eyes and weren't about to reward the girl who apologized every word back into her mouth. Her only forthright moment came when she was asked who had been her prime stylistic influence.

"Oh," she answered, without thinking. "My father."

She relived for them then the days of window-shopping on Fifth Avenue, hour seeping into hour as Black Jack stopped before each mannequin to comment on the cut or the fabric, all of it building to the hushed moment when she would try on a frock of her own—a frock that her father, out of his accumulated wisdom, had chosen.

Oh, you're right, Daddy, it's lovely.

As Jackie warmed to her tale, she could feel the Condé Nast women regarding her in a changed light—as if she were a mannequin herself, sputtering into life. When she was done, the personnel director leaned across the table and, with the tiniest signal flare of a smile, said, "Congratulations."

In that moment, it was as if the sloth and confinement of the past months had been only an apprenticeship, training her toward this moment. She had only to say yes, and it would begin.

WELL, THIS WAS the journey that Janet Auchincloss had unknowingly launched but, upon hearing the news, she was in no hurry to claim authorship.

"Darling," she said. "Be a dear and tell us when you were *going* to tell us."

"I was coming around to it."

"And that was going to take how long? Two days? A year?"

"I don't know."

"While we were busy calling in every favor, prostrating ourselves before Allen Dulles's shrine?"

"I didn't *know* you were—"

"No, you were embroiled in the *tortuous* act of coming around."

"Mummy . . ."

"The only thing I want from you now is an explanation for your duplicity. Your sin of *omission*, if you like, and don't you dare tell me it's a lesser sin than commission. In a daughter, it's rather worse."

Mrs. Auchincloss had yet to raise her voice, but the barometric pressure of the dining room was mounting all the same. The server held back, the cook bided her time in the kitchen, and Jackie's younger stepsiblings consulted their napkins with deep intent. It was Hughdie who, in keeping with his conciliatory character, ventured the first softening notes.

"Well, New York won't be so bad as all that. We know plenty of people there."

"Not *those* people," said Janet. "Photographers. Models. The *very* finest bookies, your father knows them all. I assume you told *him*," she suddenly added. "First thing."

"No," lied Jackie.

"Won't he be happy to get his hooks into you at last? Why, you could stay with him the whole time. Meet all his tramps and help him crawl into bed every night and clean the vomit off his shoes. It'll be just like old times, won't it, darling?"

"My dear," protested Hughdie. "The children."

"No, I want them to see! Little darlings, this is what a *socialite career girl* looks like. I don't blame you for saying nothing; she'll be a conversation stopper with every man she meets. She'll end up as barren as a Carmelite, and aren't we pleased? I can bring home all her magazine articles from the beauty salon, and you can line your sock drawers with them. Wave bye-bye now, darlings. Say bye-bye to Jackie."

The next Sunday was Mother's Day, and it was precisely to escape her own mother, whose reproaches trailed her like exhaust, that she ventured out to Charlie Bartlett's Georgetown row house, where she met a disheveled Congressman from Brookline, whose every response, right up to and including following her out of the house, suggested he'd seen something in her she hadn't, that she wasn't really looking to escape to New York or Paris but to settle down right here in her adopted town with the first handsome and eligible man who made eyes at her. The presumption both baffled and offended her—in part because there was a chance it had originated in her—and after she'd dropped the never-to-be-seen-again Michael O'Sullivan at his group home in Clarendon, she drove back up Chain Bridge Road with the gloomy sense that she'd been following her mother's dictates after all. It was only when she reflected upon the nature of this particular Congressman that she concluded Mrs. Auchincloss would hate him and his arriviste origins just as much as her daughter's pursuing a career, and that cheer carried her all the way to the following afternoon, when he did, in the end, phone, just ten minutes before the dinner bell. She took the call on the upstairs extension.

"How nice to hear from you," she said.

"I—ah—I hope you don't mind, I asked Charlie for your number."

"Not at all."

"It was a real pleasure meeting you last night."

"You as well."

"I told Charlie you were far and away the best charades player. Except for me."

Her laugh was brief and spasmodic. "Well now, I believe that remark demands a rematch."

"By all means. I understand you're moving to New York."

This caught her short. How had it been leaked?

"Oh, I guess so. In a week or so. I mean, it's just a little job with *Vogue*. Mummy's perfectly furious, I don't know why. I mean, I might be back any day, it's hard to know."

If he says don't go, I won't. And felt in the very voicing of the thought how wretched a woman's life was.

"Well now," he said. "I'm sure you'll have a great professional success and become a real credit to your education, and I—ah—I wish you the best of luck, Miss Bouvier."

Miss Bouvier. What surer sign that she had been scratched off his list? Even now his finger was scrolling down the memo pad to Miss Hickey Sumers, that *other* option from the Bartletts' dinner party: her lips war-painted, her very name a provocation. *You're so good to make time for us, Congressman. What an honor.* Ten to one she was already, from pure prescience, moisturizing herself in anticipation of the call.

Well, there was no point in heaping scorn on poor Hickey, not when the memory of her own words was such a torment. *Little job with* Vogue. *Might be back any day.* She'd all but copied out her own declaration of dependence. Meanwhile, Janet Auchincloss was reconsidering her strategy. Perhaps it was better to meet a daughter's resistance with tacit surrender, the better to conserve one's energies for the long game. Thus, she became quite suddenly a font of solicitude.

"Darling, do you need any help with the packing? Are you sure? Well, do let me know, and is it all right if we drive you to the station tomorrow? It's such a bother getting a cab, and Hughdie can help the redcap with your bags."

Jackie answered curtly, in her usual fashion, and was surprised to find, upon boarding the Congressional the next day, that the sight of Mummy waving goodbye produced a clutch in her throat. Since graduating college, she had gazed upon her mother simply as an obstruction, and she was seized now by the thought that, the entire time, without either of them knowing, Mrs. Auchincloss had been a joist, a load-bearing beam that, once disassembled, left a girl unsure where to set her weight. Who would ever hover over Jackie in the same smothering and infuriating way? Be driven by her to the same murderous rages? If that wasn't love, what was? And so, as the train pulled out, Jackie found herself waving quite frantically and then, at the sight of her mother's own constricted face, pressing her gloved hand to the window.

FIVE

*T*hat week with *Vogue* is, for me, one of the more mysterious interludes in Jackie's life. There she was, ready to embrace this destiny that had fallen from the Condé Nast skies. Every day, she rode up the Graybar Building elevator, sat at her swivel chair and typewriter table with the stack of interoffice memo sheets and the pot of African violets. She was taken to lunch, given free ballet tickets, invited for cocktails at a Park Avenue apartment house, where she drank vodka straight for the first time and jitterbugged and ended up on the balcony with a young man in a leather jacket who played his ukulele for her.

Think what *this* Jackie might have gone on to. A life of lingerie boutiques and skating at the Garden and standing

on some Sutton Place balcony, watching boat lights blink on
the East River. That Jackie might have formed a straight line
to the lacquered, manor-born creature of today who gets ferried back and forth to Doubleday and flicks away the public
gaze like a cobweb and who only barely resembles the girl
arriving in 1951, a terrapin without its shell, oozing doubt
from every pore in a city that makes you doubt ten times
harder.

In her youth, of course, Jackie had traveled from high-
rise to high-rise and had always been able to float above, like
the Chinese lanterns at one of the debutante parties she frequented. *Working* there put you at the bottom of the canyon.
The smell of burning chestnuts, the dragon fumes from the
subway. In those days, Reds were still screaming at you from
lecterns in Union Square, trying to save the Rosenbergs, and
cabbies actually drove after you if you undertipped, bellow-
ing about their kids, and even the newspaper kiosks were
yelling. The only tranquil figure in the mix was Black Jack
Bouvier himself, who had cut short his six-week stay at
the Silver Hill sanitarium and strolled back to his bachelor flat on East Seventy-fourth. Financial straits had forced
him to give up the limousine and chauffeur, but he still had
the Mercury convertible and a reserved late-night seat at
the Racquet Club bar, and as he staggered to the breakfast
table every morning in boxer shorts and garters, he looked
from one angle as if he'd actually been taken to the cleaners
and, from another, like the harem master of his own fancy.
"Jacks," he'd say, "pour me another coffee, would you? I've
got a bastard of a headache."

Shortly after, she would hear him heaving like a barge in his bathtub and, at intervals, shouting out to her: "Let's go to Cap d'Antibes! . . . Have you ever been to the Dublin Horse Show?" By sundown, whatever plan he'd had in mind had evaporated. Strangely, the one subject that seemed to rouse him now was her matrimonial prospects. "Jacks," he'd say, "what kind of men are you meeting at this job?"

"Well, there's the art director. He's a lovely gentleman from Russia."

"Is he the type to take a girl to dinner?"

"He's married."

"What I'm wondering is if there's anybody there who'll take a pretty girl to dinner."

"One or two."

"Would they *try* something after?"

"Don't be crude."

"Jacks, I'm just trying to save us all a great deal of time. You know, if this magazine business doesn't work out, you can always come work for me. We'll land you a sucker before the week's out. A ribeye-eating fellow with a cottage in Montauk."

It was confusing when he spoke of work because she so rarely caught him at it, but more confusing to hear him suggest that only a sucker would marry her. She wasn't such a bad catch, was she? Bev Corbin, a Harvard boy with an Owl Club address, had told her when she was just sixteen that she was "rife with witchcraft" and had sulked for months because she wouldn't kiss him in front of his friends. In Paris, a tall Russian émigré named Arkadi, at sight of her, had ripped off his shirt and danced with her to "Music, Music, Music" and gifted her a portable record player as a token of his esteem. She could feel, as a matter of daily course, men's gazes trailing after her; the only question was whether to gaze back, which required a deciphering of intent that she had not quite mastered.

As for Black Jack, what would *he* be asking of her in the months to come? She knew she wasn't his only link to the world. Her sister, Lee, currently in her final year at Miss Porter's, was a regular visitor. There was a maid to make his coffee and send anything that smelled of pee to the cleaners, and there was some kind of Canadian girlfriend (not much older than Jackie) who wandered in now and then. But Jackie sensed that Black Jack had come *loose* in ways that no one had anticipated, and although she considered herself a daddy's girl, she could not welcome the job of triage nurse. Even if she got an apartment of her own, as her father was already encouraging her to do, wouldn't she always be waiting for the next call? The *last* call?

Meanwhile, Janet Auchincloss was calling regularly to make sure she had everything she needed. "Are you *sure*? We can ship you anything you've forgotten." She wanted to know which issues Jackie was working on so she could grab them the moment they came out. "I'm not even going to wait for the beauty parlor, darling, I'm going to drive to the nearest newsstand. Wherever it is." It wasn't until the third call that she took advantage of a brief lull in the conversation to bring up Arthur Krock, the dean of Washington newsmen and a regular enough presence at Merrywood that Jackie, from her earliest years, was encouraged to refer to him as Uncle Arthur.

"I wouldn't even mention him, darling, but he says he's pretty sure he can line you up with a job."

"With the *Times*?"

"Oh, no, darling, the *Washington Times-Herald*. It's a Hearst paper so you know it's on the right side of things."

"When would it start?"

"I don't know, next year."

"Next year?" Jackie paused to recalibrate. "Well, that shouldn't interfere with anything."

"That's exactly what I was saying to Hughdie. I said, *Uncle Arthur can wait, and so can Lee.*"

There was a long pause before Jackie asked what her sister had to do with anything.

"Oh, I was only asking her what she wanted for her graduation gift and she—well, it won't surprise you to learn she wants to go to Paris."

"You'd better send her."

"Of course we will, it's just . . ." A beat. "Now don't you *dare* tell her I told you."

"Tell me what?"

"She wants you to take her. Oh, I know how the two of you bicker, and I know she's not very respectful—I've *spoken* to her about this—but she understands how fluent you are and how sophisticated and—well, I'll admit that, as a mother, I would love you to be there, too, because (I would never tell her this) she doesn't have your *command* of things. And I've already said too much, so, to help her save face, I should just tell her to hold her horses until next summer, when you'll be free. *If* you're free. I mean, autumn in Paris is exquisite, we all know that, but I don't think the summers get too infernally hot, do they? It's just the tourists that make it feel that way."

That weekend, Jackie came back to Merrywood, but purely to pick up some of the items she'd forgotten to pack. Saturday, she sat brooding in her room. Sunday, she began typing out a letter to the *Vogue* editor. She went through at least a dozen drafts, she told me later, trying to find the right balance, but there was no balance, and the final draft was a master class in equivocation. She would be staying home for the time being, but perhaps she'd come back in January, if there was an opening, as she was so hoping there would be. Or perhaps the following spring when the fashion shows began. Or perhaps not at all?

Very sincerely, Jackie Bouvier.

ONE OTHER THING happened that week at *Vogue*. She was asked to help edit a nine-page Irving Penn photo essay on Famous People of Washington. At the time, she had zero standing to make any kind of stink, but after seeing the orderly procession of Kefauver and Krock, she wondered out loud why there was no Kennedy.

"Isn't he a bit done?" said the photo editor. "I mean, that PT boat sank years ago."

The remark left a quiet sting. Like most Americans in those days, she knew the story of that boat. And of its brave young lieutenant, who refused to surrender after being rammed by a Japanese destroyer and who, despite his badly injured back, led his crew on a grueling three-hour swim to the nearest island, towing a badly burned but still living crewman the whole way. The next day, he swam another two miles to try to hail a passing boat. The day after, with food running short, he led his battered and starving men to another island—a four-mile swim against a fierce current—still biting down on the life-vest strap of that burned crewman. The next day he swam out again and brought back a canoe, food and water. Nearly a week passed before they were finally rescued by another PT boat, and it was the consensus of the survivors that they would have perished without their skipper. Handsome and gaunt, he was lionized in headlines and newsreels, awarded a medal and a Purple Heart, but in the midst of the idolatry, he had the grace to shrug his shoulders and say that, when it came to being a hero, he'd had no choice. "They sank my boat."

The tale had long since passed into legend, and it irked Jackie more than she would have guessed to see it devolving into a joke. But where was she to put her umbrage? Surely she couldn't call up the Congressman on his office line—not with the memory of her own weasel words still fresh. The *little job with* Vogue. She had all but prophesied her own doom, and if you were to ask me why Jackie kept her distance from the Congressman in the months ahead, I would say it was because she didn't want to admit to him that she had cut and run.

SIX

*W*ell, being new to the Kennedys, she didn't yet know that they can cut and run, too. I say this from experience. My Manhattan sofa used to be known as Hyannisport West because, on any given morning, you'd find a young Kennedy sleeping there. Bobby Junior, most of the time, but sometimes his brother David would come along, or Chris Lawford. Nobody ever *made* them sleep on the sofa—there's a perfectly usable guest room—but after scampering to their various boroughs, they always came back looking for the nearest horizontal surface, and, once they were asleep, they were the most prone specimens you've ever seen. My housekeeper Sheila used to dust around them as if they were houseplants.

These days, the axis lies empty more often than not, and I do find myself missing—oh, the tangle of them, I suppose. Elbows and knees jutting up where you least expected them. The profundity of their slumber, and behind it, a pure sort of trust, for they grasped at some unconscious level that they were well and truly safe, and this assurance extended to their parents, who would know, wherever they were in the world, that Uncle Lem was on the watch. Even today, if Ethel wants to know where one of her kids is, I'm the first one she calls.

In short, I am of use, and what better purpose could there be for my golden years? Oh, I can look back with pride on various professional achievements—I am known in certain circles, for example, as the Father of Fizzies—but it seems to me when all the noise of the marketplace has died away, when the last rat has run its race, it's the human connection that lingers most. Indeed, as the days dwindle down, I find myself curiously wishing I had more humans to connect with. Sometimes I'll even read those silly gossip columnists on Page Six just to see what the Kennedy boys are up to.

Of course, it's silly to argue I'm alone. Eunice calls practically every day. My friend Raul calls, too, on occasion, until he remembers why he's mad at me. And, of course, I have my Dalmatian, light of my life. Really, if you were to ask me the thing I regret most these days, it's that, with the bursitis and asthma and querulous ticker, I can't walk Ptolly as much as I'd like. But if a day is feeling slacker than it should, I will sometimes force myself out of doors, even invent an errand if need be.

Most days, though, my exercise is delving into the archives. I've made a whole scrapbook, for instance, devoted to Jackie's Washington career. Which began as just an entry-level position with the *Times-Herald*. Was there anyone less qualified to be a secretary? She disconnected calls and lost messages and, because she couldn't bear asking people to repeat themselves, misspelled names and botched phone numbers. But her resilient good cheer also endeared her a little to the managing editor, and she built that patiently into a rapport, so that, when a position opened up, she lunged for it with a velocity that surprised her.

"You want to be the Inquiring Photografer?" her editor asked. "Do you even know how to use a camera?"

Not yet, she told him, but she would. And if, after a month, she proved to be a bad fit, he could fire her with no hard feelings. "And besides," she said, "you don't want me handling your phones anymore."

So, for the sum of forty dollars and fifty cents a week, she got to harvest the opinions of Washington's populace. Every day, rain or shine, she strolled the streets with a five-pound Graflex Speed Graphic, sidling up to pedestrians and asking the kinds of anodyne questions that would cause no one alarm. "Are beauty operators and barbers entitled to tips?" "If you were put in solitary confinement and could take only one book, what would it be?" "Would you rather make a lot of money or have a lot of friends?" "Should men wear wedding rings?"

Introverted by nature, she found it a challenge to but-tonhole strangers, but it was her unfeigned shyness that disarmed their suspicion and allowed her to reproduce words and images, hot and steaming, for the next day's paper. Her feet ached from walking six days a week; she ran through heels and gloves faster than she could replace them; on a couple of occasions, the darkroom fumes nearly overpowered her. But she persevered and, every two weeks, deposited an utterly exotic paycheck in her savings account. She even talked of renting a pied-à-terre in town to cut down on her commute. And whenever she began to suspect that her work was at heart trivial, she tossed in, out of nowhere, a question of more substance. "How should health care for the aged be provided?" "If you secretly found out you had married a former Communist, what would you do?"

Things were advancing on another front, too. Another John had entered the picture.

JOHN GRINNEL WETMORE Husted Junior (Johnny to his friends). She met him at a Valentine's Day dance in New York. He was a Yale graduate, and he was—this was important to her back then—tall. He was handsome, too, in a birthright sort of way, seething with follicles. His sisters went to Miss Porter's with Jackie; his father was a partner in Brown Shipley; his mother was a Harkness, with all the promise of deferred wealth that name carried. He himself (Jackie was dismayed to learn) was a stockbroker, but his conversation, while limited, was conducted with gusto, and his smile had an impregnable, because unexamined, cheer, and though he was her senior by several years, he stared at her as woundedly as a prep-school virgin. For a girl who had not yet taken her final exams at George Washington, the dawning sense of her own power was in itself erotic.

She and Johnny talked by phone, exchanged letters, and whenever he flew down to Florida to see his mother, he made a point of stopping in Washington on the way back up. Their first date was at a dancing class, where he was the right mix of suave and awkward. He was tickled pink to learn about her job and begged to know when he might tag along. After some hesitation, she suggested a Saturday in October—and regretted it from the first moment, for it was one thing to have a young stockbroker clumsily tailing you through Washington's streets, it was another to let him catch up. "You won't have *this* to do much longer," he'd say. "My mother likes her hobbies, too," he'd say. By the end of the day, she was more exhausted than usual, and she realized it was because she'd been running the whole time. She had nothing left for him but a squeeze of the hand, a pair of lips grazing off his cheek. He called her all the same as soon as he got home and demanded to know when she would come see him in New York.

She stalled—stalled for many weeks because she grasped that she would be more vulnerable on his terrain, all the more so for having lately vacated it. But he kept pressing, by letter and by phone. Her mother pressed, too, and even her father, so that her going there began to take on the certainty of an Old Testament prophesy. In the second weekend of January, Johnny met her in the bowels of Grand Central with a box of roses. He had the good sense to wear a camel coat and a white cashmere scarf, wrapped and tied with that perfect balance of care and indifference. He took her to Ciro's for drinks and dinner, then to the late show of a Broadway movie, then to a nightclub to hear an alto saxophonist. At some point, it occurred to her that this was their first real date. They capped off the evening with a short walk through the chill of Palisades Park (she was glad to have brought her squirrel muff) then a cab to the Polo Bar in the Westbury Hotel, where, in lieu of making a move, he merely grinned and said, "How about it?"

"How about what?"

"I guess . . ." He plunged a hand into his coat. "I guess I figured if you came all this way to see me, I should come a ways, too."

Out it came, in a hinged box. A single white sapphire and a single diamond. Jackie's mind went to work at once, parsing the symbolism. The sapphire for tradition? The diamond for prosperity? Not gaudy but aspirational, was that it? Then she heard him say: "It's my mother's."

THEY WERE TO be married in June.

HE WAS A type she was already familiar with. He read the *Herald Tribune* for news, the *Daily News* for sports, the *Journal* for everything else. He played squash to win. He said things like "hotter than Hades" and "goddamn Reds," but, although he'd voted for Dewey, he would tell you after a couple of martinis that he was really a radical. His objective in life was a square brick edifice in Norwalk, where the tires of his Buick convertible would crunch on blue gravel and where the wife—she would be "the wife"—would have the cushions waiting in his armchair and the whiskey-and-soda on the side table, along with the evening ration of five cigarettes, laid out like caterpillars.

Yet, as an individual, he was scarcely to be known. Each time she saw him, he seemed no more familiar than the last. The ring was a larger puzzle. After getting it resized for her finger, she wore it from dawn to dusk—slept with it, even—expecting it to transform her by the sheer weight of it against her skin, yet she could go hours without knowing it was there, only to be astonished all over again by the glint of it in a lamp or a window. *My ring*, she thought, but no amount of vocalization made it real.

It didn't help that Mrs. Auchincloss herself, after warmly approving the match, seemed now to be cooling by half degrees. "Darling, you'll have to trust me," she said. "You could do worse." As if to quiet her own qualms, Janet began clipping and saving articles from *Woman's Day* and *Ladies' Home Journal*. "Matrimony: The Keystone to a Full Life." "A Successful Wife Is a Career in Itself." "Help Him Understand Why He Needs You." But Johnny had already come to that conclusion, and weren't the vast majority of Jackie's classmates from Miss Porter's and Vassar flashing rings of their own? None of them had put up a fuss, so why should she?

The larger question was why Jackie, having embarked on the career she'd fought for, should be entertaining the very sort of marriage she'd been swearing off since girlhood. Lacking a better explanation myself, I fall back on the uncomfortable, intractable, confounding, emasculating explanation of money.

The *encompassing* explanation, you might say, only how hard it is to pin it down, for it fractures into a million stories. I'll go first.

My father died at the height of the Great Depression. In a single brutal stroke, this left my family without means and forced me to go on scholarship through most of Choate and all of Princeton. Not such a privation, you'll say, except that, unlike Jack and the rest of my peers, I was conscious at every moment of every day where every penny was flying. I knew that if Uncle Luther didn't toss a penny or two my way every so often, I wouldn't have any. That if Jack invited me to Palm Beach for Christmas, I'd have to invite somebody with a car to take me there or I couldn't go. That if Jack wanted to meet up at the Stork Club in New York, I'd have to put on a rented suit and thumb for rides on Route One. That if he failed to invite me to Hyannisport each summer, I'd have nowhere else to go. Not even Pittsburgh, for that was now a walled city.

Jack, of course, had never concerned himself too much with logistics, his own or anyone else's. This was the luxury that wealth had given him, so he couldn't know that largesse is defined by its limits or that those limits can change with the flap of a wing. And if Jackie and I had anything in common, it was simply that we knew what it was like to be without money from a tender age and to be, at the same time, always proximate to money. It was the tinnitus-like buzzing that never left your inner ear. *Not yours.* Or, to quote Jackie's mother as they once gazed across Merrywood's green prospect: "Don't get attached, darling."

Jackie took the hint. Any property that had Auchincloss on its title could never be hers. So I don't think I got the wrong impression that first time I saw her, frozen in the high beams of Jack's car. The sense, I mean, that, in the midst of this vast and unbarricaded estate, she was still an insurgent and, for that reason, could never be *free* of money like her stepsiblings. (Or Jack, for that matter.)

Well, by now she'd been working long enough at the *Times-Herald* to grasp how the marketplace worked. If you pulled down forty-two dollars a week, that was the distance between your having something and having nothing. If a stockbroker chose to join his income to yours, the distance became larger, and *You could do worse* meant only *You could find a worse reason for marrying.*

In the end, curiously, it did come down to money. Hughdie made belated inquiries. The Harkness fortune, it seemed, was not flowing as freely as had been thought, at least not down this particular channel. Johnny Husted, upon direct interrogation, admitted he was pulling down just seventeen thousand a year. "Dear God," said Mrs. Auchincloss. "Your no-good father was earning three times as much, and that was 1928!" With no small embarrassment, Mrs. Auchincloss came to see that this prosaic and unpromising young man, through mere name and connections, had stolen this close to a prize that should never have been his. She knew better than to deliver the conclusion straight to her daughter but trusted instead to time and distance.

And still Jackie held on, long after everyone else in her family had let go. Was it simply the mineral fact of Johnny Husted's ring? Sometimes, in the middle of the night, she would wake to find it snagging in her hair. There were days, too, when she was raising her Graflex to snap somebody's picture, and the ring would catch on the camera strap, and she would be forced to remark on it all over again. It seemed to be somebody else's ring on somebody else's hand.

SEVEN

*J*ackie's column was being more spoken of now. Even friends of the Auchinclosses were reading. And, having now established politics as a fit subject, she could take the next logical step of interviewing politicians. It was from here an equally logical step to the Massachusetts congressman who had once followed her out onto the Bartletts' stoop.

Or was it? She hesitated for many weeks, and when she at last crossed that bridge, she made the appointment through his scheduler, Mrs. Lincoln, taking care to spell the last name ("No, B-o-*u* . . ."). On the day in question, she showed up at the Cannon House Office Building in new heels and new stockings. Her hair had acquired blond highlights from a local salon. She would have liked to believe herself a more sophisticated spectacle than the last time they met, but she would have settled for grown up.

Rather shockingly, he was just as diminished as she remembered. Had nobody been feeding him? The jacket still hung from his shoulders, the Arrow collar still drew away from his throat. The skin was a curious blend of tawny and ash, and the eyes were smudged in shadow. *He's ill* was her first thought, but his great good humor was intact, and judging by the way he leaned back in his burgundy leather chair and laced his hands behind his head, he was ready to pick up where they left off.

It was the first time they'd occupied a room alone, and the conversation was halting. When he learned that she'd been in Paris last fall, he asked her, drily, if she'd seen President Auriol. "No," she answered, and several agonizing seconds went past before she thought to say that Piaf and de Gaulle took her out for a drink and declared her the very flower of American maidenhood, and another several seconds passed before Jack said, "Don't you mean *fleur*?" And then more silence, and by the time he asked if Gene Kelly and Leslie Caron had been there, too, whirling around in perfect Technicolor, all chance of humor had perished.

"We're going about this all wrong," she said at last, drawing a reporter's notebook from her bag. "According to my job description, I'm supposed to ask *you* the questions."

"That's what it says?"

"It practically has the force of law. Which, as a congress-man, you're—"

"Sworn to uphold, yes. I was there." He leaned back even

farther in his armchair than she would have guessed possible. "You know, whenever I conduct an interview, my press secretary is supposed to be here."

"Mm," she said, softly frowning. "I don't suppose we could pay him to look the other way."

"He does that quite a bit but—the law is the law."

She made a show of considering.

"Maybe we could come up with our own little law. Just the two of us, for this occasion."

"I'm listening."

"Let's say for every question I ask you, you get to ask me one."

"Sounds fair."

"Now, Congressman, perhaps you could tell our readers how you enjoy living in our fair town."

"You're referring to the city of Northern charm and Southern efficiency?"

"I believe you've answered my question with a question. Unless, of course, that's your on-the-record answer, in which case our readers will be interested to hear it."

His eyes narrowed a fraction. "*On* the record, Washington couldn't agree with me more. I get down on my knees and thank God every night for the privilege of living here until such time as I can return to my district, where it is an equally great privilege to live."

"Do they swallow that line there?"

"There is no line. You are receiving my deepest, most urgent thoughts. And now it's my turn. Please define for me the object that rests on your finger."

In that moment, she didn't blush, nor did she glance at her hand, though she came within a hair of doing both.

"It's a ring," she says.

"That would appear to be a self-evident answer."

"I don't believe the nature of the answer was mentioned in our arrangement."

"Are you sure?"

She gave her throat a light clearing. "What is it you most like about being a congressman?"

"Nothing."

"Nothing comes of nothing."

His smile broadened now into something frankly admiring.

"My turn," he murmured. "To whom does the ring on your finger belong?"

"Me."

"That's equally self-evident. Let me rephrase," he said and, with a soft vehemence, raised his chair to a seated position. "Who's the fellow put it there?"

SHE HAD BRIEFLY considered slipping it off and tucking it in her purse, but she'd rejected the idea. She wanted him to see it. Or see if he saw it.

But toward what end, I've always wondered. Was it rescue she was looking for? Johnny to save her from her mother and then someone to save her from Johnny? Or was it just that, in her brief experience of Jack, she had seen how aroused he was by challenge? The higher the barrier, the harder he would work to clear it. Part of me wonders if that ring wasn't Jackie's version of a dare. "Can you clear this?" she was asking.

Or else it was something more buried. It was Jackie sensing that her future was curving away from her—or, if you like, she had peered into Schrödinger's box and found an alternative reality flickering there—and she knew enough by now about Jack's situation to sense that he was likewise curving, toward a future he didn't quite own. That ring was her way of saying: "Here we are, the two of us, being created by others. Why not do it ourselves?"

Nobody intruded during that half hour in Jack's office. Jackie left without an interview or photograph. Maybe all that was kindled was a tiny prick of light, out there where their two parallel lines—thanks to the laws or, better to say, the lies of perspective—were actually converging.

THROUGH OLD HABIT, she went to Mass for guidance, prayed hard. The letters from Johnny grew more importunate, her replies more formal. She kept the calls shorter, hedged about coming to New York again. One night, she suggested pushing back the wedding by six months. "Why?" he asked. She was just so busy with work, and she'd promised her editor to stay through the year, and she didn't want to leave them in the lurch, they'd gone out on such a limb with her. His response made two truths vivid. She had driven him beyond the bounds of frustration. And he had been harboring a certain thought about her career.

"It's not hard to take somebody's picture."

That night, as she lay in bed, it seemed to her that Johnny's mind was like a miner's lamp, cutting a very bright straight line but otherwise surrounded by darkness. She had admired that at first, the linearity of him, but now she could see how many radiating avenues it closed off, and the thought of crowding into that single beam made her ache down to her bones. Her mother, wisely, was not pushing her in either direction, so when Jackie announced that Johnny would be staying with them the third weekend in January, Janet made the necessary preparations and greeted him with unusual cordiality. The couple spent Saturday, per usual, trolling the streets of Washington, but on Sunday morning, Jackie made sure that Nellie cooked him a crown roast, and she volunteered to drive him to National Airport. They were about half a mile out when she told him he was one of the kindest people in the world. Even Johnny Husted knew what that meant. In the end, there were no tears. They stood for a while, gazing out at the airfield, watching his plane trundle through the rain. A final kiss, then goodbye.

The ring he didn't find until he got home. She'd slipped it into his pocket.

EIGHT

As soon as she woke the next morning, she began canvassing herself for regrets, self-reproaches, second thoughts—and found none. If anything, just relief, registering at first as a faint trickle and swelling into a full tide. Was severing a tie really as simple as all that?

Certainly, nobody at Merrywood was rushing in to console or commiserate. She might have wondered if it had happened at all if her mother, at the breakfast table, hadn't paused in the act of spooning her grapefruit to murmur:

"I'll send the correction to the *Times*."

Somehow or another, she had got herself clear, and the sense of her own escape buoyed her, so that the girl who showed up for work that day was both a lighter creature, able to parry the flirtations of the criminal-courts reporter without a thought, and a more determined one, stalking the salesmen and hausfraus at the Home Show to ask them what features they'd most like to see in a new home. *Three bathrooms*, she scribbled on her pad. *Screened-in porch. Doric columns.* And with each word, with each lofting of her camera, the disapproving specter of Johnny Husted seemed to recede into the mist. After filing her column, she reached into her desk drawer and took a draft of the peach schnapps she kept for special occasions and sat for a while, contemplating the future. Then, still riding the fumes of her alcohol, she picked up her phone and dialed the Congressman's office.

She told his press secretary she had to pin down some key facts with the Congressman before her article could go to print. She was less amazed by the effrontery of her lie—for, of course, there was no article—than the coolness with which she told it. Less than half an hour later, the Congressman called her back.

"I find I have important news to share," she told him.

"Go on."

"It appears that a certain engagement of which we briefly spoke is no longer an engagement."

"I see," he said. "Does anybody need to be socked in the jaw?"

"No."

"In that case, Miss Bouvier, I believe a celebration might be in order. A girl doesn't get herself unengaged just any day."

"No, it's quite rare."

"Say now, I'm leaving town Friday, but are you free Thursday night?"

Already, in her mind's ear, her mother's voice was sounding. *Don't leap at the first offer. Nor the second. Pretend you have such a vast chain of social engagements you can't pry yourself loose till August. Make him earn every minute you give him.*

And perhaps it was because Janet Auchincloss wasn't there in person that Jackie heard herself say:

"Thursday should be all right. Why don't you pick me up from work?"

THE CAR WAS a five-year-old leased black Cadillac, driven not by a chauffeur but by a House gofer. The Congressman sat in the back, riffling so distractedly through memos that it wasn't until he and Jackie were seated at the Occidental Grill, their menus thrust at them like sacred tablets, that he raised his eyes to hers.

They settled on cherrystone clams for appetizers and, for an entrée, fried soft-shell clams. The Congressman crooked a finger at the nearest waiter, while Jackie did a slow scan of the walls: framed photos of ex-presidents and ex-generals and (she was guessing) ex–cabinet officers, spaced at such regular intervals and gazing out with looks of such equivalent starchiness they all seemed to be the same man.

"What are you looking for?" she heard him ask.

"*You,*" she said. "I figured you must be up there somewhere."

"You'll find me in the kitchen, next to the dishwasher. Now maybe you'll tell *me*," he said. "What's a nice Catholic girl like you doing in a town like this?"

Catholic girl. He knew that much about her.

"Well," she said, "I grew up here. When I wasn't staying with my father. As for the religion thing, I try to keep that on the hush-hush."

"Between you and God."

"Something like that."

He began at once to quiz her. Family, education, career goals. It was no different than a job interview, really, only he would take any datum she lobbed at him and spin it into a whole line of inquiry. A casual mention of Cork, Ireland, for example, became under his interrogation a travelogue of her time in Europe. The tale of staying with a family in the Rue de Mozart expanded to include her twenty-first birthday, commemorated with sandwiches and red wine, and veered from there to braving the outhouses of Spain and being detained by Soviet troops in Vienna. No matter where she wandered, he was ready with the next question. He seemed, however, to discourage lines of inquiry about himself, as he did flattery. "You know," he said, "we're all just a bunch of worms over there."

"Consequential worms."

"Only to our districts, and only when we bring home the pork. I couldn't even tell you all the members of the House Foreign Affairs Committee. Or even the Education and Labor Committee, and I sit on that one. At least I think I do."

Perhaps because he seemed so indifferent to the impression he was making, she felt freer over their next two dinner dates to form her own. She noticed, for instance, how he favored Italian food over French and fettuccini over everything. How he liked his vegetables pureed and his drinks mixed. (Straight-up liquor didn't agree.) How he descended a set of stairs even more slowly than he ascended them and how, when he was concentrating on something, he would tap his front teeth with his index finger, like a miner seeking ore.

How often, she noticed, did he find a way to touch himself. The gesture not so much nervous as existential—was he still there? The fingers flying to necktie, to jacket flap. To the hair, most of all, which he guarded like a miser with a golden hoard. His was the kind of male beauty that improved with acquaintance because it had nothing to do with regularity. The ears jutted; the Fitzgerald teeth had never completely settled into their Kennedy jaw; and, of course, in those days he was painfully thin in his two-button suits. But he was tall in a way that surprised her, and he was what the Victorian novelists used to like to call "well-knit," and although the sickly ash color hadn't quite left his skin, the steady diet of weekends at Palm Beach had scrubbed it into something like virility, a tawny blend that brought out the beautiful tapering of his fingers, the green-gray seascape of his eyes. It all added *up* somehow, and he was not unaware that it did, he simply carried it with him—carelessly, unthinkingly—the way you might half tie a sweater around your neck and forget it was there.

When he walked into a restaurant, for example, he was inevitably seated at the best table with the best view and the most conscientious waiter. The notion that any of this might have turned out otherwise seemed never to have crossed his mind, and it was this casually lofted privilege that left him queerly helpless at times. He had never once had to make his own dinner reservations, book his own tickets, clean his own clothes or make his own bed. He was driven as much as he drove and was told at most hours of the day and night where he needed to be. One evening, Jackie watched a napkin flutter from his lap to the floor. She waited, expecting him at any moment to snatch it back up, but he stared at it, as if to ask how it could have done such a thing, and then they both waited in a kind of anxious suspension until the waiter rushed forward with a replacement.

Now, it could have been that Jack's back wouldn't let him bend that far, but I don't think she was wrong in detecting, beneath his composed exterior, a sense of limits and a certain anxiety about crossing them. She remembered that single retreating step he had made upon entering the Bartletts', and her heart warmed again at the thought that such an attractive and famous man might need someone to comfort or reassure him. Once, in the act of listening to one of his war stories, she was even moved to rest a hand lightly on his forearm. He glanced at it, then glanced away. For a man with such a playboy reputation, he was surprisingly reticent with her: a handshake after their first dinner and a European kiss to the cheeks after the second. Yet, for all the absence of skin, there was something pleasingly illicit about these encounters. A more conventional suitor would have picked her up at home and been permitted to leave only on the condition that he have her back by ten. But congressmen weren't necessarily subject to bourgeois standards and, at twenty-two, Jackie was too old for a curfew, and as much as some part of her wanted the world to know, a larger part didn't.

He was no less secretive about her. Their dinner dates were arranged privately by Mrs. Lincoln, and if by some chance a minor Washington figure stumbled over to their table to pay homage, the Congressman never paused to introduce her, never even allowed his gaze to slide her way. Was it possessiveness, she wondered, or rudeness? Or simply distractedness? Days would go by without a word from him and then, from nowhere, he might call her at her desk and chat with her as amiably as an old school pal. More than once he surprised her by having read her column. "I'm amazed," he said, "that anybody even thinks about what their last meal on earth would be. If you're about to go to your reward, why bother eating?"

She asked him then what he would do in his final minutes. There was a pause, and then:

"Put me down as 'pray to God.' In less polite company, I'd be more truthful."

It was the first time he made her blush, and she realized that the telephone lines, rather than keeping them apart, produced a deeper kind of intimacy. His voice, shorn of a body, had a way of insinuating itself into her ear, and if she closed her eyes, she could summon the body, too: leaning back in his swivel chair, his lips forever flirting with a smile.

The calls grew longer: two minutes, four. Once they were interrupted on his end by a series of pulsing alarms.

"Time to vote," she suggested.

"I guess."

"So you have to go."

"I guess."

Yet he stayed, even through the second round of pulses, leaving her to wonder if politics really was his vocation. If anything, his tendency was to tug toward the personal. One afternoon, he began unaccountably speaking of a dog he'd run across in Germany.

"Dachshund puppy. We found him somewhere between Munich and Nuremberg, and we named him Dunker. He was supposed to be a present for a girl back home, but we both grew so attached to him that we were trying to figure out how to smuggle him across the English Channel. But then, wouldn't you know it, my allergies kicked in. I couldn't breathe, my face got puffy. Fever, hives. By the time we reached the Hague, we knew we'd have to find him a new family, so we found this couple sitting out by the Noordeinde Palace, and thank God, they spoke English and they were ready to step up. So Dunker went off with them, and we stood there waving goodbye, and that was—God, fifteen years ago, before the war, and I still find myself thinking about him, isn't that funny?"

"No, it's sweet," she said, and waited a few seconds before inquiring who the other half of that *we* was.

"Oh," he answered. "Lem."

Just the barest syllable, with no further explanation, not even a gender, but it was followed by:

"You'll meet him."

Thus, weeks before she'd laid eyes on me, I had become in Jackie's mind a milepost of sorts. For it seemed to her that if a man was prepared to introduce a girl to his friend, he had begun thinking of her in a new and more serious light. Yet if this was the case, he had yet to share it with her, and in the absence of any other sign, she began, in her own indirect way, angling to meet Lem.

"What does he do for a living?" she asked.

"Advertising."

"Does he have a wife?"

"God, no. Who'd marry that chump?"

"Maybe he'd like to meet us after work sometime."

"Ehh. He lives in Baltimore."

She persisted nonetheless, spacing her inquiries at intervals wide enough to avoid suspicion and assembling in the process a piecemeal portrait. A big, bespectacled guy who'd been pals with the Congressman since the third form of Choate and had somewhere along the line been drawn into the wider Kennedy bosom so that no family holiday could be considered complete without him and no party could really get under sail until his high-pitched cackle came sailing across the room. *Lem's here!*

"I kid him all the time," said the Congressman, "but he's the gayest soul I know."

Would he be gay for her, too? Jackie wondered. The

longer he remained offstage, the more significant he became.
So clearly was he fixed in her sights that perhaps she failed
to see the obstructions she had already cleared, and it was
during one of their irregular late-afternoon conversations,
the Congressman, casting about for something to say, said:

"Could you stand meeting family?"

The word came welling up at her.

"Family? Sorry, you don't mean your parents?"

There was a soft chuckle.

"I like you too much to do that to you. I was thinking
further down the tree. Bobby, let's say. Would that be all
right with you?"

"Uh, sure."

"I'll get back to you with a date."

SHE REMEMBERED READING in Emily Post that men were
frightened by presumption in women, even more so if they
had yet to declare themselves. Now, more than ever, was the
time to play cool. So, when presented with a possible date in
March, she took a certain amount of time in responding—
went so far as to invent a conflict that she let fall away—and
in the weeks leading up to the event, she confined herself to
cheerful practicalities. St. Patrick's Day weekend, she wondered. Should she wear green? No, that was "stage-Irish."
Should she just wear something nice? Whatever she liked.

The problem, she soon discovered, was less what to wear
than how to be. Had she posed the dilemma to her mother,
it would have become, with terrifying swiftness, how to succeed. Mrs. Auchincloss would have gazed upon the whole

ordeal with such a dreadful clarity that the only options left would have been winning or losing.

And what, in the context, did that even mean? The Congressman had taken her to dinner half a dozen times, had called her perhaps a dozen more—on his schedule, never hers. Suppose now she were to meet this family of his, do her pretty little dance, and suppose they had the poor taste to dislike her. What would *that* mean? All she could say was that she had come to depend on the sound of his voice, the rhythm of his conversation, the way he alternated between astringent doses of teasing and the barest dab of honey. The buzzing he produced in her skin. Take that away—drag it into the light of a St. Patrick's Day Massacre at Bobby and Ethel's—what would be left? Just the indelible feeling of having lost something.

On the Saturday in question, seeking distraction, she drew out two sheets of smooth Bristol and wrenched open the window, straining to find something she could sketch, but the river wouldn't stay still. Two hours before the Congressman was due to arrive, she pulled up her stockings and slipped on a lavender linen dress, bare about the shoulders, applied the Chateau Krigler 12 behind her ear and along her collarbone, then wrapped herself in a shawl. She didn't bother saying goodbye, and as she waited outside, she smoked six Pall Malls in quick succession, mashing them into the gravel drive just as the beams from the Congressman's Crestline came scything through the darkness.

The car paused. A bearish figure extricated itself from the front seat. Lem, she soon discovered, though in the darkness of the car's interior, he registered mostly as a voice, high and elfin. Jackie had nearly forgotten he was there until they were crossing Chain Bridge and, for want of anything else to say, she asked the Congressman what color his car was. It was then that Lem piped up with "pomegranate."

NINE

*B*obby, if we're being technical, was the first Kennedy family member to greet her that night, and I've always considered it an unfortunate accident of timing that the second was Bobby's wife, who, if we're to remain technical, wasn't a Kennedy at all but a Skakel, a rawer, scrappier thing. Ethel in those days was devout as a nun, combative as a Cape buffalo, not above swiping an older sister's boyfriend (which was how she came to be a Kennedy in the first place), and then, having smuggled her way into the compound, quicker than anyone to bar the gate. I once called her "more Kennedy than thou," and she glowed as if I'd set a tiara on her head. The night she hosted Jackie, she strolled up to me after dinner and said in a voice she believed to be a murmur:

"She's got big feet."

I confessed I hadn't noticed.

"Big hands, too."

I hadn't noticed those, either, and when I made mention of Miss Bouvier's slender hips, Ethel blocked it like a fullback. "Can't imagine them popping out kids, can you?"

She was vain on the subject. She had already birthed one child—another in the oven—nine *more* waiting to be thrust into a godless world, as she surely knew. Ethel's ovaries could have populated whole nations, and even at this young age, she was dressing like a matriarch—nautical blouses and lily-of-the-valley perfume—*walking* like one, too, with the fetus of Joe the Third pushing her back on her heels. Imagine her, then, having to watch Jack's date swan in on a cloud of chiffon, erect as a centaur. It had to gall a little. Or a lot, if you go by how often she called the interloper "Jack-*leen.*"

"That's not her name," Bobby pointed out.

"Oh," answered Ethel, "I just thought since it rhymes with *queen.*" And burst into her usual scream of laughter.

She'd sensed the thing that set Miss Bouvier apart, which was less a matter of carriage than mystery. With every jangle of bracelet, Jackie declared herself *other*. It was, when I think about it, an exoticized version of how Jack greeted the world, and, like Jack, she was both half-conscious of and wholly dependent on her effects. The same pipsqueak voice that was impossible to hear in an open convertible became the wellspring of her charm in a living room. You had to lean *in* if you had any hope of hearing, and once you'd done that, you were drawn into the most private of conspiracies.

When it came to after-dinner games, Ethel was particularly fond of Categories and no more willing to cede ground here than anywhere else. The game actually stopped for three minutes because she insisted that Tung was Mao's *first* name. Like many indifferent students, she stockpiled facts like a quiz-show contestant, and she wrote down her answers before anybody else and then sat with glittering eyes, waiting for the egg timer to wind down.

"You *do* write slow," she told Jackie. "It doesn't have to be pretty, honey."

Well, you don't compete on the Long Island equestrienne circuit and rack up national championships by the time you're eleven without developing a robust competitive instinct yourself, so Jackie didn't set her pencil down until she'd filled every category, and when Ethel challenged her on the word *okapi*—to be specific, said, "What the hell's an okapi?"— Jackie answered, dry as you like: "It's a giraffe native to the Congo." Light pause. "I can fetch a dictionary." Lighter pause. "If you've got one."

By now, she was drinking pretty fluently, one sloe gin fizz after another. The effect, though, was exclusively in her eyes, which began to soften, then harden. She just about made it through round five before asking where the ladies' room was.

"This ain't a restaurant," said Ethel. "The *bathroom*'s around the corner."

"Everything all right?" Jack called (not moving an inch).

"Oh, yes . . ."

The game was held on her account for five minutes. Further than that the hostess would not venture.

"Gee whiz, let's play without her."

"Maybe she's ill," I said.

"She's fine."

But I had glimpsed a note of light affliction in her face as it flashed past, and I thought again of that girl sitting alone in the headlights of Jack's car. "Maybe I should just check on her," I suggested.

Ethel was about to retort, but Jack gave me a silent nod.

The bathroom was empty, and after poking my head into the kitchen and the pantry, I found her on the back patio, sitting on a garden wall beneath a cedar of Lebanon. It was the first time I'd seen her with a cigarette.

"You know you can do that inside, if you want."

"I know," she said, flushing. "It's just a habit I picked up from my mother. She was always embarrassed to be seen with a cig, so that made *me* embarrassed, so now we hide it from each other and the whole world and—" She paused. "That must be about the silliest thing you've ever heard."

I said there were sillier. She nodded absently.

"That Ethel must have played a lot of field hockey," she said.

"Sharp elbows, you mean? When the umpire's not looking?"

"There is no umpire."

I felt a light twinge.

"She's just a little protective," I suggested.

"Of whom?"

"Well, the family."

"They're not even her family."

"They are *now*, they're the people she loves. Isn't that how families work?"

Her reply was to flick a hunk of ash onto Ethel's patio.

"Tell me about your first time," she said.

"My—"

"With *them*."

"The whole family, you mean?"

"I want to compare notes."

Smiling, I cradled my hands behind my head. "If you must know, they boiled me like a lobster."

She clapped her hand over her mouth, but a single laugh had already broken free.

"I do not lie," I said.

"I don't care if you're lying, I want to hear."

It was my very first weekend in Hyannis. Summer of '34, and I was sweating hard from being stomped into the tennis court—Pat was responsible—so I excused myself and ducked upstairs and stepped into the shower and, still a little flushed, reached for the cold-water faucet. Blame the plumbers who, without meaning to, had switched out cold with hot. The jet of scalding water met me like a fist. The next second, I was flat on my back, scrabbling for purchase in the claw-foot tub, listening to what sounded like a fire alarm—which, on closer inspection, proved to be my own voice, scaling higher. It was Mrs. Kennedy herself who came running, ears thrumming to an alien frequency. When she

whipped the curtain open, I hadn't even sufficient presence
of mind to cover my nakedness, but after she'd turned the
faucets off, I was able to thank her.

Here's the deal. If you sustain second-degree burns in
Hyannisport, you get a private room in Cape Cod Hospital.
Sustain them in the company of Kennedys, you get a running spigot of visitors, from Mr. Kennedy on down. Even
eight-year-old Bobby, writhing with shyness, was heard
to wish me a speedy recovery. I like to think now it was
their kindness that buttressed me through the dressings, the
redressings, the skin grafts, the applications of tannic acid.
In my more painful interludes, I imagined myself a war pilot
shot down over Bretagne, but if I were to be honest, in the
exact moment of scalding, I could only think I was the family's dinner.

And, if I'm to be honest, meeting them for the first time
was indeed like being dropped into a lobster pot but with
the crucial difference that, after the first shock of immer-
sion, you found the waters merely warm, not hot, and that
their secret plan was not to eat you but give you your own
corner of the pot, from which you would never be budged. I
don't know how much of this last part I was able to convey
because Jackie's first response was:

"They burned you alive."

"Well, they didn't mean to."

"That's what Joan of Arc said."

I smiled, hung my head a little. "I guess what I'm saying
is it's hard coming into any strange family."

"What do you do when you're not being a best friend?"

"I'm in advertising."

"One of those big New York firms?"

"Oh, no, no, no. The Emerson Drug Company of Baltimore."

"I don't know them."

"Yes, you do. Bromo-Seltzer."

She stared at me. "That's you?"

"Well, the ads are."

"But *everybody* knows Bromo-Seltzer. Why do you need to advertise it?"

"Because there's also Alka-Seltzer."

"Oh," she said. "I've always thought they were the same thing."

"That's why I have a job."

She rested her hand very lightly on my right wrist. "You're nice. Nicer than them."

"No, I'm just the friend."

"That's a nicer job than family."

"It's easier. Why, it's the easiest thing in the world, really."

Being Jack's friend, in particular, I wanted to say. As natural as rolling down a hill.

"You're much quieter with me," she said.

"Well, it's just the two of us and—I can adapt."

"I like you quiet. But I like you noisy, too."

"That's a relief."

"Would it be terrible," she asked, "if I told them I had a headache?"

"I won't stop you."

She gently laced her arm through mine, and together, we stood and walked toward the house. As we were opening the kitchen door, I leaned into her and whispered, "Bromo-Seltzer's great for headaches."

"Always on the clock," she whispered back.

TEN

To be fair, she did have a headache—that's what tribunals will do—though it had less to do with the hazing than the Congressman's silence through it all. She knew enough of romance novels to know that, when a heroine is being ill-treated, the hero will fling down his cravat and say, "I won't stand for this a second longer." He might pause on the brink of declaration, but it would only italicize the feelings he was at pains to suppress, and the heroine could turn a braver face to her oppressors.

By contrast, the Congressman sat the whole evening in the wing chair and said virtually nothing. Perhaps some of his imperviousness rubbed off on her because, having made the resolution to leave, she allowed nothing to dissuade her.

To her surprise, the Congressman rose at once and fetched her shawl and guided her to the car. It wasn't until he closed the door after her that she let her face go utterly slack and dropped her head against the headrest. The alcohol rushed through her in a fresh tide, and the air around her seemed to flicker like hornets. She thought of asking him to put the top up, but the wind distracted from the motion inside. The closer they drew to Merrywood, the more clearly she could see their leave-taking. Vague promises to call again. *Work's awfully busy. Nation's business. No telling when I'll get sprung again.* She wanted none of it. If there was to be a death, she wished to be interred with no service.

Somewhere just south of Langley, she became perfectly persuaded that she would vomit. Envisioned it with such clarity that her mind nearly became an accomplice to the act, and she found herself pressing a hand against her eyes to drive the vision back.

"You all right?"

"Of course," she said.

The car took one last sickening swerve and relapsed into stillness. She peeled her fingers from her face, gazed out in wonder. Merrywood.

She glanced at her watch. Just a few minutes shy of ten.

The Congressman was already strolling around the car, guiding her to her feet. She felt a pleasantry froth on her lips—then felt, more distinctly, something circling her waist. He was drawing her toward him. For what purpose she had no way of knowing, she could only think: *What a strange way to break it off.*

The kiss lasted no more than a second. Next moment, they were staring at each other.

"Good night," he said.

"Good night." She took a backward step in the gravel. "Good night, Jack."

IT WASN'T THE first time she'd addressed him by his first name—he'd encouraged that from the start. It was merely the first time she felt herself claiming it. A couple of hours later, she was writing it across a sheet of stationery—JACK—then watching as her hand, seerlike, appended the letters I and E. How suggestively they'd been entwined all along.

She lay in bed with the lights off, swallowing down coffee and smoking and trying to still her brain, her stomach, everything that kept her from isolating the graze of lip, the soft pressure of his chest through his coat. Had she passed whatever test lay embedded in that dreadful evening? What would be the consequences? If she could have piled them in columns, she would have brightened at the thought of more Lem, shuddered at the prospect of more family, but there was a larger consequence that her brain kept groping toward. He would be calling her again, at some to-be-determined point in the near future. Once more, his voice would buzz in her ear, and with that the buzzing in her brain became only an extension of him.

IN FACT, HE called two days later, pretending in a not-very-disguised voice to be an anonymous State Department informant.

"Oh, sir, I'm sorry," she said, "but I should probably refer you to one of my reporter colleagues. I'm just a columnist."

"Communist?"

"No, sir, *columnist*. You may have read my work."

"I don't read fifth columnists, thank you very much. I report them is what I do."

On it went, his voice shedding its last layer of pretense as the old gibing rhythm returned. They had picked up exactly where they'd left off, and this was both a comfort and a disquiet, for it seemed to her that the one-second interval on the gravel drive should have lofted them to some new level, where a man addresses his girl in changed tones. But all he said in conclusion was:

"Off to make sausage."

HE CALLED AGAIN two days later. Again the following Monday, again the following Friday. If she were to map each call against the next, the pattern would scarcely have deviated. A slighting reference to whatever congressional business he had just sloughed off. An item from that day's newspapers. From there, her latest column. "Well now," he'd say, "if *I* found out I'd married a Soviet agent, I'd just get Cardinal Spellman to annul it . . . Geez, beauty operators and barbers are *completely* entitled to tips, just not from me." One afternoon he phoned her in a higher degree of merriment, having read a *Times-Herald* article that likened Washington bachelors to barnacles.

"It says here that by virtue of being the so-called 'hunted sex,' we have caused outbreaks of sexual promiscuity and increased requests for marriage counseling. I mean to tell you I had no idea. I thought I was just helping out."

"It's not your fault you own a dinner jacket," she assured him.

In the brief suspension that followed, she wondered if this was a roundabout way of asking her out again. Instead, he let out a trailing sigh and signed off with "The salt mines are calling."

She knew she should be grateful for a great man's attention, but it seemed to her that every joke, every tangent was an attempt to deny her clarity. What was she to him? He to her? At times, his ironic remove was such a goad that she would sit listening in a kind of coiled fury, the blood pulsing so loudly in her wrists and temples that she imagined it to be audible on the other side of the newsroom. One afternoon she had just hung up the phone with him when a city editor sidled over to her and said, "Tell your mother to stop calling at work." She assumed at first he was joking. Then she thought back to the just-concluded conversation and realized that Jack could have had the same one, word for word, with any of the men in the newsroom.

A more experienced or confident woman might have cut the calls short or declined to take them at all—withdrawn just far enough—and it was in these moments, more than ever, that she wished for a confidant. Her mother, of course, wasn't to be trusted. Neither, after some thought, was her father or sister. With a twinge of surprise, she found her thoughts cohering around Lem.

Hadn't he been exceptionally kind to her at Bobby and Ethel's? Wasn't he uniquely qualified to explain Kennedy mating rituals? Maybe he might volunteer to be her guide into this strange new land.

So she began, as before, introducing his name into the conversations. "I saw a Bromo-Seltzer commercial last night and thought of Lem . . ." "Oh, hey, does Lem know how to dance? They're looking for men at the Dancing Class . . ." "Does Lem wear fedoras? Hughdie's got some he's never worn, and they need a home." Each time Jack answered neutrally, and she had no notion she was making any headway until one afternoon, he replied, in a tone of mild peevishness:

"If you want to date Lem, why don't you just say so?"

So, without too much effort, he'd been prodded into mock-jealousy, which was near to the real thing, and for the first time in their acquaintance, he had used the infinitive *to date*. Baby steps.

"Don't be that way," she teased. "Lem isn't the dating kind, is he? But he's a perfect dear, and you can tell him I said so."

ELEVEN

I feel for this Jackie—*my* Jackie—I really do. She was waiting, and who could blame her, for the kind of declaration that makes a girl have a hard discussion with her mother. Something like, *I know he's shanty Irish but he's a war hero and there's loads of money and possibility and have you seen him?*

She was in no position to know that hard discussions were already beginning around her. I was party to one of them. The morning after the Bobby-Ethel affair, I was heading back to Baltimore, and Jack took the unusual step of driving me to Union Station. We had just about slipped free of Georgetown's grid when he said, in a voice of enigmatic blankness:

"Well?"

"Well, what?"

"What do you think of Our Miss Bouvier?"

"Oh," I said, "it's *our* Miss Bouvier? In that case, we find her dear."

"Dear . . . "

"I mean in a way that's opposed to . . . what you . . . customarily go for . . . "

"That was tortured."

"Well, don't blame *me*, you never ask me about your girls. I mean, why would you when they're all gone by cock's crow?"

"You never told me my cock was crowing."

In spite of myself, I laughed. And then, irritated at giving him the satisfaction, I stared out the window the rest of the way. It was when I was climbing out of the car that he said:

"We're in a different era, Lem."

THE PHRASING WAS just vague enough to make me think he was referring to McCarthy. Only because McCarthy was on everybody's mind in those days (fifth columnists, indeed), and because he and Jack were the weirdest sort of pals. But no, there was something else afoot, and the fact that Jackie and I were both so slow to pick up on it speaks to the fact that neither of us was a political creature. Which is why, in the spring of '52, we were apparently the last people in the Western Hemisphere to grasp that Jack had his eyes on Henry Cabot Lodge Junior's Senate seat.

Lodge had his eyes on it, too. Like Jack, he had a handsome face and a glittering war record; unlike Jack, he had a family membership in the Boston Tennis & Racquet Club and a name that had been around since the Puritans. The very shape of his mouth was a reproach. On top of that, he'd taken on pretty much every mick who'd been thrown at him—Curley, Walsh, Casey—without a break in his stride, and there was no reason he wouldn't do to Jack what his papa had done to Jack's grandpa back in 1916. Take it from me: Brahmins don't give up their possessions easily because heaven wouldn't care for it. *The Lowells talk only to Cabots, and the Cabots talk only to God.*

"I bet I'm a better lay," said Jack one night, over a bottle of Scotch in his office.

"No doubt that's true," I said.

"Do you think Lodge screws with his socks on?"

I said probably, yes, though I can't, for the life of me, recall a time when I've screwed with my socks off. Who's noticing?

"I'm telling you now," said Jack. "We'll sweep the whole goddamn state from Boston to Stockbridge."

It's funny, when he first got into politics, it seemed to me he was just biding his time. I figured he'd hold out until the next bright thing caught his eye. A motion-picture studio, like his dad, or a major-league franchise. Maybe he'd do nothing at all—that's what I would have done in his place. So it caught me off guard, I admit, to see him training his sights higher, and I couldn't help feeling a little displaced, for it was one thing to run a startup campaign with old ladies and one-armed vets in Cambridge (as I'd done for his first House campaign); it was another to wage a statewide war and be hectored by every concave-chested, chain-smoking, rosary-clutching pol in Massachusetts. Even if I'd wanted to help, I was living in Baltimore with my mother, on the rung that lies just above genteel poverty, and I was making a career that involved paying the closest possible attention to the market share of Bromo-Seltzer and going to bed with those numbers dancing in my brain like Dia de Muertos skulls.

God knows Jack wasn't begging me to sign up. In fact, I heard nothing at all from him for a spell. Then, sometime in April, he called up to say: "I need you to take Jackie to the National Gallery."

By now enough time had elapsed that the name didn't quite register.

"Miss Bouvier," he said.

To be clear, I hadn't forgotten her. I'd simply ceased to associate her with Jack, for the simple reason that she was most alive to me during that brief tête-à-tête in Bobby and Ethel's backyard.

"When is this to happen?" I asked.

"Saturday. I promised her we'd go but now I have to unpromise."

"Because . . ."

"The Franklin County selectmen are meeting in Springfield."

I smothered my laugh. "What about Sunday?"

"Red Cross drive in Fall River."

"Friday, then. The House is always off on Friday."

"B'nai B'rith in Haverhill. You know, you'd be much better company, anyway. I told her this shit is right up your alley."

"*This shit?*"

"I believe I said, 'Lem is a perfect savant when it comes to the French masters.'"

"Italian, but . . ."

"The point is when I mentioned your name, she said, *Ooh*. Just like that. It escaped her. *Ooh, he's nice.* Clearly she doesn't know you."

This is what comes, I thought, from taking pity on a girl who wanders away from a game of Categories to have a furtive smoke.

"I wouldn't know what to say," I hedged.

"Start with hello. If you're feeling venturesome, ask how she is."

"What am I supposed to discuss?"

"What people do."

"What am I *not* supposed to discuss?"

"Christ, Lem, I know it's been years since you've been on a date, and I know it's because no girl who isn't blind or clinically insane would have you, but I figured you could be depended upon to look at pictures and make conversation for a couple of hours. A mop could do as much."

THIS IS SOMETHING Jack never got about me. An exhibitionist is not necessarily an extrovert. I'll give you an example. When I strolled down from Union Station to the National Gallery that Saturday, I found Jackie sitting at the top of the Mall-side steps, as still as when I first beheld her. At the sight of me, she smiled and gave a slow beauty-queen wave. That was all the impetus I needed to start strutting up those steps, knees pumping, arms flung wide—climbing my stairway to paradise. I could see the tourists staring; at least one child pointed and laughed. But having reached the top of the steps, I was suddenly at a loss. I was half an hour late, owing to the trains from Baltimore Penn. Even hello was a little beyond me. Jackie, bless her, said:

"My, how you move on that marble! I get as nervous as an old lady."

I offered her my arm, but once inside, she gently detached herself, and traveled from room to room, alone, in her crepe tunic dress, the exhibit brochure dangling unread by her side. If I'd been timing her, I might have said she lingered longer over the Vuillard and Matisse than the Renoir and Bonnard, but she meted out to each canvas a quantum of respectful attention, then moved on. She didn't need an escort, I remember thinking. She just needed someone to leave her alone.

That freed me, you might say, to wander on my own recognizance, and after passing through a couple of rooms, I paused before Monet's portrait of his wife, Camille. She was standing in a garden with another painter, name of Bazille, who wore a sack suit and a felted-wool bowler, and the wife had on a white cotton promenade dress with a postilion jacket, but what made it unusual for an Impressionist work was that the psychology was more interesting than the composition. Madame Monet gazes off into the middle ground—at a plane tree, a lark—but her companion has eyes only for her. You could almost hear his voice in her ear.

"They look like lovers," said Jackie.

She had sneaked up behind me.

"They're hiding something," I said. "That's for damn sure."

"Imagine if they were having an affair, and Monet knew all about it and painted them anyway. All but captured them in the act."

"And they let him do it! Say, do you believe in prescience?"

"I once had a dog who was prescient."

"A dog?"

"He'd always run out of the room exactly two minutes before Mummy was about to blow up."

"Like those dogs who leave town before earthquakes."

"Exactly!"

"Well, the reason I bring up the subject is Madame Monet there—she's going to die before too long. Cancer. And Bazille, he'll be dead in a few years, too, thanks to the Franco-Prussian War. So when I look at them together like this . . ."

"Ah." I felt her gasp feathering my neck. "They're not philandering, they're *commiserating*."

"About what's coming, yes."

"Poor things. And all that beautiful dappling . . . it's just mortality, isn't it? Closing around them."

"Well, that's one idea anyway."

Frowning, she studied the canvas a while longer. "They can still be lovers, too, can't they?"

"Just doomed ones."

"The best kind," she said. "Maybe we should get a drink now."

In those days, there were precious few taverns on

Constitution Avenue, so, at Jackie's suggestion, we took a cab to La Salle du Bois at the corner of Eighteenth and M. A swanker place than I usually frequented, but, at four in the afternoon, the silver fox coats were still a few hours off, and we had the place all to ourselves except for a bartender in a white duck uniform. I ordered a scorpion, she ordered a grasshopper, and we sat there in the parchment-shaded glow of wall lamps.

"They've got the best crêpes suzette," said Jackie, but when I suggested we order some, she said, "What, so I can be fatter? No, thank you."

There was, of course, nothing remotely fat about Miss Bouvier, but that commonplace did call into focus the contradictory elements of her. Male and female, you might say, warring in the same way Jackie's parents had. Willowy arms barging out into large and capable hands . . . a stem of a neck poking out from rangy shoulders . . . and then the flattened, almost boxer-like profile of her nose, as if someone had brought a fist to it in utero. It was a lot to reconcile, and it's possible I was staring at her too hard.

"Where did you learn all that stuff?" she asked.

"What?"

"Bazille and Mrs. Monet."

"Oh . . . my misspent youth, I guess. I was a no-good art and architecture major."

"I won't hold that against you. Who'd you study?"

"Tintoretto."

Her smile was encouraging enough, the rum persuasive enough, to go further.

"If you want to know," I said, "I've always believed he was the first Impressionist."

"Three centuries ahead of schedule?"

"Damn straight. Look at any of his canvases, what's he doing? Exactly what the Impressionists were doing. Grabbing the light, the *moment*, before it gets away. He doesn't scrape down his paint to make it look presentable, he doesn't have the time. Have you seen *Il Paradiso* in the Doge's Palace?"

"It's vast."

"And *intimate*. Every square inch pouring out of him as you watch. He's just the poor fool trying to capture it all."

A slow smile. "You're an admirer."

"Oh, he was the greatest of the Venetians."

"Not Titian?"

"I guess, if you like your technique *perfect* and harmonious and . . . *regular*. If you like your artists all *Hellenic* . . . "

"What's Tintoretto?"

"Hebraic. Spirit over form. He's looking for the spot where spirit is *erupting* through flesh, and all he can do is try to get it on canvas, and it's the *only* thing worth doing, really, because—" I stopped, half defeated. "Because why else live, I was going to say."

She looked at me with a new intentness.

"Do you ever talk like this with Jack?"

"Oh, he'd have no interest. I mean, we went to Venice when we were college kids. San Marco's, the Bridge of Sighs, the whole nine yards. And Jack was a good sport the whole way, *grateful* to be there, no question."

"But . . . "

"Well, he went at it the way normal people do, that's all."

"You mean he wouldn't stand gawping in the Scuola Grande."

"Or the Chiesa della Madonna. He'd just get his fill and wait for me outside. Which is how most humans operate, I recognize."

"Not you, though."

"Well, that was then. Now I'm just another working slob."

She smiled. "It's still nice to look at pretty pictures."

I drew out a packet of Pall Malls, offered her one, which, upon reflection, she took.

"Jack told me you were in the war," she said.

"Well, I *tried*. I couldn't get into the service because of my eyesight, so Mr. Kennedy pulled strings and got me in the Ambulance Corps. Don't you love how the Army thinks? *Blind as a mole. Let's give him wounded soldiers to ferry to safety.* After a couple of years, the Navy drastically lowered its standards, so in I went. Course I wasn't a *hero* or anything. Nothing like Jack."

"You keep saying all the ways you're not like Jack."

"Well, there are many, as you can probably perceive. I've been on enough double dates to know that."

She quirked her brow. "I guess that's just how best friends work."

"Why, sure. I bet when you talk about *your* best friend, you—"

"I don't have one."

"There's a sister," I suggested. "Or a brother."

She thought.

"My stepbrother was the first boy I ever kissed. But that's not what you meant."

"Well."

"I think I need training in this friend business."

"Okay."

"And, Lem, let me tell you, I'm a quick learner, ask anybody. And I take perfect notes, and you can invoice me every month."

Even now, all these years later, I'm not sure how serious she was. Whenever I looked at her, levity and solemnity lay entwined, and if her eyes were widening farther than I would have thought possible, it might have been the crème de menthe.

"You're in luck," I said, stubbing out my cigarette. "After a couple of drinks, I do pretty much anything for free."

"That was my hope."

TWELVE

On the train ride back to Baltimore, I may have flashed back to an exchange or two or wondered what it would be like to have a friend who unfurled the words *Scuola Grande* when you brought up the subject of Venice. And it's true that, over dinner that night, Mother asked me what I was smiling about, and I didn't realize I was smiling.

It's true, too, that I was sort of hoping Jack would call to ask me how it had gone only so I could revisit it in the telling. But, of course, he was now in full politicking flight, and I had seen enough of campaigns to know they had their own minute-to-minute exigency. God help whatever affair of the heart was trying to break through the Chamber of Commerce luncheon or the VFW picnic.

I don't think it's too much to add that I was also distracted by my own career. Emerson Drug was just the latest stage in a journey that had progressed from passing out free samples of Juicy Fruit to selling Coca-Cola to New Jersey drugstores to finding feet for General Shoe of Nashville. Anyone who's hiked that long is still hiking, and that lends itself to ragged days and long nights and tense moments. You can't imagine, for example, how much artifice goes into a fifteen-second spot at the eight-minute mark of *Howdy Doody*. That's why, once I'd resubmerged myself in my Baltimore life, my afternoon with Jackie began to recede a bit—life was rolling back over it like a breaker. So when Jack called a couple of weeks later and asked if I'd come down to Washington for drinks—that very night—I was only put out at the timing.

"You want me to drop everything," I said. "On a Wednesday night."

I did, of course, pliable beast. We met at Longchamps, a knockoff of a New York restaurant chain that was already a little knocked off itself. Simulated-leather banquettes, plastic-topped tables. The kind of place that served bowls of glazed nuts. Jack was late, as usual, and by the time he staggered in, necktie listing eastward, I'd already staked out a corner booth as unlit as a confessional. Even in the shadows, I could make out the dark smears under his eyes.

"This is the Happy Warrior," he said, lowering himself as if by crane onto the banquette. "This is he."

It was the usual discursive chatter: Stalin and some starlet Jack was hot for after seeing her in *Bird of Paradise* and what she would look like without a sarong, and I was distracted enough that my eyes drifted over to a pair of young men, in salt-and-pepper suits, facing each other across the table. One of them kept taking off his steel-rimmed spectacles and rubbing them on his tie, and I had to fight off the strangest urge to wander over.

"Do you still find Miss Bouvier dear?" asked Jack.

"Oh, well . . . better than that. No, she's charming."

"She's been promoted, then."

"Two or three pay grades."

"I'm glad to hear it. Unaccountably, she liked you, too."

I leaned back in the booth, studied him for a second.

"So that's why you dragged me here? To uncover my thoughts about Miss Bouvier? We could have settled that in a ten-second phone call."

"There are no ten-second phone calls with you. Any other thoughts besides charming?"

"Um. Elegant."

"Okay."

"Quick on the draw."

"Fine."

I thought for a bit more. "Lonely."

"Ah, yes. No one to talk to but the cook and the chauffeur and the ghosts of the ancestral dead. Listen now, LeMoyne. Given that you seem to approve of our Miss Bouvier, I think it would be a gesture of kindness—a humanitarian act, if you will—for you to draw a little closer."

I took a sip of my Manhattan. "What does that mean, *draw closer*?"

"In plain English, be her friend."

"There are a million people her own age who could do that."

"But how many of them do I know?"

My finger sketched a circuit of the cork coaster. Then another circuit.

"So is it a *friend* you want me to be, Jack?"

"What else?"

"A secret agent."

"I'm shocked you would suggest anything so sinister. This is simply a case of me being gone a lot, and what's so wrong with having somebody I *trust*—somebody I know won't be making any moves because he's hopeless with ladies—checking in with her now and again. Keeping my name in the conversation. Reminding her I'm not a total loser if it comes to that."

"Why would she need reminding?"

"Well, obviously, she wouldn't, but we want her to feel like she can stay the course, Lem."

"*What* course? What are we even talking about?"

Jack signaled the bartender for two more Manhattans.

"You're putting up a lot of resistance," he said, "to a very simple request."

"But you've never made it before. Back at Choate, did you ever leave me alone with Olive Cawley so she and I could get acquainted? Of course not. Back during the war, did you ask me to sweet-talk Inga Whoever-She-Was? You didn't want me within miles."

"I was only thinking of you. She was a suspected Nazi."

"And what about Betsy Finkenstadt? And that blonde, the Malcolm girl? The one who said she eloped with you."

"She didn't."

"Of course not, nobody ever got you that drunk, but you sure as hell never asked me to—God, take them to art galleries. Usually, the only time I ever speak to your girls is on their way to the cab."

"Just pretend the cab is a little farther away."

"What I'm asking, Jack—what I actually need to know—is what distinguishes Miss Bouvier from her predecessors."

He was quiet for a space. Then he reached into his pockets for loose change.

"Let me enumerate her assets," he said, sliding a penny in my direction. "She comes from a good family."

"Oh, that."

A nickel came toward me. "Arthur Krock speaks highly of her."

"I'm sure he does the same of Madame Chiang Kai-Shek."

A quarter. "She's Catholic."

"From Newport?"

"They let us in now and then. My point, really, is there's nothing *not* to like."

"That's a double negative but . . ."

"A *positive*, arithmetically speaking. And with *that*," he said, sliding one more quarter forward, "I believe I've answered your question."

He hadn't, of course. I waited until the next round of drinks had arrived, then gave mine a few tight swallows.

"Shall I walk you through *my* thoughts?" I said, sliding his coins back to him, one by one. "You are a contented bachelor. Nobody has ever been contenteder."

"True."

"You've never in your life wanted to be married. You always used to say, it's not the ball and chain—"

"It's the chain on the balls, yeah."

"You said those were words to live by."

"They are until they aren't."

"So, at the risk of introducing the subject of ethics to a Boston pol . . ."

"Yes."

"There's no point leading on *any* girl when you have no intention of . . ."

The word wouldn't even climb to my lips. *Marriage.* As forbidden as *Yahweh* to the Hebrews. And as if to expel even the thought of it, Jack reclined against the banquette, gave his back the tiniest of stretches, and said:

"There are higher calculations going on here, LeMoyne."

"Which you can't divulge."

"Which I must not divulge."

"Because my poor brain wouldn't."

He stared at the coins on the table, then swept them back into his pocket. "I don't have any more cash on me, can you cover the drinks?"

In this respect, I guess, the rich really are different from you and me. Jack was always pestering you to pay for his lunch, tide him over with a loan he'd never pay back. If you were one of his staffers, you might be out of pocket ten bucks by the end of the week with no hope of reimbursement.

"Look," I said. "If you're going to send me on a secret mission, I need to know who my spymaster is."

"Christ, Lem."

"Is it you? Is it the boss man in Hyannis? Who am I working for? To what end?"

He held his tumbler in his palm, gave it a light oenophile swirl, then drained it in one pass.

"Dad thinks I can't get elected if I don't have a wife."

"With all due respect, he's crazy. You've been elected three times."

"He doesn't mean the House."

"There are bachelor senators."

"He doesn't mean the Senate, either."

THIRTEEN

*I*t's hard, I know, for today's younger folks (my friend Raul, for example) to understand how American politics used to work. They've seen a Mephistophelean Quaker, a lusting-in-his-heart peanut farmer, the husband of a divorced ex-dancer, and an actual divorcé stroll into the Oval Office, all without much fuss. *How difficult can it be?* Thirty years ago, it was nothing but difficult, and the White House was the last thing an Irish Catholic boy could aspire to. If your people had grubbed potatoes from the soil, if one grandfather was a saloon keeper and the other a pol who sang "Sweet Adeline" and made time with a cigarette girl named Tootles, there were only so many rungs on your ladder.

That history lesson never quite took with Mr. Kennedy. Tell him he couldn't go to Boston Latin or Harvard, he went anyway. Blackball him from a country club, he made his own, exclusive to Kennedys. Tell him he couldn't run for the land's highest office, he went after it anyway. Deny him the office on the basis of fascist sympathies, he passed on the dream to his firstborn son. Kill off that son in the war he himself never stopped opposing, he passed it on to the son who lived.

As to what *that* son wanted, well, that's where I always ran aground with Jack, trying to imagine his stake in anything, beyond the almost grudging spectatorial interest he took in watching it unfurl. My truest, deepest impressions of him were formed at prep school, and *that* boy couldn't have given a shit about being respected or popular or anything. The one title he coveted, oddly, was Most Likely to Succeed, and strictly to thumb his nose at the headmaster, and he only won because he bought the votes. Growing up in Joe Junior's shadow gave him—well, the room, I guess—to compete in the stuff that didn't much matter and to take himself out of the competition that did, if only to show how little it mattered to *him*.

So it was always surprising to learn that something, or someone, mattered. A few nights after I saw him in Washington, for instance, he phoned me up and said, "Billings, do you still fit into your suit? Or have you gotten too fat on Mama's home cooking?"

"The last time my mother cooked was when yours did."

"So never. Listen, Jackie wants to go to a fashion show next Sunday. The—uh . . ." He paused, as if he were translating from Aramaic. "The *Elizabeth Arden* collection."

"That's not fashion, you scurvy bastard, that's cosmetics."

"It's Greek."

"And you're out of town, naturally."

"Even if I weren't out of town, I'd be out of town."

"Why does she need an escort?"

"Apparently, she doesn't want people to know she's taking notes."

"Why is she taking notes?"

"I have no idea."

I told him there had to be somebody a hell of a lot closer who could step into this breach. Billy Sutton, maybe or Dave Powers . . .

"Dave's from *Charlestown*, Lem. And you seriously want Billy Sutton rubbing against Northwest matrons? Anyway, I told her you'd do it. Said you'd dress up nice and purty and be a perfect gentleman."

"Probably the only gentleman."

"Aw, Washington's full of emasculated husbands. Just don't embarrass me."

IN FACT, ON that particular Sunday, the only men on view in the Shoreham Hotel's Blue Room were practitioners of the cosmetic arts. Otherwise, the crowd consisted of a hundred ladies in gray silk floral prints, cultured-pearl necklaces and cameo brooches. The hats were enormous, and there was a muff or two, for all that it was seventy degrees outside, and

enough L'Air du Temps perfume for all of France. In short,
it was a roomful of rock-ribbed Republicans gathered for
what the event's hostess, Mrs. Gladstone Williams, called
a "checkup from the neck up." For a good half hour, an
Elizabeth Arden clinician spoke of the benefits to the mature
complexion of foundation, rouge and powder, even as she
piped home the message that a happy and contented wife
was by her essence beautiful. The afternoon's high point
came when a stylist applied something called Italian Duet
lipstick (confusingly, a single column) to the pliant mouth of
a cosmetics model, who sat so still beneath her smock I felt I
was in an operating theater, and I was startled to see passing
signs of sentience: a blinking eye, a twitching finger.

Jackie sat to my right, taking methodical notes in a steno
pad. I can see now this was her way of keeping in touch
with her vocation, but at the time, I'm afraid, I was just
wondering how to break it to Jack that this girl of his cared
deeply about the merits of Love That Red versus Bachelor's
Carnation. I must have checked my watch four or five times
before Mrs. Gladstone Williams, smiling like an expensive
Persian cat, strolled back to the front of the room.

"Ladies and gentlemen, what a stimulating afternoon it's
been! And what a treat we have in store for you. Won't you
please welcome our special guest *chanteuse*?"

Well, this was Washington in 1952, so the young woman
who came sailing out from the wings in a velvet off-the-
shoulder gown, the ash-blonde who had stuck a gardenia
in her hair and was beaming like a Con Ed plant, required
no introduction. Miss Margaret Truman. Who, in those

days, carried a certain whiff of danger, entirely owing to her father, who had once threatened to castrate a critic for panning her concert. It seemed wholly possible that a White House minion was even now scanning the room, taking down every grimace, so I was steeling myself but good when the accompanist rolled out the opening chords of "Believe Me If All Those Endearing Young Charms."

In the interests of charity, I should say she wasn't as bad as her press clippings suggested. A smallish but clear soprano, reaching for the melody line and *holding on*, as if it were a pony's mane. What impressed me most was the unaffected joy she took in performing, and it made me a little sad that, after playing venues like Constitution Hall, Miss Margaret Truman should now be pouring her effulgence on a blue-hair salvation show. Now, I can't say exactly when that went from being sad to funny, but somewhere in the middle of the second verse, I leaned into Jackie and muttered: "Where's she singing tomorrow? A nail salon?"

Well, as anybody will tell you, I can't really do anything under my breath. I heard a hiss like wet logs as the two august ladies in front of me angled their heads toward me. To my right, Jackie gave her head a rough shake and slipped away.

I sat for a moment—pinned, you might say, by Jack's admonition. *Just don't embarrass me.* In the next second, I was stumbling after her, tripping on folding chairs and doing passing violence to a straw hat and feeling the entire ill will of the Truman administration piling upon me as I left the Blue Room behind. I swung my head toward each end of the hallway and found her, at last, crouched by an Art Deco cigarette urn, her shoulders shaking. I was already composing my apologies, so you'll have to imagine my surprise when she lifted her face to mine and, after a quick survey of the hallway, burst into the purest form of laughter. Not her usual coo but something richer and freer.

"Oh, my God, Lem. Oh, dear God. I was thinking the same thing. And the—" The next wave of laughter caught her with such force I thought she might topple. *"The gardenia!"*

FOURTEEN

I wish I could say we were brought together by some-thing higher-minded than church giggles, but what's more adhesive? On one of our Sunday afternoons, we went to see a rotten Loretta Young picture called *Paula*. We sat in the back row of the Ambassador Theatre, which was empty as only a 1,700-seat house could be, and started laughing from the moment Loretta Young clocked some kid with her car. It was funny, you see, because the triangular pendant she was wearing in that instant had such a rageful key light fixed on it you'd have thought she was a locomotive comin' round the bend. Well, in the picture, Loretta drives on, but she gets to feeling guilty, and when she learns the kid can't speak anymore, she invites him into her home and gives him speech therapy and the love he's never had, and you know it's just a matter of time before he realizes she's the one that clocked him, *but how will he figure it out?* Jackie was betting on straight-up confession. Me, I had my money on that radioactive pendant, and sure enough, the boy sees it, and it's the *one thing* he remembers from that terrible night, and I gave a shout of triumph that echoed all the way out to Eighteenth Street, and Jackie was laughing all the harder because she believed that Loretta Young's wig, under the stress of the moment, had skewed a half-inch west, and I said no, it was just a little tousled from despair, and this is how two shameless hours slip away, ladies and gentlemen, without your even knowing.

Now, I don't want you to think we were always slumming. One weekend, we went to see lithographs by Toulouse-Lautrec. Another time, it was Eskimo art at the Whyte Gallery and Peruvian tapestries at the Textile Museum. The National had just reopened, so we caught Ethel Merman in *Call Me Madam* and then, a few weeks later, Carol Channing in *Gentlemen Prefer Blondes*. Washington in those days was a sleepier, more palmetto kind of place, but you could still stumble across jazz singers at Loew's Capitol or the National Guard Armory, and there was a National Ballet, though I can't recall what it was doing, and once, operating merely on rumor, we found a concert version of *The Magic Flute* in the bowels of the Agriculture Department.

Rather gradually and then rather completely, Sunday afternoons became our time. We never exactly defined them that way—certainly we never consulted Jack—but in the act of dropping me off at Union Station, Jackie might suggest something for the following Sunday, or I might suggest something back, and by the time I'd hopped on the train, we would already have set the coordinates. It had to fall somewhere in the District of Columbia—no Mount Vernon tours, no Skyline Drive excursions—and we had an informal rule that, if either of us got second thoughts over the course of the week, we'd phone with a definite alternative. "I'm not feeling gung ho about Karl Knaths, but there's a William Walton exhibit at the Corcoran." Or "Listen, it's been a week, and I don't think I'm up for *Okinawa*. Can we watch *Skirts Ahoy!* instead?" Where possible, we steered clear of tourists, but we strolled with great contentment through the Dumbarton Oaks garden and circled the Wright Brothers' plane in the Arts and Industries Building. In late May, on an impulse, we forsook the Freer for the lowbrow joys of the Ringling Brothers, which would have been the first and last time I ever saw Jackie with cotton candy. It took her unholy hours to get it peeled from her skin, and she claimed to have carried it all the way to work the next morning, along with her ceramic Ringling Brothers tankard, which disappeared under still-unexplained circumstances.

As I write it down, it sounds frenetic, but the parts that truly linger in my memory are the still points, the after-moments when she and I would gather to discuss what we'd just seen. I remember Jackie, for instance, diligently putting in a good word for Grandma Moses—"mysterious charm," "taproots of myth," that sort of thing—and me sailing back

with "Madison Avenue rube" and "world's most commercial
primitive artist." But the thing is I *liked* Grandma Moses,
much as I hated to admit it. As for Jackie, I think it's fair to
say the old lady's canvases did not get mounted on the White
House walls while the Kennedys were living there.

One conversation in particular comes to mind. We
had got to talking about Ingrid Bergman, a beautiful and
acclaimed and, I don't think it's going too far to say, sancti-
fied actress (hell, she played Saint Joan) who had made the
surprising decision to leave her husband and bear a child
with an Italian film director. This was in the late forties,
and the news did not go over well. She was evicted from
Hollywood, denounced from the Senate floor. To judge from
the gossip columns, America would have stoned her to death
if it could have found an arena convenient to all. "And what
for?" asked Jackie. "She wanted to be with another man."

"She might have told the first man first."

"Oh, you mean like all those *husbands* who tell their
wives?"

This was the first time I felt her to be standing in Janet's
shoes, and maybe she could only do it by proxy.

"So," I said, "you're telling me a famous husband
wouldn't get the same business for leaving his wife?"

"Ask my employer, Mr. Hearst."

"All I'm saying is if you follow your hot pants out the
door, people will have an opinion."

"Oh, hot pants. That's not why a woman leaves a man."

"Why then?"

"Freedom."

Well, I had a bit of a laugh, I confess. The idea that a millionaire movie actress with a swimming pool and someone squeezing oranges for her every morning was in some way unfree, but Jackie kept insisting that was *money*, not freedom. We went back and forth, and then she fell quiet for a space, and at last she smiled, very indulgently, and rested her hand on mine. "Don't take this the wrong way, Lem, but you're a man. Freedom is what you know."

For the first time in our still-young acquaintance, I had the feeling of falling short. Of a standard I didn't yet know existed. I suppose I could have listed for her all the ways I wasn't free, the interlocking manacles of family and livelihood—I could make a pretty good list right now, but I get tired just thinking about it.

The topic of freedom reminds me of another Sunday we spent together. She'd phoned me a few days prior to beg off because she'd been called into work. "That's all right," I said. "I'll tag along."

She wasn't an easy sell on this point. Probably she was thinking of the time Johnny Husted had dragged after her like a thousand tin cans. I assured her I would be discreet, wouldn't look her way, wouldn't let anybody know we were connected. Her final condition was that I couldn't laugh.

We met at the corner of Fifteenth and K. She was already in position with her new Leica, so I repaired to the nearest newsstand, where I made a show of buying the *Times-Herald*'s chief rival, the *Post*, and reading it in public view. Only then did I realize that the newspaper formed a perfect blind for tracking her as she sauntered down K Street, curling her gaze north and south. To this day, I can't be sure what she was looking for in that trout run. Maybe just a flicker of kindness before she reeled in the line.

A celebrated journalist once told me that, when he went to interview people in their homes, he always brought the chunkiest, clunkiest reel-to-reel tape recorder he could find and spent the first ten or fifteen minutes being completely defeated by it. His object, he said, was to bring himself down to the level of his interview subjects so they would lose whatever inhibitions they had. Jackie, of course, wasn't famous in those days, but there was still something about her that needed, like fame, to be disarmed. The extreme femininity, for instance, by the ponderous masculine camera. The satin gloves by the not-entirely-unfeigned look of panic in her dilated eyes. Who, they must have wondered, was this gentlewoman fallen on such hard times? What did she want of us? At first, they would have no way of knowing for the voice was scarcely audible. In the usual manner, they would lean forward and keep leaning until the hook was in.

The hardest part, she told me later, was getting the photograph because, in those days, strange to relate, one paused at the prospect of being in the paper. The older women, especially, had to be coaxed along, but if they were still of a certain age, Jackie could seal the deal by murmuring: "You know who would love to see this? Your mother."

Before she threw in the towel that day, she must have interrogated a good two dozen people about what they thought a woman desired the most. I remember asking her why she went to such trouble when the column only had room for five. "Oh," she said, "most people don't even know what they think. About anything." That principle must have been in particular force that day because she wound up falling back on the doormen and taxi-stand drivers, whose occupations she loved above all others because they didn't allow for movement. The Alexandria hack, for instance, who shouted from his rolled-down window: "I know what my wife desires most! Another husband."

We took that same driver's taxi back to her office, and I planted myself in a chair between the cuspidor and the water cooler. The *Times-Herald* was then just a few years away from being swallowed, and I've always believed that the closer a newspaper is to its grave, the more gaily it gleams. The *New York Times*, then as now, was a gray lady, but Jackie's paper was Camille, fluttering all the way to its last cough. Phones squealed, typewriters hammered, editors bellowed for the rewrite man, the copy boy. There was a tattered coverlet of cigarette smoke; ink rose up like swamp mist; you smelled glue and soot and despair.

The only remaining question was where Jackie fit in. The lone woman in the city newsroom, she sat hunched over an Olivetti manual, stabbing at each key as if to drive it back to whatever fen it had bubbled up from. It occurred to me then that this was the same paper Kick Kennedy had made a go of during the war, reporting for the Did You Happen to See? column or reviewing the occasional play or movie. She used to stuff her fur coat into a paper sack before she came upstairs, where she was welcomed, perhaps, in the same respectful spirit as Jackie and, by respectful, I mean they didn't hit on her in public and didn't blow smoke directly into her face. Jackie carried her two hundred and fifty words of copy to the assistant city editor, then disappeared down a corridor. Came back a half hour later, with the smell of darkroom chemicals wafting from her skin.

"Don't you like my manicure?" she asked, extending her hand.

I stared down at her fingernails, bilious green from the developing solution. The words were out of my mouth before I considered the implications.

"This is a real job."

She angled toward me, as if I were just another man on her street.

"You don't think freedom comes free, do you?"

FIFTEEN

Freedom. What a word. Even now I grapple with what it means. Looking at myself in a full-length mirror, for example, I see a body that was once vigorous enough for heavyweight crew and now sits, a scuttled hulk, on the Upper East Side, pondering trips it's in no position to take. My last automobile ride was to see Mother's grave in Pittsburgh; I didn't even drive and still came home as wrung out as a wet polecat. When I want to take laps these days, I add codicils to my will. And yet within the mossed-over prison walls of my self, I feel paradoxically free. Perhaps only now, staggering into my sixty-fifth year, do I know what it *is* to be free, which of course has nothing to do with one's temporal condition and everything to do with one's

mind. Thus I sit, end-stage Lem Billings, at perfect liberty
to rage, mourn, love, spend it all down as slowly or quickly
as I please.

The other night, my friend Raul came by and found me
watching *The Robin Byrd Show*. Now, if you don't live in
New York, you would have no earthly way of knowing this
is a nightly public-access chat program where the hostess
lolls around in a crocheted bikini and interviews porn stars
and strippers. Sometimes she does more than interview
them. Miss Byrd has bronze skin and white teeth and
remains the soul of cheer no matter what's going on around
her. I sometimes think she has found the secret to happiness,
and when she's performing her signature tune, "Baby, Let
Me Bang Your Box," I find myself wishing Jack were there
to witness the New Woman, the kind who requires no chas-
ing, no persuading. "Where's the fun in that?" I imagine
him saying.

Well, Raul didn't begin to understand my interest. "Papi,"
he said. (It's not a nickname I particularly care for, but it
does reflect the difference in our ages, and Raul, who is a
New School professor, would tell you it's an ironic reconfig-
uring.) "Papi," he said. "You must see she is the perfect wish
fulfillment of colonialist heterosexual male desire."

"She seems happy."

Though, even now, the word I'm groping toward is *free*.

Well, Raul soon grew bored with the argument and
asked me how much I pay my housekeeper and why doesn't
she even dust the scrimshaw. I told him I hire housekeep-
ers less for what they do than for what they overlook.

Hypodermic needles, puke. Sheila cleans *around*, and I'm grateful.

Grateful, too, for memories. How could I not be, thinking back to that spring and summer of '52, back to *my* Jackie, who was still counting her pennies then and shopping at Woodie's and Hecht's more than she would have liked and working with a local seamstress to make knockoffs of the latest designs. She wore every kind of thing. Cotton pinafores. A plaid gingham frock with a billow skirt and an organdy petticoat. As the weather grew warmer, a navy pima cotton sleeveless blouse. A chambray plaid gown with a wide whirl skirt. Sunback dresses, sometimes with jackets. Whatever it was, she wanted my opinion. Not a mere up or down vote, either, but a point-by-point critique, the kind she'd gotten as a girl, strolling Madison Avenue with Black Jack.

She loved it, I remember, when I said that her white sleeveless shirt-dress reminded me of Elizabeth Taylor's in *A Place in the Sun* or that her alligator-leather handbag was the same red as the Virgin Mary's robes in Tintoretto's *Paradise*. But there were times she'd have made up her mind before I got there. The terry coatdress had already been written off as the opposite of smart, and nothing I said could dissuade her. There was one skirt I wasn't even allowed to look at because it was too "swashbuckly" and would have to be burned at sunset with her in it.

She was particularly bothered that summer by her hair. Very much against her father's wishes, she had got a poodle cut before the rest of the country caught on, and she was dismayed now to see how prevalent it had become. ("Lucille *Ball*'s got one.") But, hard as she tried, she couldn't find her way to a clean break. She consulted the magazine oracles and poked her head in at K Street salons. She stopped women on the street, under the guise of Inquiring Photografer, to ask them what they'd had done. The way was no clearer by July.

"*I'm* the problem, Lem. My hair can only frizz out or sag all to hell. No medium ground. I think I should just shave it off and start over again . . ."

She could be quite clinical about herself, I remember. "Well, obviously, my sister got all the curves, and don't think I don't hate her for it. I guess I can look slim enough if I get the cut right, but nobody's going to hire me as a swimsuit model. I'm a little tall for my liking, and my chin juts out a bit, and I don't exactly have Cinderella feet so I have to be *very* careful about my shoes. And my eyes are so far apart it takes me three weeks just to order a pair of glasses because they have to custom build the bridge. God help me if I ever lose a pair."

Not that I ever saw her in glasses.

I realize, in setting all this down, I'm giving the impression of vanity or narcissism, but I don't think that's quite true. Jackie—like Jack, in a way—subscribed to an aristocracy of beauty. Beauty in this case being not the raw elements but the way you chose minute by minute to recombine them. There was no better illustration, really, than her own face, a study in disproportion that I had lengthy intervals to study. It was her father's square head, of course—the vast

omniscient eyes, the Mediterranean mouth—held periodically hostage by her mother's Northern European nose and
brows, and there were times when those features seemed
engaged in a kind of ancestral war. Then, through some tiny
act of will—a tart remark, the slightest plumping of lip—
she would call them back. Not into uniformity, exactly, but
something better.

These moments might flash by in a second or, depending on the elements, extend for hours. One Sunday she got
us into an early-evening reception honoring the first lady of
Ecuador. Her lipstick was fresh, her hair recently curled, her
neck and collarbone resplendently naked in the chandelier
light. It was, I think, the first inkling I had of her power, for
it wasn't just the trust lawyers in worsted suits and the senators' wives in flowered prints, all craning for a view, no, it
was the Portuguese attaché, who gave her the up-and-down
and then did the same for *me*, as if to ask what latent powers
I must harbor to own such a woman.

I got so used to observing her—in all lights, against all
backgrounds—that it rarely occurred to me she might be
observing me, too. But she was, down to the aglets of my
wingtips. There was a particularly steamy day in August, I
remember, when she demanded to know why my seersucker
wasn't wrinkling. I hedged as long as I could and then confessed, with some embarrassment, that it was nylon. She
looked at me with changed eyes.

"How real it looks."

As she got a better handle on my own tastes, she began
bringing me things. Nothing fancy. Black enamel cufflinks.

A Princeton tie. (I already had three, but I was touched.) Once she snuck me one of her stepfather's old watches—a Swiss Super Roamer, with a cognac leather wristband.

"Hold on," I said. "You *took* this?"

"Well, he wasn't wearing it anymore because he thought it was broken. But that's only because he's deaf and can't hear it ticking."

"It's a hot watch, Jackie."

"Oh, I'll take the fall if it comes to it. Hughdie can never stay mad at me."

Another time, she met me right at the station with a box and a broad grin. "Jack won't wear hats," she said, "but I know you will, and this is coconut straw with an India-print hatband. I've always thought men look well in coconut straw, don't you?"

It was, to be clear, a porkpie hat, which I had never in my life worn, and I wondered if for once she had misstepped, but a single look in the men's-room mirror persuaded me that her eye was true. I wore that hat for another ten years, and not just in her presence. Once she gave me a tartan-plaid handkerchief, and I muttered something about how she shouldn't be spending her hard-earned money on me.

"But who better?" she asked. By now, she was on her third Aperol spritz, which may explain why she reached for my hand. "I like you to have nice things because you're so nice to look at."

"If you incline to Mr. Magoo."

"Take off your specs," she ordered.

"All right."

"And stop squinting."

"I don't think I can."

She traced a slow arc around my face. "*Look* at you. Beautiful bone structure. Rippling jawline. Gorgeous eyes, gorgeous mouth."

"You should tell Jack," I suggested. "He used to call me *Pithecanthropus erectus*."

"What does that mean?"

"Uh, walking ape man, something like that. I think he was referring to my—I've a high forehead, you see."

"It's a powerful forehead. That's why the Congressman was jealous."

"If you insist."

"Stop it. I'm sure plenty of girls have made fools of themselves over you."

"If they have, they never told me about it. Anyway, I'm kind of busy for a social life."

"All work and no play," murmured Jackie. "Well, it's a good thing I'm already spoken for."

Her lashes took a particularly luxurious downward turn, and I realized that this was as flirtatious as she had yet been with me.

"Yes," I said. "You're spoken for."

SIXTEEN

*S*ometime in my early forties, I was working an ad shoot when a Leo Burnett casting director sidled up in a grimly salacious way and asked if I was talent. "Hell, no," I said. "I'm *wrangling* it." "You'd be a perfect Marlboro Man," she said. Well, I laughed to beat the band, but she only pressed her card more firmly into my hand and urged me to call her office for an appointment. I gave it a thought or two, but I couldn't get past the image of me on a horse. Squinting at a butte, trying not to cough. I've always maintained that advertising is as much truth as lie, and a Marlboro Man who doesn't, in some part of his soul, believe himself to be a Marlboro Man would never pass muster. All the same, it would have been gratifying to sit out with the Kennedys in their Palm Beach redoubt, leafing through the latest *Life* or *Fortune*. "Why, looky here," I imagine myself saying as I thrust the full-page ad in Jack's direction. Given time, he composes a crude response—something about horses—but the joke, by its very nature, imbues me with a new stature. For he respects publicity.

I bring this up because it was a queer sensation to be *looked* at in the way this casting director did. Through the lens of glamour. The closest I've come probably was escorting Jackie that summer around Washington. Put a pretty girl on your arm, I'm telling you, and the glitter rubs off. Whether it's a coat-check girl or a streetcar driver, every wink, every arched eyebrow declares that you must be somebody more than they first thought.

This was not my usual way of traveling through the world, and I couldn't help feeling like the impersonator in *The Prisoner of Zenda*, waiting for the true Ruritanian king to return. Yet Jack, having brought us together, had long since stepped away. In those days, whenever he called me— and this would have been two or three times a week—he'd speak of everything *but* Jackie.

The Massachusetts Senate race was no longer a Honey Fitz campaign but a national concern, combed over like entrails for the opinion pages, pondered every Sunday morning by *Meet the Press*. No matter where you plunged your hand in, you could find a theme—Irish versus Wasp, upstart versus establishment—and still push out eight hundred words by deadline. Jack, being in the thick of it, could only see ad buys in Newton. Should Bobby be allowed to speak?

Would Ethel's obvious pregnancy attract the housewife vote? We never hashed things out at great length because he was always so exhausted. Some nights, I could actually hear the squelch of bathwater beneath him, and I realized that my contribution to the Kennedy campaign was to let him drift off to sea like an empty dinghy.

Now and then, he would pause and ask, apropos of nothing: "All is well?" "All is well," I would reply, without knowing exactly what I was replying to. And it was because we never spoke of Jackie that a feeling of illicitness began to attach itself to my encounters with her. Every time the switchboard operator at Emerson Drug put through one of her calls, it came prefaced with "Your friend is calling." Water-cooler conversations halted as I approached. Bucky McAdoo began clapping me on the back as he sailed out the door. "It's awfully late, Lem. Don't you have somewhere better to be?"

One Saturday morning, I was reading the paper on the back patio when Mother came out with a wondering expression. "Somebody on the phone."

It was Jackie, of course. She'd needed to make some last-minute change in our plans and, knowing I wouldn't be at the office, had taken the unusual step of calling me at home. The whole conversation took less than a minute, and I thought no more about it until Mother brought it up over lunch.

"That girl. Is she the reason you go down to Washington every Sunday?"

"She's one of the reasons."

Mother stared into her wineglass. "Would I know her family?"

"Not unless you know the Auchinclosses."

The name landed somewhere behind her eyes.

"No. I'm afraid I don't."

"Mother," I said, "it's all right. I'm just entertaining her. She's Jack's girl."

Strange to hear it spoken like that.

"He knows you're seeing her?"

"Of course. It's his idea." I made a point of tugging up the ends of my mouth. "There's nothing improper going on, dear one."

"No, I know."

"Then what?"

"I suppose it was how she said your name."

"How was that?"

"Like a geisha."

Nothing outwardly changed. We woke every Sunday for the 8:30 Eucharist at Old St. Paul's. If the weather was fine, we took coffee and pastries at a Charles Street café and an early-ish lunch at home. When the taxi pulled up a little before one, she would tell me to have a nice time and call if I was running late, and I'd kiss her on the cheek and climb into the cab. The only difference was that she'd wait until the cab had gone before heading back inside.

But whatever constraint I carried onto that train was gone by the time I got to Washington, and over the course of that summer, my outings with Jackie became less a mission and more the filling of a vacancy, which had predated her and which I had not even necessarily grasped about myself. To be sure, I had friends in those days, family, work, all the attachments one can expect to form, but in my experience, a man doesn't always understand he has a vacancy until somebody begins, however inadvertently, to fill it. This is maybe just a way of saying I was a little lonely myself that summer and that our time together could make an hour pass more quickly than it was in the habit of doing.

I think, for instance, of how we used to swan into La Salle du Bois, Jackie already scattering her Sorbonne French. *"Bonsoir, Messieurs! La table dans le coin, s'il vous plait, pour deux. Et peut-être une carte des vins? Ah, vous êtes si gentil."* With any other girl, I suppose, it might have sounded affected, but it made the mere act of being seated before a white-linen tablecloth eventful.

Wherever we went, she knew the maître-d', the assistant maître-d', the headwaiter. Joe at the Hi-Hat, Stephen at the Congo Room. The night chef at Duke Zeibert's. "You get out a lot," I once suggested.

"Oh, I just write them up sometimes."

The one place where she had no pull was Harvey's on Connecticut Avenue. On our first voyage there, we arrived a little after five and had to wait nearly two hours for a table. Our reward was a side view of J. Edgar Hoover, alone at a corner table, jowly and bison-shouldered and dining on white toast, grapefruit, cottage cheese and Bibb lettuce.

"Do you think he has stomach trouble?" Jackie mused. "Somebody should sell him Bromo-Seltzer."

"It won't help, he's being consumed by his secrets."

"No," she insisted. "He's eating them himself."

"Of *course*. He has to eat them or they'll pass into enemy hands."

That was all the premise we needed to plot out J. Edgar Hoover's Diet of Secrets. A list of Red sympathizers for breakfast. A list of Red agents with midmorning coffee. Perverts for lunch. Philandering Cabinet officials for high tea. Radical Jews for cocktails, Negro-lovers and folk-music listeners for appetizers, and for dinner—well, we thought about what was piled on that lettuce and came up with naked postcards of Bess Truman. Then, having still a lot of time on our hands, we theorized there must be an FBI agent tasked with catching the secrets when Hoover passed them out again.

"Very delicate task," I suggested. "Far above GS-6."

"Major security clearances. And asbestos gloves. Of course, it's widely considered a plum job."

"A road to *power*. He who sifts Hoover's stool . . ."

"Charts America's course."

"Exactly."

It seems to me now we were all but daring him to turn our way—without, of course, fully appreciating that we didn't merit a dram of his attention. A biographer might speak to the irony of Young Jackie beholding the man who would play such a key role in her own life, entrapping her husband's secrets like flypaper. I find it more interesting to ponder Jackie on the other side of Fame, pressing her *nose* to it. Was it as lonely as it looked?

* * *

HOW LITTLE WE spoke of Jack, though neither of us had exactly stipulated that. If anything, Jack had instructed me to keep his name in the mix, but the conversation seemed to flow more easily without him in the middle. If ever we drifted his way, Jackie would call us back. "No," she'd say. "Not yet."

Sometimes, to be sure, she came at him in a roundabout way. Was it true, she once asked, that I'd proposed marriage to Jack's sister? I explained that every man who'd known Kick Kennedy had proposed to her at some point because she was the best pal and *livest* live wire and you'd have done anything to keep her around a bit longer, only marriage was the stupidest way to go about it. If you'd asked me to call one person back from the dead, I said, it would be Kick. Jackie was quiet and then said:

"He misses her, too."

One night, over screwdrivers, she volunteered that she'd first laid eyes on Jack not at Charlie Bartlett's row house, as everyone (including Jack) believed, but at the Syosset wedding of Charlie's brother a full two years prior, and she might have missed him altogether had it not been for another wedding guest. Gene *Tunney*, of all people, the ex-boxer, who was still a fit specimen in middle age (he raised Hereford cattle in Stamford) and who was disposed to like her, he said, by the fact that she wasn't smoking (though she'd binged three cigs before coming) and who, in the midst of inveighing against tobacco, paused to point out, with grudging approval, the only other guest who was abstaining. "You see that fellow there? I happen to know he has the spinal column of an eighty-year-old broncobuster. No, it's true, he can barely stand, let alone walk, and would you know it to look at him? The picture of health, and that's because his lungs are pure."

But not his thoughts, Jackie silently added, for the gentleman in question was conversing with a blonde in a gray foulard dress, and from the unhurried precision of his movements, the coolness of his stare, there seemed only one possible outcome.

Even then, of course, Jackie knew who he was. Could have recited in a vague way his war record, some of the East Hampton slurs about his provenance. This was the first time she had ever paused to consider him. She paused a little longer than she meant to and might have crossed over into staring had Gene Tunney's voice not drawn her back.

"Listen now," he told her. "You'll want to watch that one."

But I am was her first thought. It was then that the former heavyweight champion of the world curled his fingers around her arm as far as they would go (boxing) and angled her away.

"Find yourself a banker," he said.

SHE SHOULD HAVE listened. For a few months, she did. How else to explain Johnny Husted?

"But I've never met a banker," she told me, "as attractive as Jack."

Having ventured that far, maybe she couldn't find a way back, for she said, in a voice almost defeated:

"Can you tell me about him?"

SEVENTEEN

*T*his is what I told her.

The first time I ever met Jack Kennedy was when he walked into a Choate yearbook meeting and said, "I want to go out for the board."

I can still hear him. *Bo-wuhd*. It's hard, though, even for me, to see him as he was then, a hundred pounds wet. The frailty of him. The knot of his tie was half as wide as his neck. He looked as if he'd just raided his father's closet. Any moderate wind could have toppled him, and I remember, in the midst of my amusement, feeling an urge I would consider nearly parental to gather him up. Not too different, I'm thinking, from how Jackie felt, watching him stroll into the Bartletts' row house.

At fifteen, Jack's identity was defined by not being his older brother, Joe Junior, who was one of the Choate elect. Star baseball player, a student of electromagnetic intensity, casually strapping, handsome—and, as such boys often are, rather savage, one of the sixth form's most chilling despots. There was no avoiding him, whether he was wrapping his arm around your shoulder or holding you down on the floor for a paddling. Whereas Jack, you might say, slipped in the side door. An indifferent student, not terribly coveted, too reedy for American sports. I don't think the majority of the third form could have named him at sight, for all that the family name was known. Yet here he was, striding into the yearbook office as if—well, as if there were no reason *not* to. As if some lark was in the offing.

I'd only been on the board myself for a year, so as the junior officer, I was tasked with telling him that he'd have to sell fifty dollars' worth of ads before he could even be considered. "As it happens," he answered, cool as gin, "I've already got sixty-one dollars in commitments from the Hyannis Grocery and Oxford Meat Market. As well as definite interest from JPK Enterprises."

Now how was I to know that Oxford Meat was where his family shopped in Palm Beach? Or that JPK Enterprises was the hub of his dad's business empire? He wasn't in any hurry to offer documentation, he just figured we'd believe him. So we sent him back into the hall and took a vote, which surprised me by being six-to-one in his favor. It surprises me now to recall that mine was the dissenting vote. Was it just the prospect of some sloppy punk kid, a year younger than me, waltzing in like he already owned the place?

Naturally, I was the one who had to go out and tell him. He took the news with perfect aplomb because, of course, there had never been any doubt in his mind. But there was nothing smug about him either, and whatever reluctance I carried into that hallway vanished when he put out his hand and said, "This'll be swell, Lem."

I had no idea he even knew my name. He always knew your name.

What brought us together, what made us the very best of roommates, was that we both hated Choate. In all its nasty, prudish, brutish, regimented, upwardly aspiring, faux-British faux-Christianity. You weren't to drink. You weren't to smoke. You weren't to swear. You weren't to talk back or come late to class or doze off in chapel or bring your luggage up at the wrong time or bring it down at the wrong time or keep a sloppy room or leave your room with your shirt untucked. Whatever tasted of personality was their business to snuff out. One night I was backed up against a fireplace and yelled into tears by our housemaster for making an expression he judged to be "a face."

Honestly, it wasn't the rules, it was the rule enforcers. Worst of them was our headmaster, George St. John, who once told Mr. Kennedy that if Jack were his son, "I believe I should take him to a gland specialist." In our final year, St. John gave a chapel talk about how five percent of Choate students (don't think he didn't give us the eye) were no better than "muckers." By which he meant the Irish laborers who

cleaned shit out of rich folks' stables. The very next day, Jack
and I and, oh, Rip Horton and Maury Shea and a few other
sixth formers came together to form the Muckers Club. We
had little gold shovels made for twelve bucks apiece by a
Wallingford jeweler, and we talked about bringing horseshit
onto the Spring Festivities dance floor, and we must have
had a rat in our midst because St. John called us each into
his study and told us there was a train leaving somewhere
between five and six o'clock and we were to be on it because
we were no longer students of Choate.

Cooler heads prevailed, and we were only kept over
for Easter vacation. Surely it didn't hurt that Mr. Kennedy
offered to buy some film projectors for the school, although
when St. John's back was turned, he leaned toward Jack and
whispered, "If that club had been mine, it wouldn't have
started with an *M*."

In a nutshell, this was the crypto-fascist regime Jack and I
were up against, and we didn't like it one bit and didn't care
who knew. After a while, our housemaster got so sick of our
antics that he recommended separating us and sending us
down to the younger houses, but film projectors weren't easy
to come by, and so, by hook or by crook, we held fast. I even
stayed on for a year after graduation just so Jack could have
company in *his* final year. That's how tight we were.

WELL, I CAN'T begin to tell you how eagerly Jackie lapped
this stuff up. Jack, of course, had told her nothing of his
childhood, and she loved the idea, I think, of capturing him
in this larval stage. It was like wrapping her arms around

him when he wasn't looking. Tell me, she'd say, about Jack's electric Victrola. About the semester you both got out of compulsory public speaking by joining the Dramatics Club, only to spend countless hours as beefeaters and gentlemen of Japan while Gilbert and Sullivan raged on all sides. (It's why I can still sing the whole *Mikado* score.) No matter what story I dredged up, Jackie would listen with the deepest attention, like an musicologist tape recording folk songs. What a curious phenomenon, I remember thinking. We stockpile memories of a person without ever imagining they'll have free-market value, only to learn we've been squatting on a golden hoard.

"Oh, my God," she'd say. "You tried to enlist in the Foreign *Legion*? Like *Beau Geste*? Was that Jack's idea? . . . You mean you switched seats while the car was still *moving*? How is that even *possible*?"

Over time, it was true, she began to home in on specific themes.

"I bet you had lots of girls in your room."

No, I explained, we didn't dare. We would have been expelled.

"But boys used to sneak over to Miss Porter's all the time. You're telling me it didn't work the other way?"

Oh, I said, there were dances, of course. Olive Cawley used to come over.

"And what was Olive like?"

Oh, you know. Angular, striking. Like Katharine Hepburn but more teeth.

"How big were they?"

How big . . .

"Her teeth."

I couldn't say.

"Was she sweet?"

Very.

"Did they ever slip away?"

Her teeth?

"No, Jack and Olive. Did they ever disappear behind a tree or something?"

If they had disappeared, I wouldn't have seen them.

I think Jackie had her eyes on Olive because she figured that was to whom Jack had lost his virginity, but in fact, that story had nothing to do with Olive, and I knew better than to share it. The truth was that Jack and I lost our virginity together. Or that was the plan.

You see, we'd made a pact that we would be initiated by the same girl. We didn't care who she was, really, as long as she would take us both. Of course, it doesn't take much to see what kind of girl will do that for you, and the prospect of *that*—well, I was still a momma's boy from Pittsburgh. I didn't believe in hellfire, but clap? So I wasn't exactly clamoring, but just a week or two before Jack's seventeenth birthday, Rip Horton jumped the gun and lost *his* at a bordello in Harlem. Dirt cheap, he said. Like falling off a log.

Jack hated to be one-upped, so he declared that he and I would be heading to that same bordello the next weekend. I should probably point out that Harlem wasn't what it is now. For swells like the Kennedys, it was practically a stroll up the Rialto. Not worth driving the family convertible but certainly worth the cab fare from Grand Central. We started the night with a corner peep show, but the real show was the rich young dames in ermine who kept tumbling out of white limos, dancing over piles of garbage on their way to Basement Brownie's. They were in no mood to be pestered by a pair of prep-school lads, so Jack and I swallowed down shots of schnapps and strode, arm in arm, to the three-story brownstone on 133rd Street.

A toothless old woman was leaning out a second-story window, and men were shooting craps in the vestibule. We were convinced Rip Horton had given us the wrong address, but then a lady in a silk dress came processing down the carpeted front staircase like an ancient Ziegfeld girl. "Good evening," she said. "We ask that gentlemen pay in advance." After tucking our six dollar bills into her bosom, she led us in measured cadences to the third floor, where we found a row of girls in wooden chairs. They wore silk dresses, too, with spike-heeled patent-leather pumps and red velvet hats, some of them with bird-of-paradise feathers. Jack took his sweet time choosing—walked up and down with his hands folded behind him like Rommel inspecting tanks—then settled (surprisingly) on the plumpest one, a girl of maybe sixteen or seventeen years with a full bust and scullery-maid shoulders. She rose from her chair and strolled into the adjoining room. Jack gave me a single glance, then followed her inside.

Sitting there with all those girls, I remember being quite grateful for the masculine accent of my bowler hat and for the way it concealed my lap. A minute passed, five. As I felt the soft hammering of my heart spreading out to my skin, I began to wonder if I was very slowly dying, and I wondered, too, what Jack would do with my body and who would notify Mother and how would they phrase it and would they bury me next to Father. Questions of the most morbid intensity, so it was a great relief to see Jack amble out of that room, as whole as when he walked in, and it was in this spirit that I rose and shouted: "That was fast!"

His face reddened as though it had been slapped.

"Your turn, asshole," he muttered. And shoved me inside.

The first surprise was that the girl was not in bed but standing by the window. The second was that she was still half clothed, in a cup bra and high-waisted bloomers. I stood there smiling cretinously in a wash of fuchsia light. Probably I made some joke or commented on the weather. Her response was to come away from the window and seat herself rather heavily on the mattress. With a sense of obligation, I joined her there, taking care to keep a forearm's width of space between us. I could see that one of her brassiere straps had slipped off her shoulder, and I guess it says something about my state of mind that I very nearly slid it back up, the way you instinctively right a painting that's hanging off center.

"What's your name?" I asked.

"Lenore."

"Lem," I said, though she hadn't asked. "I always like to come to Harlem," I said. "My friend—the fella who was just here, he's—you know, he's seriously ill. We don't know if he'll make it another year, so I told him we'd come here and make his dreams come true, if you know what I'm getting at. Because we don't . . ." Hadn't I said this? "We don't know if he'll live another year. But I said I'd be there for him because that's what a best pal does."

In memory, the monologue swirls between truth and fancy and settles into a kind of halftime pep talk. Lenore was unroused.

"What I'm driving at," I told her, "is that I really don't need anything. I'm squared away myself. In that department. So maybe we could just sit here for a few minutes, if that suits you."

My nostrils picked out the faintest thread of rose water amid the tobacco. My ears picked out the sine curve of police sirens.

"Okey-doke," she said.

Her voice was more girlish than I expected, and after a stretch of silence, she actually began to hum, very softly. I couldn't have told you what the tune was—medieval plain-chant, for all I know—but to my ears, she was somehow *describing*, in musical terms, what had just happened in this room. And with that, the thing I couldn't imagine was all I could see. Lenore pressed against the wall. Jack driving in, groans spilling from his narrow chest, eyes clouded, neck arching. My hand, under cover of my bowler, crept toward my zipper, and one thing led to another, and then, just like that, it was done. A palmful of spunk. I wiped myself clean with my handkerchief and said thank you to Lenore and fixed a grin on my face and strode out of the room. "Strike another one off the list," I called.

I wish I could say Jack and I floated back to Choate on clouds of priapic glory, but neither of us had brought rubbers, and Jack got into a terrible panic and insisted we grab every cream and lotion the hospital pharmacy had in stock. He tracked down some terrifying miniature whisk that you stuck down your Johnson to clean it out. One night, he even rang up his family physician—this would have been one or two in the morning—to describe the exact condition of his willy. "See, Doctor, there's a broken blood vessel in the—I think you call it the *glans*? I really can't say how it got there, I just noticed it in the shower . . ."

So this was not a story to be shared with a girlfriend, but I do sometimes wish Jackie—*my* Jackie—could have seen *that* Jack. Not a conquistador, I promise you. Just another scared kid.

THERE WAS SOMETHING else I didn't bring up with her because I knew he wouldn't want me to. What I'd said to that Harlem girl was true. Jack, for as long as I'd known him, was dying.

Or at least felt himself to be. He'd barely made it past the scarlet fever at three, and he caught just about every childhood germ or virus a body could. At Choate, I once saw him faint dead away at chapel, and I was there the next day when they carted him off to New Haven Hospital. A wasting disease, we were told. The whole school was instructed to pray for him. Even I, hellbound Christian, got down on my knees. I did the same when he transferred from the Gothic spires of Princeton to the sterile climes of Peter Bent

Brigham Hospital. By then, I'd seen him in and out of so
many clinics and wards he told me I should write his biography and subtitle it *A Medical History.*

It alters your sense of scale watching someone go through
that. I remember friends asking me during the war if I was
worried about Jack cruising in the Solomons. "No more than
usual," I'd say. He and I used to have these very calm, rea-
soned discussions about the best way to go. Freezing? Slow.
Hanging? Uncertain. Drowning, wet. Poison, messy. "Death
by boredom," I once suggested. "You mean Congress," he
said.

The point is he never, never once, became morbid. "Eat,
drink and make love," he once wrote me, "as tomorrow or
next week we attend my funeral." So when he got himself
elected to Congress, I truly believe he thought of that as his
endgame, and I believe I agreed with him, and it was this
particular dappling that lay over my summer with Jackie.

"You know what?" she said one afternoon. "I may not
have been his first, but I'll be his last."

"Yes," I said. "I think you will."

EIGHTEEN

She enjoyed hearing me talk about Jack so much because it created the illusion of his being there. For, in truth, she saw even less of him that summer than I did. Even when the House was in session, his campaign followed him back to Washington. She held out hope for a lunch date in the House dining room, but weeks went by without so much as a phone call, and every inquiry she lodged with Mrs. Lincoln was met with "I'll be sure to tell him." It was the same feeling that had enveloped her at the Bartletts'. She was to take her place in a vast sisterhood, lapping up whatever spoonful of attention dribbled down. Hadn't she resisted that role then?

There was a night late in June when we were sitting on the Washington Roof, drinking mint juleps in frosted chrome cups. The air was tight and sultry, and Jackie was smoking like a condemned killer—four Newports in quick succession, each one jabbed like a shiv into the eye of the ashtray. I did my best to keep the chatter going, but in retrospect, I can see that whatever came out of my mouth just added to the pressure building inside her.

"Lem," she said. "Do you think I'm pathetic?"

"Of course not."

"Are you sure? I mean, if *you* were waiting for some boy to call you all the time and he never did, wouldn't you qualify as some kind of sucker?"

"Well." I felt a light prickle in my face. "Not if he was running for the United States Senate."

"Put that aside . . ."

"But you can't, darling! He's a public figure, and that means he has to take care."

"Of what?"

"Reputation. Not just *his*, of course, but yours. I mean, Jack is a gentleman, he doesn't want your picture snapped by some cheap photographer or your name . . . bandied about in gossip rags."

She was quiet. Then came her smile, as quiet.

"Don't think poorly of me, Lem, but I'd love to be bandied. No, it's true, I'd settle for being an anonymous brunette in Earl Wilson's column, because at least I'd be in the same room, wouldn't I? Do you know the other night, I was wondering if I knew anybody at NBC who could smuggle me onto the set of *Meet the Press*. Just to see him, I mean. That's what I mean by pathetic."

"Oh," I said. "I know it's hard. The political life, it's hard on everyone."

She was silent a longer while, a lip of ash forming at the end of her cig.

"Would you tell me, Lem?"

"Tell you what?"

"If it was time to give up."

I hadn't been drinking so much that Jack's words didn't come right back to me. *We want her to feel like she can stay the course, Lem.*

It was the closest thing to a mission I'd been given, but so many weeks had passed that I couldn't honestly say in that moment what the course was or how anyone could be kept on it. For some seconds I dithered only to fall back on the simplest response.

"Don't give up."

"Why?"

I moved closer and, in a tone wavering between reassurance and mock-reassurance, said, "They also serve who only stand and wait."

A single blue vein welled from her forehead.

"You mean I'm to be a servant?"

Well, I tried to explain as best I could, as I try to explain it now. When I use the word *service*, I don't mean *obedient* or *lesser*. I mean simply recognizing the world as it is. The vast majority of us are destined for the plains. We troop along, gazes fixed, groping for happiness where we find it. A small minority, by grace of God or luck or heredity, are afforded a different path. What they see along the way is something we can't imagine, but now and then, one of the chosen might actually look *back* and pluck an unelected soul to be his companion. And this last class—the plucked—why, they're the rarest of all, for they must have a foot in both worlds and never once lose their balance. It takes doing.

This is a theory I've had the luxury of elaborating over time, so it's quite possible that I hadn't thought it all the way out. I say this because Jackie gave her cigarette another stab and said, half under her breath:

"I'm not like you. I can't just be somebody's minion."

SHE GAUGED HER error at once. There followed a fugue of apologies and reassurances. I told her it was quite all right, but I needed to get back. She offered to pay for my cab. I told her that wasn't necessary. With a catching voice, she offered to give me the rest of her cigs, though I barely smoked. "No, it's fine," I kept saying. "I'm fine."

I slept the whole way back on the train and woke in Baltimore Penn Station with just a dim sense of rupture. It was only when I was putting the key to the house door that the word came sailing back. I drank a couple of Scotches before bed, and the next day, over lunch with the art director, I took an extra martini, which reduced the word to a small whine in my left ear. That night, my mother came and found me in the study.

"It's her," she said simply.

I took the call in my bedroom. Waited for Mother to hang up and then raised the receiver to my ear. Her words came rushing out at me.

"Lem, I'm so sorry."

"No, you—"

"Please let me finish. I said that to you because it was how *I* was feeling and—it was wrong, Lem, because that's not how I feel about you, and I love our time together, it's the brightest part of my week—no, it really is, I wake up every morning and count the days, I do—and if all that should stop because of something childish I said, I don't think I could bear it, I couldn't *bear* the idea that I'd separated us, Lem, it tears me up, you see, because I love you."

A run-on sentence, if you want to be technical about it, but the point, really, was where it ran *toward*. Those treacherous words. I suppose, in my thirty-six years on Earth, I'd had them flung at me from some direction or other, but if I'm to be rigorous, they usually came with a *we* attached. I can recall, for example, the Kennedy girls or even Mrs. Kennedy saying, "How we love you, Lem," or, "Lem, what would we ever do without you?" But "*I* love you," that wasn't quite as common. I could think of nothing better to say in reply than "I love you, too," which was nearly as nice to say as to hear. I was actually smiling a little by the time I set the phone back down. Marveling, too. So this was what all the fuss was about.

NINETEEN

The next time I saw her, Jackie had a Bloody Mary waiting at the table, plus a silk bias tie she'd bought for me from Garfinckel's and a manila envelope with a month's worth of her columns. "Only if you get frightfully bored on the train," she said. "Otherwise, use them to wrap fish." She laughed extra loud at my jokes and let her hand rest a fraction longer on my sleeve, and I alternated between being touched and being at a loss, for surely this was the sort of reception a girl would give—well, a *man* friend. It got even more uncomfortable when Jackie, in an impulse of domestic intimacy, folded her hands over mine.

"Mummy wants to meet you."

A dry patch formed at the back of my throat. "Why?"

"She's been badgering me to tell her who I spend my Sundays with, and I was keeping it a mystery just to annoy her, but that was getting dull, so I just up and said, 'If you must know, he's Lem, and he's divine.' So she said, 'Let's have him over then.' 'Well, I said, he can only do Sundays as he's extremely busy.' She said, 'In that case, Sunday lunch.' And the only reason I even agreed is it's the only day in the week we don't have to speak French at table. If you're going to be thrown to these particular wolves, you should be able to speak your native tongue."

Wolves. But I wasn't the prey, was I? For days after, I labored under the presentiment that some Kafkaesque mistake had been made, that Mrs. Auchincloss (and, by extension, her husband and the world) was preparing to accuse me of crimes I had never even conceived of. More than once, I asked Jackie if this was really the best idea.

"Oh, it'll be fine, Lem. We're all God-fearing people."

It seemed, then, that Pittsburgh *would* come to Newport, and all that remained were logistics. I would have to leave earlier than usual on Sunday, which meant missing church with Mother. It took me half an hour just to choose a bow tie, and the whole way from Baltimore, I was in a stew over whether the straw boater was preferable to the Panama hat. I had some notion of ducking into Lansburgh's to find something more suitable, but the sight of Jackie's Mercury convertible idling outside Union Station—the sight of Jackie herself in the passenger seat—closed off that avenue. It was Merrywood or bust.

My second trip there, in contrast to the first, was conducted in the light of day, a gunmetal-blue sky with fat
freighters of cloud. This time I could appreciate the way the
oaks and maples towered over us, the quiet belligerence of
the magnolias and weeping cherries. Even the rhododen-
drons were flexing their shoulders.

"Look here," I said. "Your mother knows, doesn't she?"

"Knows what?"

"We're just friends."

"I don't know what she knows."

"Does she know about Jack?"

There was a pause. "I don't think she's impressed by
him."

"But she's never met him, has she?"

"Mummy can be quite abstract about her loathing."

The sun fell back behind groves of first-growth beech,
chestnut, oak. We passed a red-clay tennis court, a green-
house, a horse paddock, a pool, a Cape Codder dog kennel.
At last, the driveway, with a soft exhalation, curled to a stop
before a mock-Georgian edifice. Only a few decades old by
that point, but the ivy had long since run wild, and the red
brick was turning to chalk, and the palisade of boxwood
looked as though it had been standing for centuries. So, too,
did the butler, who opened the door and passed my hat to
the housekeeper and asked if I wanted refreshment.

In those days, Merrywood was as populous as it was
vast. Nine bedrooms, eleven full baths, a staff of easily two
dozen, a quarter of them groundskeepers. It would have
been natural to cower before such scale—surely that was

the founding intention—but for someone like me, there was something nearly atavistic about the broad staircases, the plaster moldings, the outsized oil portraits, even the pink soap balls in the powder rooms. I could almost believe, stepping into that foyer, that I'd been granted an alternative destiny in which good Dr. Billings lived and the Depression never was. As if to affirm the illusion, came Jackie's stepfather, Hugh Auchincloss, bearish and amiable, pumping my hand as though I had a county seat of my own. Next came Janet Auchincloss, slight and tawny and ductile, with a single strand of pearls and a palette of flaming red nails, giving me a tolerably firm handshake of her own and telling me I had time for a quick dip in the pool if I wanted to cool off before lunch.

"But I didn't bring any trunks," I said.

"Oh, we can certainly lay hands on a pair of Hughdie's, he never wears them. No? Are you sure? Well, *next time*."

Yes, it was a bit like being the prodigal Wasp, but even as I was letting down my guard, Jackie was dragging it back up. Eye rolls. Squeezes on the wrist. In retrospect, I wonder if she wasn't simply testing me, waiting for me to bolt. (Where?) Seconds before we traveled into the dining room, she whispered: "The stepmonsters and half-monsters are joining us, too. So sorry."

Nothing about the meal that ensued, though, was different in form or spirit from the Sunday lunches of my youth. The flocked silence, broken by crystal clinking against china. The atrial ticking of the grandfather clock. The beef bourguignon (gout special, Jackie called it), prepared in direct defiance of the warm weather. As for the stepmonsters and half-monsters, they seemed not terrified but bored. If they'd been encouraged to think of me as Jackie's suitor, the prospect had failed to rouse them, and the whole meal would have passed without incident if five-year-old Jamie hadn't announced between courses that he'd eaten a frog and let loose with a belch of such force that every fork stopped in reply.

"You may leave the table," said his mother.

He tossed his napkin onto his chair and made for freedom. No one was more envious than Janie, aged seven. "I told him he shouldn't," she said.

"Boys aren't always educable. And what about you, Nini?" said Janet, wheeling on her stepdaughter, seventeen. "Have you any reptiles you'd like to introduce?"

"Frogs are amphibians."

"Your expensive education is such a comfort. Tommy?" She turned to her stepson, fifteen. "Perhaps you have something to impart besides baseball cards."

"I don't think so."

"Nothing for the good of the cause?"

"Nope."

She gazed at him fondly. "This must have been how Madame de Sévigné felt, presiding over the great salons of the Place des Vosges. Mr. Billings, I don't know if you've noticed anything in particular about our staff."

"I can't say I've—"

"Unlike our Southern compères, we don't believe in colored servants."

"I see."

"Now I myself have a family tree stretching back to Richard Henry Lee, but I don't take cover in ancestry, I *know* how things work in our modern era. One can't have colored servants for the simple reason that one can't give them what for. Nini, sit up straight. I don't need to tell you how fraught it's become. If you tell your maid she's not up to snuff, the very next minute, she's calling some Jew lawyer . . ."

"Mummy."

". . . and, next morning, you're in violation of the Fourteenth Amendment. Janey, hands in lap."

I suppose I should note here that Mrs. Auchincloss never once raised her voice and never differentiated a political from a personal statement. She was, from first to last, making conversation. As for Hughdie, he retained the same mask of benign cheer at dessert that he'd worn during the appetizer. Only later would I learn he'd switched off his hearing aid.

The young people were released after pie, and the adults took coffee in the outdoor garden room. The heat was bearing down by now, and more than once, I had to tease some sweat off my brow with my napkin. The talk straggled toward the Gold Cup, then dwindled into pleasantries, then dwindled once more into the difficulties of maintaining a clay court. I was taking an unusual interest in the arc of a red-tailed hawk over the tree line when Mrs. Auchincloss pushed away her saucer.

"Jackie, you should take Sagebrush out for some exercise. The poor dear's pining for you, and you know it's perfectly vile of you to monopolize your friend the whole afternoon. Go for your ride, and Mr. Billings and I will take a stroll, how shall that be?"

Hughdie begged to know if he would be joining us.

"No, dear, it's nappy time."

"Are you quite sure?" asked Jackie.

"What do you think I'm going to do, feed him to the bears? I wouldn't do that to Eleanor Roosevelt." Hearing no further objection, Mrs. Auchincloss slipped on a pair of duck boots and called for her two King Charles spaniels.

It wasn't the formal tour I might have expected but a mostly eastward trek that followed the lawn as it sloped toward the bluff. From this distance, the river seemed to bifurcate: a still and brown crawl on the Maryland side that rematerialized on the Virginia side as a froth of whitecaps. Across the water came the first hint of a breeze, spiced with pollen, and the sound of the season's first cicadas, rattling and buzzing like Stukas.

"Do you hunt, Mr. Billings?"

"Not well."

"Shoot skeet, perhaps."

"Less well."

"We've a badminton court, if you like that sort of thing."

"I'm afraid I've never played."

"Nor I. It was all Hughdie's idea. I have to grant him at least one wish a year, you see, or he'll come up with more. I've found the trick is to keep each wish within bounds."

"And who grants *your* wishes?"

"I do. Which means they can be of any size."

In the smile that peeped now from her mouth, one could see a hint of the society nymph who had inveigled two such radically different men to the altar.

"You can't have much to wish for out here," I said. "It's heaven."

"I do still pinch myself, it's true. To be in all this *wildness*, and the city just eight miles away. Do you know," she added, with an additional pressure on my forearm, "that's as far off as I like to keep Washington." She came gradually to a halt, bent to give her dogs a scratch. Then, gazing toward the river, she said, with no darkening of tone: "You've been spending an awful lot of time with my daughter."

"I suppose that's true."

"Have I been misinformed, Mr. Billings?"

I smiled with as much robustness as I could manage. "Under the circumstances, I hope you'll call me Lem."

"I hope I shall have cause to. Jackie's been terribly close-mouthed about you two, but I mean, linen and candlelight, what's a mother to think? Never mind, she's assured me you're—well, let's just call you the boon companion. I'm now trying to find the nicest way to describe a congressman so *very* tied up with his own affairs that he must dispatch his—well, I'm afraid *boon companion* no longer covers that part. There must be some other expression."

"I don't think you need one. I'm your daughter's friend, that's all. I have no other role to play."

"Do you have a light, then?"

She offered me one of her cigarettes, and we smoked in silence, long enough for the dogs to collapse, sighing, around our feet.

"It's funny," she said. "It all reminds me of that Longfellow poem we used to read back in school. *The Courtship of Somebody.*"

"*Miles Standish.*"

"That's the one. Didn't he send a friend to do all his wooing for him? As I remember, it didn't end particularly well for him."

"It ended well for his friend."

I was gratified to catch her ever so slightly off guard.

"Well now," she said, studying me over her sunglasses. "I wonder if you're a more deep-revolving character than you let on, Mr. Billings."

"My intentions are honorable."

"Only if you mean the most obvious kind."

"I've no other. I'm not wooing your daughter on my behalf or anybody else's."

"Then what are you doing?"

"Enjoying her company."

"How *charmant*." She gave her cigarette one last drag, then dropped it into the grass and mashed it with her boot. "Tell your Miles Standish: We don't negotiate with go-betweens. This isn't the seventeenth century; a gentleman has to show his *face*. Even if he's no gentleman." She leaned in so close that I could smell the remains of coffee on her breath. "There's a limit," she murmured, "to how much social climbing one family can undertake."

TWENTY

*J*ack, no surprise, found the whole thing hilarious.

"Miles Standish? Did she really call me that? Wow, that's the first time anybody's ever accused me of being on the *Mayflower*. Ooh, but she sounds frosty."

That very night, I got a call from Mr. Kennedy.

"Listen, Lem. This girl."

"Girl, sir?"

"This Jackie."

You might say those two words were what lifted the whole business to a new level. Never in my adult days had I heard Mr. Kennedy refer to one of Jack's girls by name.

"Yes, sir."

"What can you tell me?"

Curiously, I glanced over just then and found my mother, lingering as though by contract, just outside the parlor door.

"Well now," I said. "She's very sweet."

"I'm not asking you if she's sweet, Lem. I don't care to know. What I mean is does she have the wherewithal to be a political wife. Does she have it in her?"

It amazes me now that I'd never thought to ask the question myself. As I leafed through the span of our Sundays, I couldn't recall a single political conversation. We were less likely, really, to talk about how Harry Truman might avoid impeachment than how John Garfield came to die in a showgirl's apartment. Once, I remember, Jackie volunteered that she had seen Mrs. Estes Kefauver under a K Street hair dryer, in the grips of a particularly dire permanent. Others might have ventured from there to discussing Senator Kefauver's crusade against organized crime or his electoral prospects on the national scene. Jackie and I wondered if the dryer heat was the thing that turned the faces of senators' wives into those impermeable masks captured every night on TV. From there we worked our way to a theory that Senator Kefauver's lopsided smile was caused by tiny swallows dragging up his top lip at the corners.

"Well, sir," I told Mr. Kennedy, "I would say that Jackie is a diligent student of the world. She may not have extensive experience in the sphere of politics, but she would undoubtedly take to it. If for no other reason than that she's awfully attached to your son."

"She wouldn't be the first. Or the last. The thing is, Lem, we can't afford to pin these particular plans to a shrinking violet. Ethel tells me the girl is whispery."

"I would say soft-spoken."

"There's also been some question raised as to her breeding potential."

"Ohh, I couldn't speak to that, sir. I mean, if it's any indication, her mother"—once again I glanced at my *own* mother, still stationed in the doorway—"has borne four children."

"You raise an excellent point. If she could avoid clap from the first husband and squeeze sperm out of the second, she has life force. What about other men?"

"Sir?"

"Does this girl have other men in her life?"

"Well, there was a fiancé."

"He's nothing to worry about. Any others?"

"Not that I know of but—"

"Does she seem like the type who *would*?

"Would . . ."

"Take advantage of an opening."

"I wouldn't suppose so."

"Has she ever confessed to being a virgin? Or not?"

"It hasn't come up, sir."

Scrambling then toward a safer topic, I landed on:

"She speaks languages, you know. Three or . . . it might be four."

There was a pause, then a staccato burst of laughter.

"Can she say *no* in any of them, Lem?"

"Oh, I'm sure she *could*, she—"

"Does she have any other degenerate habits? Things that, once they got into the bloodline, might be hard to get out again."

"Well, I would consider her a—a very hard *worker*, sir, if that's what you mean. I mean, she writes this column, you know, and it's not—I mean, she never misses a deadline."

"I've seen the column, Lem." His voice dropped by a minor third. "It's exactly the kind of thing a debutante would write."

I bridled a little on her behalf. Maybe because I'd seen her chemical-stained fingernails or because I'd kept the manila envelope of her clippings, which included the issue where she'd made the front page. (*"Which First Lady would you like to have been?" Asked outside of the White House.*)

"Listen," he swept on, "we're having her up to the Cape for the Fourth. Can we count on you to be there?"

I had, in fact, made plans for the Fourth with Mother, but he sallied back with:

"We wouldn't normally ask, but you seem to have gotten to know this girl better than anybody. I figured you might interpret her for the rest of us."

SO THIS WAS to be my role: Squanto, translating the young maiden for the Kennedy pilgrims. Whatever misgivings I entertained went away when Jackie called the next morning.

"My God, they've just invited me up for the Fourth. The whole Irish lot of them. Lem, you've got to go, or I'll die. I'll actually curl up like a centipede and die."

"But what can *I* do?"

There was a moment of incredulous silence.

"You can *explain* them to me."

*   *   *

THERE WAS NO compound in those days, just a white-clap-board house at 50 Marchant Avenue. To call it a cottage meant you came from a world where cottages had eleven bedrooms (four for servants) and nine bathrooms and a sewing room and a packing room and a sunroom and a four-car garage and an enclosed swimming pool and a tennis court and a huge wraparound porch with an unoccluded view of the Atlantic. I once asked Jack why they so rarely went into town. "Why would we?" he answered.

Now Jackie, child of Merrywood and Hammersmith Farm, didn't blink at any of this. What she wasn't prepared for was the relaxed dress code, which, by her standards, meant an opulently skirted champagne-on-caviar silk-taffeta dress. Imagine her dismay when, on the very first night, each Kennedy girl strolled to the table in some variation of Bermuda shorts and Capezios. The last to arrive was Ethel, defiantly casual in a plaid gingham shirt and tennies. She gave Jackie the full up-and-down and then, in a tone of manufactured horror, cried:

"I forgot about the fashion shoot!"

There I was, assuming it was a one-off joke, but Jean at once broke in with:

"I *told* you *Harper's Bazaar* was coming!"

"Oh, my God, *when*?"

"Five minutes!"

"I should really change."

"You should."

"This very instant."

"Sooner."

"What will I wear, though?"

"I'd say your best Pierre Balmain."

"I didn't bring it."

"Are you sure? It's not all balled up in the bottom of your bassinet?"

By now, Pat and Eunice were joining in from their seats, offering Ethel couture from their own closets—Chanels, Balenciagas—and, when that failed, suggesting she duck out back when the photographer got there, hide under a lobster net. The whole routine lasted no more than a minute; the voices never rose above the conversational; the gazes never once swerved Jackie's way; the intent was unmistakable.

It wasn't the hazing I'd prepared her for. No, on the train ride up, I'd spoken of my own first dinner with the family, when I had no more status in the world then than Jack's friend from school. I will never forget when Mr. Kennedy, not three seconds after sitting down to dinner, gave his napkin a snap, gazed on me with those mild eyes, and said, "I see Barrio has resigned the prime-ministership in Spain. Any thoughts on his successor, Lem?"

The laugh had scaled halfway up my throat before I could send it back down. *Barrio?* But when I gazed around that table, every face, from Teddy's on up, was turned toward mine, and every knife and fork hung suspended. Stunned, I tried to summon up Spain from the world map—a fat T, wasn't it, in Europe's southwest corner? hugging Portugal to its bosom?—but nothing about the shape translated into facts, and my mouth went dry as salt. I cleared my throat and cleared it again.

Joe Junior was the one who saved me, not from charity but impatience. "If you ask *me*," he said, giving his own napkin a snap, "this new man Lerroux will have no end of trouble with the anarchists and Communists. But, unlike Roosevelt, he'll have the benefit of a military unconstrained by democratic traditions." I was just sifting that through my brain when I heard Jack—sixteen years, a hundred twenty pounds—pipe forth that Lerroux would have an even harder time contending with the Catalan separatist movement and might soon have to make politically unsavory allegiances with the extreme right, as exemplified by Generalissimo Franco. Bobby and the girls leapt right in. Wasn't it time, in fact, to let the Catalans attain their long-cherished independence? Had they ever been successfully subjugated over their centuries-long history? And would Lerroux, in order to forestall his various insurgencies, have to make common cause with the Spanish Moroccans?

My God, I realized, *they've all been cramming.*

Jack more than any of them! Parrying each thrust. It suddenly made sense that he was the only boy at school who read the *Times*. He didn't want to be found wanting when Joe Senior came swooping in at the end of term with some poser from the back pages. No, Jack knew Joe Junior was reading those same pages, waiting his turn. Another fifty-meter sprint in the track meet that had shaped their whole lives together.

Well, from then on, in the weeks leading up to any Kennedy visit, I always made a point of picking up Jack's discarded newspapers and giving them a quick scan—I didn't want to be caught out again. Jackie did much the same thing, and that first night, when she took the proffered seat at Mr. Kennedy's right hand, she actually glanced down to see if any stray *facts* were peeping out from her corselet. Perhaps out of chivalry, he went a bit gently with her and, though he himself wasn't literary, confined most of his questions to books. Had she read *Witness*, by Whittaker Chambers? No, though she hoped it would help its author pay off his legal bills. Had she read *The Old Man and the Sea*? Why, yes, it only took an hour or two. Did she agree that Hemingway was the greatest writer of his generation? She had a sneaking fondness for Fitzgerald, but maybe that was because he seemed to enjoy women more.

During the whole interrogation, I could see Jack softly rubbing her elbow with his thumb. Encouragement or seduction, I couldn't be sure, but I think it helped to steel her. It helped, too, that they were in the heart of campaign season, and Mr. Kennedy had only so much energy to devote to people who weren't Henry Cabot Lodge, and of course, by now, the larger Kennedy uproar had taken over—all of it pointing inward. Did anybody have a worse backhand than Jack? Dear God, if Jean sliced one more ball into the woods, they'd have to name the forest after her. On and on, a fusillade of insult, wadded-up napkins, dinner rolls lobbed across the table, and in the midst of this Irish picnic, Jackie felt safe enough to give me a veiled wink across the table, which I received with almost as much reassurance as if I myself had been the newcomer.

We were halfway through dessert when Mr. Kennedy called down the table.

"Morton?"

He was addressing Morton Downey, a saloon singer from the twenties and thirties with a body made for radio and an epicene, almost castrato-like tenor that women tended to die for. He married a movie starlet and fathered a litter of kids, but as his listenership declined, he consoled himself with finding an audience of one in Mr. Kennedy, who, for all his pains to leave his heritage behind, liked to surround himself with micks—daily reminders, you might say, of what he'd transcended. Morton was far and away the most illustrious of—well, let's call them the lackeys—but that didn't make him any less obliging when the command came. Without another thought, he set down his fork and padded into the living room, seated himself at Mrs. Kennedy's Ivers & Pond and called up a swell of damp chords. Then, in a voice of maudlin conviction, he began to sing one of his old hits, "That's How I Spell Ireland," which did indeed require him to spell the damn thing at excruciating length. *E* for *Eileen* and *A* for *angels* and on and on. Just when he'd got through that first chorus and you were starting to relax, there followed two more verses, not to mention two reprises of the chorus, and when Morton got to the final line, he lingered with such ferocity on the penultimate syllable, wove such a nest of melismatic thread around it, that you'd have sworn he'd die before he struck *land*. It's no surprise that my eyes cut toward Jackie. The surprise, really, was that she was looking not at me but Jack. Whispering in his ear.

I could tell it was something wicked because of the hiccupping motion his chest made, and I remember feeling the most curious twinge, as though somebody had pulled up the ladder to a treehouse. Looking back, though, I can see this was the first time they became coconspirators. I can see, too, why it had to happen. Jackie, casting about for succor, must have realized that I was no less an outsider than she in some ways and could offer only so much protection. If she was going to get out of this kingdom alive, it would need to be under the aegis of the crown prince.

"Say now," Jack whispered to her. "This evening isn't turning out half bad."

AFTER DESSERT, WE adjourned downstairs to Mr. Kennedy's state-of-the-art movie theater. This was a carryover from his days in the film business and, you might say, a sign that his home was not a retreat from but a rival to the world. Being a devotee of grosses, he took no special interest in aesthetics, and that night's picture was a perfect stinker called *The Winning Team*. It was the kind of movie where they throw one damn thing after the other at the hero—he's poor, he injures his eye, goes to war, develops epilepsy, becomes a drunk—and he rises above every damn one with the help of Doris Day.

It would have been one thing if Jackie were a baseball fan, but she found the whole game bafflingly static: men braced for the extremely off chance that something might happen. She knew, though, there was no chance to excuse herself with a yawn or a stretch, not when Mr. Kennedy insisted on planting her in the front row—pinning her, in effect, between himself and Jack. So it must have been a relief of sorts when, halfway through, the old man tapped her on her arm and motioned to the door. In the dimness of that theater, she had some idea that the whole family would be trailing behind, but the door closed after her, and it was then she remembered—well, not the first thing Jack had told her upon her arrival but the third.

"Don't let the old man get you alone."

But Mr. Kennedy's tall, stooped figure was already traveling down that crepuscular hallway. He paused before the last door, then swung it open and ushered her inside. Darkness sprang away before an infusion of electric light, and Jackie found herself surrounded by an armada of dolls. Hundreds upon hundreds—from every clime, in every costume—frozen and unblinking in glass cases. She told me later she thought she'd stumbled into a charnel house, and the only place she could bear to rest her eyes was on Mr. Kennedy and only because he was alive.

"Did you have any dolls of your own, Jackie?"

"One or two."

"I didn't set out to be a collector, but we acquired so damn many when we were in London. I don't know why, but when you're an ambassador, people bring you dolls."

"I suppose there are worse things."

"Mm." He executed a slow pivot. "Of course, in the old days, this was just a plain old storage room. Lobster pots and fishing rods. Beach chairs." He waited no more than a second before adding, in the exact same tone: "This is where I used to take Gloria. And I do mean *take* her."

Who, she wondered, was Gloria? A secretary? A governess?

Her mind shifted through the possibilities before settling on the most neutral.

"Is that so?"

"Again and *again*. The woman was insatiable, I tell you."

In fact, as Jackie was about to learn, this Gloria had the tastiest rosebud and the tightest pussy God ever gave a female and was capable of coming six times in a single evening. She loved swallowing his semen—claimed it had curative properties—and whenever she was ready for another round, she'd nibble on his ear and whisper, "Olé."

Jackie sensed, not for the first or last time, that she was being tested. It was true that she'd heard anecdotes just as salacious, if not more so, from her own father, who, in the course of picking her up from Miss Porter's, would speak in an almost fatigued way about which of her classmates' mothers he'd fucked, embroidering every conquest down to the smallest detail. Jackie had taken it in without a peep, her dark eyes gleaming with an occult knowledge, but it had all felt, under the conditions, like a clannish rite, the Bouviers against the world. By contrast, the experience of gazing into Mr. Kennedy's gelid blue eyes, of watching him light a La Corona cigar, left her feeling like a minority of one. She could feel her skin shrinking around her bones.

"How much do you earn, child?" he asked.

She hesitated but eventually volunteered that she earned fifty-six a week from the *Times-Herald* (up from fifty-two) and a fifty-dollar monthly allowance from her stepfather.

"So a little more than thirty-five hundred a year."

"I guess."

"Does that seem like a lot to you?"

"I don't know. I suppose it's better than nothing."

"It's pretty damn close. For a girl who likes nice things."

Now, of all moments, she blushed. "I would say I care for beauty," she protested.

"That comes with a price tag, too. Or didn't anybody tell you? Even these dolls," he said, sketching a circle around the room. "It cost a small fortune to ship 'em across the Atlantic. Well, it would have been a small fortune to anybody else." His face unexpectedly blossomed into a grin. "Do you know I could sit down right now and write out a check for ten million dollars?"

I'm sure you could do it standing, she thought, and it was a mark of where she sat in the power relations that she held her tongue.

"Oh," he went on, "you'll think I'm boasting, but really, I'm putting things in perspective. You see, I earned that money so my children wouldn't have to. So they could be free and independent and do what they damn well pleased with their lives. And here's the thing, when you have a million-dollar trust fund, you can do what you damn well please with your life." He gave his cigar a speculative roll. "Take my boy Jack. He's many things—good, bad and indifferent—but the thing he is more than anything is set *up*. He's lucky that way, and the girl who marries him will be lucky, too, never having to worry about money again. Think of all—all the *beauty* she'd have at her command."

Just over Mr. Kennedy's shoulder, a doll in a red-and-white dirndl was studying her with glassy eyes of the most piercing blue.

"It sounds like . . ." she began.

"Like what?"

"A business venture, I guess."

"What's the difference? You tell me, what's the difference? A girl invests poorly, she gets nothing. She invests wisely, she gets a return. Ask your mother if you don't believe me."

He had crossed some line, she grasped this, and in a strange way, it emboldened her to hold his gaze.

"I think my mother—of all people—would say feelings enter into it, too. If the feelings are bad, money won't fix it."

"Only because there's not enough money. Ask my wife if you don't believe me. How many women her age get to spend every spring in Paris gawking at fashion shows? She buys anything she damn well pleases, ships it back overseas, and sashays home when she's good and ready. *Another* lucky girl, and she knows it, no matter how much she grouses. What I'm telling you, my dear, is that feelings are the one thing in a marriage that needn't be rushed." He paused, and then, in a voice of equivocal blankness, added: "You know, there are a lot of other rooms in this house. I'd be happy to show 'em to you."

For a few seconds, she could do nothing more than stare. At last she heard herself say:

"I'm dying to know how the movie ends."

He took a luxuriant drag of his cigar.

"So am I."

TWENTY-ONE

Shortly after eleven, she was shown to the last in an endless row of doors. Opening it, she found a curious mélange of décor: oyster white walls and a hunter green coverlet, a chintz-covered headboard and a wooden icebox, a pair of unengraved victory cups, a badminton racket and, on the dressing table, a perfume bottle, nearly empty, with a mighty stopper. The bed itself was no wider than the back seat of a car and no more comfortable. She sat, a little dazed, in the cane-bottom chair by the window, smoking a cigarette, only to stub it out when a knock came at the door.

It was Jack, poking his head around the corner. "Comfy?" he asked, closing the door softly after him.

"Oh, I'm just wondering whose room this is."

"Nobody's."

"So it's a guest room?"

"Every room is a guest room."

It was her next lesson in the Kennedy way. No matter where the family hung its hat—Bronxville, Hyannisport, Palm Beach—no child had a lock on any room. Depending on when your boarding school let out, you came back to whatever space hadn't been claimed. No point putting up a picture or squirreling away a stamp collection, not when you'd have to drag it out again a month later. You simply joined the nomad caravan. To someone like Jackie, who kept her room as sealed and curated as the British Museum, the news landed with a soft horror.

"You mean there's nothing anywhere that belongs to you?"

"Oh, sure," he answered easily. "Books and clothes and stuff. Scattered about." Then, not missing a beat: "There's you, maybe."

What a shock. To be claimed all over again. The feeling wasn't too different from what had rolled through her in that gravel driveway, only there was nowhere to put it. She rose from the chair and, after an interval of uncertainty, seated herself on the bed. He joined her there a moment later. Sat next to her, took her hand and, frowning down, said:

"He likes you."

"Oh," she said. "That's nice."

"It's what he told me, anyway."

"Then it must be true. I mean, he speaks his mind, your father."

"It's his tragic flaw."

She sat awhile, wondering how long it would take for one of her flaws to be declared tragic. Perhaps that was just the province of old men.

"Are you glad you came?" Jack asked.

"Of course. Are you?"

"Why wouldn't I be?"

Her eyes grazed toward the window. "Did you wonder if I wouldn't?"

"I guess I didn't . . . one way or the other . . . "

Something had lodged in him, she couldn't say what. She could only wait for it to jar loose.

"Did he make moves on you?" he asked at last.

"No," she answered. "I . . . no . . ."

"You're sure?"

"Yes."

"Okay."

The scene in the doll room flashed once more upon her. From that nightmarish swirl of unblinking eyes, a single question fought itself clear.

"Who's Gloria?"

There was, about his mouth, just the lightest tightening. "He mentioned her?"

"Oh, yes."

"In a euphemistic way or—"

"Not a bit."

"Huh." Jack glanced away. His mouth relaxed into a half grin. "Well, geez, you've seen *Sunset Boulevard*, haven't you?"

She stared at him. "Gloria *Swanson*?"

"The same."

"That . . . crazy old silent-movie queen with the turban?"

"Well, she wasn't old *then*, this was twenty-five years ago. As for crazy, well, she was crazy for Dad, I guess. At least that's where her career went."

"And he brought her here?"

"Sure."

"Your mother didn't object?"

"Why would she?"

Jackie took a moment to imagine Mrs. Kennedy and Norma Desmond, in matching turbans, staring at each other across the dinner table.

"I even caught them at it once," Jack said.

"Who?"

"Dad and Gloria."

"You *caught* them? Where?"

"On the boat."

She peered into his face, trying to turn back the years, the better to warm to this child who had wandered into the wrong cabin. But it was as if he had fixed himself against her exact purpose, for the old grin slid down and, when she raised a hand in the direction of his cheek, he deftly intercepted it.

"It was very educational," he declared. He held her hand for a while longer, then softly kissed each finger. "What symmetrical digits," he purred.

Then, abruptly, he stood and turned away, but not before she had glimpsed the mound pressing against his khakis. The thought landed with a brute force: *What would Gloria do?* Would she have beckoned him to her bed? Drawn him *in*, again and again, shrieking *Olé* at such volume the servants would come running? In the end, somewhat to her own disappointment, she could only be herself, sitting there on the edge of the bed in a kind of melting suspension.

"Lock the door, now," he said. "Lock the door, my little princess."

And just as she was beginning to glow at that epithet, he said:

"Try not to play on Lem's team tomorrow."

TEAM, SHE ECHOED. *Tomorrow.* Was it to be another round of Charades? Or Categories with Ethel? In fact, it was something worse. It was football.

Touch football, officially, though for the men, it was something closer to semi-tackle. The kind of enterprise in which Teddy could disembowel Bobby and Bobby could respond in kind. Ethel, being well along in pregnancy, was spared physical violence but not her husband's outrage when she dropped a pass. "It was right in your goddamn hands! Western Union couldn't have delivered it better!"

Jackie had spent most of her life blessedly ignorant of the game, but she knew enough of its rules to know they were being flouted from the first hike. Once the ball was in motion, whoever owned it could pass or lateral to anyone else anywhere on the field. Fumbles made not the least bit of difference, and it was left to Mr. Kennedy, surveying the proceedings from the porch, to intervene periodically with a finger whistle.

"Ball goes to Team Jack!" he might call down, at which Team Bobby would launch into a counteroffensive of lawyerly arguments and masculine shaming. The only one who stayed out of it, really, was Lem. He had found, through years of trial and error, the one thing he did well, which was rushing the quarterback. "One Mississippi, two Mississippi!" Then he'd charge toward the nearest Kennedy, waving his arms like an enraged bear. Once the ball had been lofted past him, he might in a general way make in its direction, but no one was more relieved when the line of scrimmage, after some debate, was reasserted and he might once again go charging forth.

Jackie, for her part, sought comfort at the perimeter. If Jack instructed her to go ten yards down the field and make a buttonhook, she didn't stop to ask what a buttonhook was, she merely went jogging in the general direction of the ocean. Once, to her great surprise, the ball actually landed in her arms. She stared at as if it were a foundling, then began running toward what she perceived to be the goal line. From behind came a stampeding of feet and a bestial grunt. Turning, she found Eunice, teeth bared to the gumline. A second later, she lay stunned in the grass.

"You're not hurt," said Eunice, drawing her to her feet. It would later occur to Jackie that every Kennedy child must have grown up hearing those same words. She herself had been thrown from horses in her brief time on Earth, but, in each case, the pain had been mitigated by the knowledge that no active malice lay behind it. When, a few plays later, she was tackled in almost exactly the same way by Pat, she

chose to embroider her contusions into an injured ankle
and make a mincing exit toward the porch where, though
she drew out her rattan chair to within a few feet of him,
Mr. Kennedy scarcely acknowledged her. It was his wife—
emerging shortly after, dressed for church and carting a
pitcher of lemonade—who beamed at her as though they
were Coliseum ladies watching the gladiators.

"How *fast* these boys are," said Mrs. Kennedy.

The next day, she was back to her usual cool self, bidding
farewell to Jackie with an outstretched hand. The Kennedy
girls, at least, were grudgingly polite and expressed the hope
that they might see her sometime in Washington, and Mr.
Kennedy clasped her in a brief, close embrace. The whole
business passed in smiles and lightly cocked heads and soft
waves, and Jackie had the decency to wait until she was on
the homeward-bound train before asking: "Why do you like
them so much?"

I TOLD HER then that, to appreciate the Kennedys as I did,
you would have had to be an impoverished Wasp from
Pittsburgh with a widowed mother fluttering like a moth
against her shrinking circumstances. I'd grown up around
horsehair furniture and auctioned-off leather-bound sets,
and my youth, it seemed to me now, was an arrangement in
black and gray, whereas the Kennedys were the full ultravio-
let spectrum. Rancor and laughter and sailing into the wind.
It didn't matter how well you played a particular game—
there would always be another—so long as you played in
earnest and raged at the outcome. I can't explain it exactly,

but the world just seemed to accelerate around them, and if you somehow found the capacity to keep up with them, it didn't matter how hard you were working to do it because they rewarded you by acting as if you'd been there the whole time. My mother always used to say we have two families, the one we're born to and the one we find. Well, I mean, to find such a family—I thought I'd hit the taproot.

That was not a feeling Jackie could share. To make sense of her three days and two nights with the Kennedys, she had to come at them like Margaret Mead in a pith helmet. Observe, she noted, the savages in their littoral clime. Charging from room to room, falling over each other like gorillas. Observe in particular how much of their humor centers on people coming to harm. With what hilarity do they speak of young Jack crashing his bicycle into young Joe's and coming away with twenty-one stitches. Of young Bobby, in response to the dinner bell, colliding with the glass partition between living and dining room. Of young Lem, for that matter, scalded within an inch of his life by the Kennedy shower. *Wasn't that a hoot?* Even the oft-repeated lore of Mr. Kennedy selling all his shares just days before the stock market crash depends for its pungency on the millions who didn't. One must conclude that this tribal culture admits of only winners and losers.

By the time she got back to Washington, Jackie had decided that the Kennedys were not to be surmounted, only sidestepped, held at *bay*, if she were to have access to one particular Kennedy. And this Kennedy had only grown in appeal now that his interest in her had ceased to be speculative and now that he was set alongside his family. She couldn't help noticing that, during the whole ridiculous family football match, he, alone of the three sons, had never been tackled. Looking back, of course, she could see this was a tacit acknowledgment of his medical status, but at the time, she felt it as a gesture of fealty, and she assumed there would come a time when the same fealty might be extended to her.

And even if it weren't, what should she care if she could have the man himself? He was calling more frequently from the road—in the early evening, when he was still relatively fresh—and on those infrequent occasions when he came down to Washington to put the squeeze on donors, he made a point of asking her to dinner. (Mrs. Lincoln handled the reservations.) Depending on their respective schedules, dinner might lead to another kind of squeeze. On the way out of The Colony, say, he might curl his arm around her waist, then very gradually tighten. The taxi would take them back to the *Times-Herald* offices where her own car waited, and there might follow another squeeze, another kiss or two. Then she would drive back to Merrywood, only a little worse for wear.

One night, he made a point of asking George, his valet, to pick them up in the Ford Crestline. The top, she noticed, had not come down though the early-August heat was oppressive.

"Have you ever been to Hains Point?" he asked.

It lay at the tip of an ersatz island, dredged up from the confluence of the Anacostia and Potomac rivers and threatening under any heavy rainstorm to return. The slow drop in elevation, coupled with the steaminess of the night, left her feeling queasily subterranean. After a few minutes, the car slowed, then lilted to a stop. The engine switched off. Jack murmured:

"How about you take a smoke break, George?"

George had neither a cigarette nor a lighter, but he was already stepping out of the car, shutting the door after him and strolling toward the river, where the lights of the capital lay trapped in air-amber. She waited. Then, as if suddenly remembering something, he curved a hand around the back of her head and leaned in. She could feel his razor stubble, lightly abrading her jaw and neck, his free hand deftly unbuttoning the top button of her dress and taking a speculative walk down to her clavicle. She recognized what her role should be—to withdraw, to deny—but the cloud of his breath seemed to find a parallel cloud in hers. A humus-like heat rose up around them, and his free hand ventured farther, and she silently called it further, and there was no telling how far things would have gone had there not come two quick raps on the window.

It wasn't George returning from his smoke break but an officer from the U.S. Park Police. A *mounted* officer, drawn by their fogged-out windows and pinning them now with the full force of his flashlight. Expecting, probably, to put the fear of God into two kids from Sidwell Friends and finding instead a young woman yanking up her bra strap and a somewhat older man suavely drawing out his House ID.

"Oh, gee, I'm sorry, Congressman! Guess I didn't see the tags. Listen, you folks have a good night!"

Jack waited until the horse clops died out, then turned back, expecting to resume, but she couldn't. The embarrassment of being caught in the back seat like a horny teenager with bobby pins flying—nothing could survive that. Jack gleaned her position at once and, without another word, rolled down the window and called for George. She gave him this much credit. He didn't sulk or wheedle or nurse hard feelings. He just packed up his lemonade stand, as it were, and carried it away.

By midnight, she was able at last to pull her bedsheets over her and recall that stolen interval with a smattering of pleasure. She recalled, in particular, his face in the car's shadows, a perfect mask of desire. Recalled, too, how powerless she had felt in the face of her own desire. She was a girl of her era and so could never be entirely free of shame, whether it came from her mother or, more comprehensively, the One True Faith, with its incense and ashes, the trapped air of its confessional booth. As secular as she was, she hadn't yet divested herself of the hope of salvation.

But what was salvation to Jack, who was all the more attractive for being so indifferent to souls, his own or anyone else's? And so as she allowed her own hand to finish the journey he'd begun—over the clavicle, down the abdomen, past the pelvic bone—it was Jack whom she conjured up. His cedar scent in her nostrils, his bony weight pressing down—not crushing so much as guiding her toward her final destination. When it was over, she lay there for some time, her chest lightly rising and falling, sweat in bands along her brow, wishing he could see her.

THE NEXT DAY, he called her at work. "Sorry about that interruption," he muttered.

Oh, she had to restrain herself from saying. *We got there.*

TWENTY-TWO

*T*hrough all this, Jackie and I were, by common consent, carrying on with our Sunday outings. Jack was never at liberty to join us, but wherever we went, his spirit followed. Jackie was always wondering if he'd like it there, too. (The answer, often as not, was no.) What would he be ordering? What kind of wiseacre remarks would he be making? She was compulsive about scanning the clothes of passing men to see which would suit him. "He likes navy, doesn't he?" "I think he'd look well in chalk stripes" "Maybe a wool necktie, just for the holidays." And I'd find myself saying things like "Not with that Duke of Kent knot" or "Double-breasted, are you kidding? It's got to be two-button or he won't look at it." But when she hit it just right, I'd cry:

"Wrap it up, missy! We're taking it home." And she'd grin like a child at a carnival.

When the talk flagged, she'd beg me to tell her something else about her new boyfriend. Were the members of the Choate Muckers *really* expelled? she wanted to know. Yes, but only for a few hours. Had Jack really bet me a hundred bucks to take off my clothes and sing a Mae West tune to Mr. Kennedy? Well, yes, but I blanched at the last minute. Had Jack really packed twice as many socks as underwear when they traveled to Europe? Yes, and there was a theory behind it that has long since escaped me. Biography was where most of our conversations stayed, with the occasional excursion to medical history. Jack was allergic to dogs, yes, and—how this pained her—horses, and was a touch deaf in one ear and longer in one leg than the other and could eat any quantity of dairy products without gaining a pound. Now and again, even as she absorbed the minutiae, she chanced a deeper inquiry. One Sunday, for instance, she surprised me by asking, apropos of nothing, "What would Jack do with a virgin, I wonder?"

Well, I knew he wasn't the type to guide a trembling maiden, step by step, to Hymen's temple. He would be in too great a hurry. Then again, he wouldn't necessarily want a girl to be a "voyager" because then she'd have too many ports of comparison. So I bluffed out some sort of reply and deduced, from the mere raising of the question, that Jackie herself was still a virgin. This, of course, was something nobody would have remarked on in 1952, except to endorse it. Girls were to approach their wedding night with no clue as to what awaited them other than what they'd gleaned from girlfriends and *Forever Amber*. I remember trembling a little for Jackie, thrust up against so much sexual experience, so many notches in so many bedposts. Oh, she knew the ways of the world, all right. She had a healthy streak of observational wickedness in her—it was one of the things that had endeared her to me—but of carnal knowledge I assumed her largely innocent. Not too long afterward, though, she gazed rather moodily in the direction of a nineteenth-century call box and asked, "Do you think it's possible to love more than one person? I mean, really love?"

I told her that I knew as much about love as I knew about leprechauns. In both cases, I assumed them to be fantasies. She smiled a little and said nothing, and then a week later, under rather unusual circumstances, told me what was on her mind. And here is where I peer into the Schrödinger's box of Jackie's life and find an utterly different path leading to an utterly different John.

SHE MET HIM in Paris during her year at the Sorbonne. She knew him by name or, rather, by his father's name. J. P. Marquand, though largely forgotten today, was one of the premier fictional portraitists of America's Wasp establishment, a caste to which he himself was a rather embittered outsider—biting, as Mrs. Auchincloss once put it, the hand that had never fed him. John Marquand *Junior*—Johnny, to his friends—was embittered in his own way and had consciously marked out a route opposed to his father, serving overseas in World War Two, then settling down in the Paris he had helped to liberate and separating himself from the entirely appropriate wife who had, in the postwar spirit of normalcy, been assigned to him. Jackie first encountered him at an expat literary salon in Montmartre, and it was in a weird way his unattractiveness that drew her. Not that he wasn't pleasing to the eye—sandy hair, bright blue eyes, declarative Anglo-Saxon bones—but he had a way of stooping and brooding and snapping. He could play the piano by ear but hated doing it and hated anyone who asked him, and he had, over his left biceps, a snake tattoo that, having long ago horrified his parents, had become a hollow mockery. Whenever he encountered her, in whatever bar or walk-up, he never looked pleased to see her or regretful to see her go. She wasn't always sure he remembered who she was.

Here, finally, was what made her soft on him: He was writing a novel.

It was called *The Second Happiest Day*, and in his mind, it would transport the dry sociological voice of his father into the 1950s while positioning John Junior—John *Phillips* was the nom de plume—as the prophetic voice of his generation, those children born on the bare limb cut from under them by war. Johnny had got the whole thing figured out, with one glaring exception. He hadn't yet grasped he would need a muse.

By then Jackie was a little late to shape the first masterpiece, which was just a few months from completion, but she wasn't above wanting to stamp herself on the next one. She had only a feathery sense of how muse-ing worked—she sensed there was some gazing involved, discussion into the early hours—and she hadn't abandoned the inchoate ambitions that had brought her to Paris in the first place (art director of the twentieth century), but she had enough sense to keep her options open. And as she and Johnny began to meet with greater frequency, drinking grasshoppers and chain-smoking Gauloises Caporals at L'Éléphant Blanc, she began to find in him tiny coral veins of warmth that might be coaxed out. It seemed to her that the mere fact that she was willing to make this sometimes excruciating effort, if only for a few minutes at a time, meant that she might be in love, a little. One night, they were dancing to "Come on-a My House," and she noticed him looking at her in a slightly less vexed way than usual. "What's more beautiful than any work of art?" he asked, and before she could answer, he blurted: "You."

It was a line, of course—she'd heard plenty like it. At the same time, it was so out of character for him that it had the ring of truth. The grasshoppers kept coming, someone was always willing to light her cigarette, and as the night wore on, she and Johnny spilled, limb by limb, onto the pavement, entangled in ways that weren't always clear. By the time the midnight bells rang out, they were tottering up the Rue du Vieux Moulin in the direction of the Left Bank. Her brain was pickled, her face half buried in his peacoat.

Johnny muttered that it was so late they might as well go back to his place, but it was impossible to believe they were going anywhere. She dozed at intervals, or forgot she was moving. Perhaps he carried her part of the way. She awoke, as if crawling from a sack, to find herself in the foyer of Johnny's apartment building. An ancient concierge with mighty forearms was gazing at her from behind a tiny desk, and Johnny, with some difficulty, was dragging open the door to the elevator, one of those ancient Parisian models with the coffin-sized cage that moved at the pace of a vast bureaucracy. Jackie followed him inside and braced herself against the grillwork as he jabbed the button to the top floor. The cage, after some consideration, shuddered into motion, and Johnny turned to face her, momentarily at a loss. Then his mouth unlatched, and his breath began to clot into staccato rasps—a sound that should have been grotesque yet she found herself leaning into it. In the next second, they were lunging at each other. It might have been comical, two immovable forces colliding, but his superior weight drove her back against the elevator wall, the whole carriage groaning at the impact. He fumbled for his fly and fumbled for her skirt. She yanked down her girdle. Then, with a stunning infusion of strength, he hoisted her off the ground.

The iron grillwork pressed vividly into her lower back, and she found she couldn't distinguish the sensation of his hands from that of his hips. Every act and reaction seemed to be part of the same hydraulic process—she could almost imagine it working without her. Johnny arched his head toward the ceiling and gave out a great sorrowing cry, and the elevator lurched to a stop, and in the remnant light of the fifth floor, they regarded each other. Johnny's thing lolling shyly against his trousers. Jackie's stockings piled at her feet. Her gloves, shockingly, still on.

She followed him into his apartment, then hustled into the W.C. and washed herself on the bidet. Out of deferred chivalry, Johnny spent the night on the sofa, and she took the bed. She woke early the next morning, memory reassembling itself. She dressed herself in last night's clothes and stood staring out the casement window, smoking one of Johnny's cigarettes. Then she walked over to the sofa and knelt beside him. Touched his hair, his face—softly, so as not to wake him. She must have loved him very much. That was the only explanation, she told herself. The only reason, too, that she was crying.

Well, by the time she told me all about it, the tears had dried up, and she had been absolved of her sin by two different priests. What was left was more on the scale of a problem. How would Jack take the news?

"What news?" I asked.

"That I'm . . ."

"How would he even know?"

"Well, there are ways to tell, aren't there?"

I had to remind her this wasn't the Middle Ages—nobody was going to be checking her bedsheets for blood. It would almost be better, I said, to go into marriage with a little bit of experience. That way, you wouldn't be in such a terror about the sex part. I was moved, too, to detail some of Kick Kennedy's unconventional romantic past, which had twice gotten her disowned by her mother but had never once deterred Jack, who'd stood by her every step of the way.

"That doesn't count," said Jackie. "She was family."

Well, honestly, how was I to know what a man wanted

on his wedding night when I'd spent my life avoiding that question? By the time we were walking toward the street-car on Pennsylvania Avenue, I was distracted enough that I didn't hear her the first time and had to ask her to repeat herself.

"I sometimes think I still love him," she said.

"Him?"

"Johnny Marquand."

"Well," I said after a space, "it's perfectly natural to love your first real beau. I mean, you don't love him more than Jack, do you? All things considered?"

She thought about it longer than I would have guessed.

"Jack needs a wife," she said. "Johnny needs me. Even if he doesn't know it. Especially if he doesn't know it."

She was still speaking of him in the present tense, and I soon found that they were corresponding regularly and that their epistolary relationship was considerably less strained than the flesh-and-blood version. In print, he didn't sulk or bridle, and she could try on different poses with him, different hats, without fear of repercussion. Whatever thread still bound them she was reluctant to sever, particularly now that his much hoped-for career was taking off. The book had been accepted by Harper and Brothers. It would be serialized in the *Saturday Evening Post*, anointed by the Book of the Month Club. Johnny had cleared the bar with room to spare, and she found herself thinking what an interesting vocation it would be to be an author's wife. Renting a cottage in the Basque country. Taking excursions to Istanbul and Dubrovnik. She'd write dispatches for *Vogue*; he'd report on

Greek politics for *Harper's*. At the end of each day, he would set before her a sheaf of typewritten fiction, and she would retire with a glass of wine and read each line with a tactful, searching, generous intelligence, leaving the lightest pencil notes in the margins.

I don't know that many people would believe that Jackie Bouvier, having tasted of a Kennedy, might dream of another slightly less public path. One that led across the ocean to an acid, irascible writer who had never once said he liked her. But in those days, some large part of her was still willing to serve as a votary of the arts, for it was in Beauty that life's deepest meanings dwelled, or so she still believed, and I didn't have it in me to disagree.

And I have to think that, if Johnny Marquand had but said the word—the *words*—the right combination of *need* and *help* and *impossible* and *muse*, Jackie would have chucked her job and, with a queer sort of relief, her Congressman and caught the next plane to Paris and showed up at his doorstep, daring him to reject her, and the second book would have got written, and the third, there would have been prizes and speaking engagements, essays for *Life*, visiting professorships, film adaptations. The two of them gay and *distingué*, a couple in the least tedious sense of the word, trailing Old World glamour after them, Scott and Zelda without the madness.

So if I'm to speak of contingency, of Schrödinger's box, I will add that this came within a whisper or two of happening.

In 1979, I was invited to a book party at George Plimpton's Upper East Side duplex. The author in question was a rather eccentric character who had struck it big with his maiden outing in the early fifties but had failed, despite years of effort, to get a second novel off the ground. Perhaps he'd needed a muse after all because all the writing in circles had finally broken him, or at least stripped away his ambition, and he had retreated into a second marriage, financially comfortable and childless, devoted to travel and exotic pets. Now, after more than a quarter-century of literary silence, he was reemerging with a brief, illustrated monograph on the subject of parrots. Indeed, upon entering the book party, you found an actual parrot perched on the author's arm. In this way I came face-to-face with Johnny Marquand. Eccentric and well-lubricated, in a rumpled Oxford and corduroy blazer, looking as if he'd come from playing bocce in Central Park. Handing him my copy of *Dear Parrot* to sign, I happened to mention we had a friend in common. I was even on the verge of naming her, but, with a beery smile, he was already sliding the book back to me. "Friends are such an agony, aren't they?"

I didn't know what he meant at the time, but a year later, I think I do. Friends are the ones who tend to be there when the portal to some alongside life opens. They see you make the choices or fail to make them, and they grasp the consequences. It seems to me now that Johnny Marquand spent the rest of his life hearing the thrumming of a different destiny in his ear, and doing whatever he could to make the sound go away.

TWENTY-THREE

I doubt I ever would have learned about Johnny Marquand if something hadn't happened to me that summer after one of our Sunday-afternoon jaunts. Jackie left on the early side because she had to be at work first thing the next morning. This gave me an hour or so to while away before heading back to Baltimore, and because the evening air was unseasonably mild, I took a little stroll through the downtown section. I ended up in Lafayette Park, where I struck up a conversation with a gentleman of about my own age or perhaps a bit younger. We were standing by the Andrew Jackson equestrian statue, and I remember speaking to him about visiting the Hermitage in Nashville. I remember, too, how he could light a match with his own thumbnail, cupping his palm around the flame, and also light a match on the heel of his shoe. Well, in the course of this conversation, I must have, without meaning to, put ideas into this gentleman's head. For, as it proved, he was no gentleman but an undercover detective with the Metropolitan Police Department. A second later, I was under arrest!

Handcuffs were slipped over my wrists, I was shuffled toward a police cruiser and conveyed to the Indiana Avenue station. I remember trying to stay in an urbane register the whole time—the tone that conveys misunderstanding, right minds will set it straight—but each step in the pilgrimage pulled out another floorboard. There was the photograph. The fingerprinting, each digit jammed into the card. The surrender, one by one, of my hat, my wallet, my suspenders, my necktie, my shoelaces. They offered me the usual phone call, but whom was I to call? I had friends, of course, of long standing—great influence, some of them. I ran through them all in my mind. Family members, old prep-school chums. It was then I realized that, for all our relatively brief acquaintance, Jackie was the one person I couldn't imagine blanching at the news. The one person who might carry on afterward as if it had never happened, laugh it all to the winds, which was the only comfort I could extract.

So I called the extension at Merrywood. I must have dialed four or five times before a maid picked up. Another five or six minutes before Jackie came on the line.

"What's up, Lem?"

Still I was striving for urbanity. "You won't believe it." "Fellow came right up to me." "Just being pleasant."

"Thought he was just some drifter down on his luck." "Next thing you know." In retrospect, I can see there must have been a hollowness at the root because Jackie cut back in.

"What's the bail?"

"Well, it's five hundred, which is totally ridiculous. I mean, there's got to be a bondsman awake at this hour. Hell, there's *always* a bondsman awake, isn't there?"

"No," she said. "It should be cash."

This gave me pause. Rich people rarely walked around with money in those days.

"I'll ask Mummy," she said. "She's got cigar boxes salted everywhere. I just have to figure out where they are. I'll be there as soon as I can."

Strange, it was only then I realized I'd been carving divots out of my scalp, so deeply that blood now blazed like war paint from my fingertips. I must have made some cry because she asked if I was all right. I nodded, stupidly, as if she could see me. Then I asked if she could call my mother.

"What should I tell her?"

"Oh, just . . . tell her I'm not feeling so hot. Tell her I'm staying over at Jack's. And . . . you won't tell Jack, will you?"

"Of course not."

WELL, THERE MUST have been a lot of cigar boxes scattered around Merrywood because hour massed on hour. My cell was twelve-feet square with a single toilet, unflushed, unflushable. My cellmates were a young boy charged with firing a pistol and a drunk of no clear age who slept through the night except to vomit. The contents of his stomach formed a steadily welling pool around him that drove me finally to the furthest corner, where I sat, speaking to no one. I *grieved*, as though the world had already sawed out a circle beneath my feet. I thought of my mother, my sister, my colleagues at Emerson Drug. But the image that gave me the sharpest pang was Jack. How many thankful prayers did I cast up that my actual, hated first name—the name on my driver's license, the name on the booking card—was Kirk. Only somebody well versed in Billings genealogy could travel from there to Kirk LeMoyne, thence to Lem, thence to Lem's friend. No matter what happened, I kept reassuring myself, Jack would never be touched.

But the night bled on and the concrete dug in and the smell of rot fixed in my pores, and my mind, sprung from the cage that contained my body, sprinted toward every calamity. Cameras at my arraignment. My picture, pinned by flashbulbs to every front page. For some reason, it was Mrs. Auchincloss I envisioned, pausing in the act of sprinkling Worcestershire on her shirred eggs to squint at my half-toned image. *By God, he looks familiar!* The dawning would be gradual but ultimate and would be followed by phone calls. The news would fan out until there would be no square left in Christendom to harbor me.

Well, one way or another, I don't think I got more than five minutes of sleep that whole night, but if I didn't exactly doze, I *dazed*, until I heard my own last name, piercing the clay of evening-morning-afternoon.

"*Billings.*"

My effects were waiting for me in the anteroom. So was Jackie, dressed for work in a tailored blue linen suit with a tiny white check. She could not have looked more foreign to her surroundings, yet she fairly beamed to see me and hooked a hand through my arm and walked me past the interrogation department and the booking station, chattering the whole way, as if we'd just met up at Harvey's or the Occidental.

"Oh, Lem, what an awful bore for you. Now listen, I've found a lawyer. He's very well connected—son of a congressman—and he gets *every*one off. I mean, he strolls into court and prosecutors throw up their hands. So here's his card—he said to call him when you get back. Not from the office, of course. Oh, and I talked to your mother, and she says you should only come home when you're feeling up to it. I told her it was probably just one of those twenty-four-hour affairs, and it didn't sound like she was at *all* fretting. But maybe call her from Union Station to let her know you're on your way."

Her speech, it seems to me now, was a kind of flume, rushing us past each obstruction (the complaints department, the information desk) and sweeping us clear of our linoleum surroundings. We let the door close behind us and came down the stone steps, my trousers bunching under my feet because I hadn't stopped to refasten my suspenders. There wasn't time. If I could have, I would have walked straight back to Baltimore, trousers dragging behind me like a silent-film comic's, but I only got as far as the street before I . . .

Broke down is the best way to describe it. The *systemic* failure that left me collapsed on the nearest bench, head in hands, weeping volcanically. Sobs of such an extreme pitch that I quailed before them, for they seemed entirely independent of me. A broken levee that could never be patched.

"It's all right," said Jackie. "Let it out, darling. Let it *all* out."

WELL, IT'S BEEN true all my life. If one has been—has been *bared* in some painful, involuntary way, one's friends will often, in the spirit of compensation or fellow feeling, reveal something about themselves, as if to say: "Let's be naked together, shall we?" So it was with Jackie, who chose that moment to tell me about Johnny Marquand and the elevator and the whole messy business. And how strangely healing it was to hear it.

There's no point dwelling on the legal outcome of the Lafayette Park incident, except to say that, thanks to Jackie's lawyer and the three hundred dollars I handed to him in an unmarked envelope during our one and only meeting, the charges against me were dropped. I never had to set foot in a courtroom.

Of course, I paid back Jackie in full, and it was only later, almost in passing, that she told me of another kindness she'd done me. It seems that, without my knowing, the criminal-courts reporter for the *Times-Herald* had been tipped off to my situation and was set to publish a squib in the metro section. It would have had the usual identifiers—name, age, home address—for, of course, that was common practice in those days. Jackie kept a close vigil and, as soon as she learned something was in the works, talked her editor into spiking it. Told him I was the exact opposite of a deviant, and it would have been worse than a crime to have my name rubbing against muggers and murderers. She must have been persuasive because nothing ever ran, and the Auchinclosses never had to read about me over shirred eggs, and Mother's only response, when I finally dragged myself home Monday afternoon, was that, if I stayed away from hot dog vendors, I wouldn't come down with stomach flu.

As for Jack, he was none the wiser, so far as I know. I do remember that some years later, he asked me why I always insisted on leaving the White House by the southeast visitors' entrance. I couldn't tell him that the sight of Lafayette Park affected me in a particular way, so I made up some old family superstition. It's a curious thing that, as many times as I've been to Washington since then, I still can't wander by Lafayette Park.

The only person I've ever told about what happened is Raul, and I immediately regretted it because he insisted on parsing the whole thing.

"So you are telling me it was all a misunderstanding," he said.

"Of course."

"You went to Lafayette Park, which, as even I know, is a place that has always attracted a certain kind of man."

"Well, how was I to—"

"You began to make conversation with a stranger."

"It was called being friendly."

He asked me then how many other men I'd been friendly with in Lafayette Park or elsewhere. There was nothing particularly aggressive in his tone. I told him I'd had lots of friends of all types, male and female. I could neither count nor categorize them.

"Papi," he said. "Tell me where we first met."

"At Grand Central."

"Why did we meet?"

"You were coming back from a trip."

"And what were you doing?"

"Admiring the architecture."

"Ah. Was it the ceiling you were admiring? Or the Guastavino vaults?"

"Both."

"You are a lover of Beaux Arts."

"As you know."

"And all those years ago, when you were in Lafayette Park, you were looking at—what? Statues?"

"There was a statue, yes."

"And it was the statue that made you stop?"

I could feel my hackles rising, one by one. "I was out for a stroll."

"Ah."

"That sounds so *knowing*, and I don't know what I'm supposed to know."

"You *do* know. You just won't say."

"Say what?"

"What and who you are. It has a name."

Oh, I've told him more than once: Spare me your names.

There's a serious misapprehension going on in today's culture that actions are the same as identity. The Greeks understood that a man may do many things without being simply one thing. I'll never forget the time Raul invited me to his beloved Pride parade. Scowling lesbians, boys in crotch-high shorts, transvestites waving like Mississippi beauty queens from convertibles. They have an inalienable right to dress as they like and go where they will, but I cannot accept their acts as expressive of me. If you gave me the same number of Long Island matrons, I could commandeer a few blocks of New York once a year, and what would it signify?

The plain truth is I don't need an identity for the simple reason that I long ago found it. So I disclaim this club, even if they do, for some perverse reason, want me as a member, and Raul—well, he doesn't exactly disclaim *me*, but he does periodically despair. It's touching, really, how much he wants to save me. I get pamphlets and monographs and, though I have no car, bumper stickers. I get dragged to lectures on Bleecker Street, I get referred to therapists and, where that fails, theorists: Theodor Lessing on Jewish self-hatred, Anna Freud on denial, somebody named Foucault, who leaves me arctically cold. Even in our calmest moments, I can feel Raul combing through my words and deeds for the thread that will unravel me. He thinks it highly significant, for example, that I listen to Joan Sutherland and watch *Magnum, P.I.* Once, I happened to refer to some fellow in passing as "a Mary Louise," and Raul sat straight up, like a mariner putting a finger to the wind.

"'Mary Louise,'" he said.

"What?" I answered. "That's how we say it."

"Who is we?"

"People of my generation."

"Like *friend of Dorothy*? Do you also say this?"

"On occasion."

"Do you always speak in code? About these matters?"

"I consider it a wink."

"At whom are you winking?"

"The people who would get it. I don't know why you're making it so complicated."

"What I'm suggesting is that there is no need to wink anymore."

"No need not to."

His mouth folded down a fraction.

"So what you are saying is you are still scared."

You can see how impossible he can be. I demanded to know exactly what I should be scared of, and do you know what he said? "Whatever scared you *then*. Jail. Ruin. A mother's tears. Oh, please believe me, I am sympathetic, but you are a retired gentleman living comfortably in Manhattan. No one can touch you. Why should you hide behind codes?"

I believe I may have said something about decorum not being the same as hiding—decorum, to the contrary, being one of the building blocks of civilization—but I could hear my voice once more climbing to its highest register, and that to me is always a sign that (drawing a metaphor from a sport I despise) I have landed in the rough. What this means in practical terms is that we have regular fallings-out, Raul and I, and we withdraw to our respective corners of the city.

Weeks, even months go by before one of us sends out a conciliatory phone call. Nothing is said of the previous argument (I don't always recall what it was about) and we carry
on in our way. Given the difference in our ages, I suppose I
should be grateful he still considers me a project of interest,
and I try to find ways to let him know I'm not completely a
lost cause, even if I do draw the line at Foucault.

No, all in all, I consider it a good thing that we hav-
en't had a complete breach, only because the house has been
a little echoey since Bobby Junior went to law school. He
calls every so often, reversing the long-distance charge from
Charlottesville, but it rarely ends well. We had one particularly testy exchange last winter that ended with him yelling:
"Christ, I'm not *him*!"

Well, did I ever say he was? From the beginning, all I've
ever maintained is that Bobby Junior, foremost among his
siblings and cousins, has the intellect and charisma, the
innate qualities of leadership, to carry America forward. As
Jack manifestly did. And if I can be a part of helping him
realize his God-given potential, then I am happy to serve. It's
what I've always done, and it's what I've always said. Every
great leader needs a great friend.

After some introspection, I can see that Jack was, in
one respect at least, the lucky one. He didn't have a raft of
Kennedys getting there before him. A boy like Bobby Junior
looks around now and sees nothing but footprints, all deeper
than his own. That creates an enormous pressure, and I can
see how carrying on, as I like to do, about his father and
uncle—being the repository for family lore that I've always

been—well, that might add a little bit to the pressure. So, for now, I hold my tongue, I keep my distance.

But here's the thing. When you throw in your lot with a Catholic family like the Kennedys, you're never alone for long. Relation after relation comes your way. They stay in your guest room, they ask you up for the holidays, or they just ring you out of the blue to seek an opinion on a trestle farm table. I talk to Eunice practically every day, and I just helped the Smiths decorate their Bridgehampton place. Michael and his wife want me to do the same with their house in Virginia. I had a swell time with Courtney and her husband at Trader Vic's, and when Timmy Shriver graduated from Yale recently, I even threw a little celebration *chez moi*. A lovely evening—I believe I sang *The Mikado* all the way through, swords and everything, and I wasn't even drunk. It's true that I'm well on in years—sixty-five next month—and I can't exactly hack my way through the Colombian bush or gallop across the *llanos* as I once did with Bobby Junior, but I can still remember and, more to the point, still *remind* these young people, dear to me all, of the legacy they will one day fulfill. If that doesn't give a life meaning as it straggles toward its end, if that doesn't impart a legacy that will endure long after I've gone, then I don't know what could.

TWENTY-FOUR

All the same, I find myself lingering in my bathrobe longer than I should—some days I never take it off. Some mornings, too, I stay in bed a bit longer than I need to; I don't always open the blinds. There are times I'll hear an amusing joke from Carson, or I'll read about the two pandas trying to get it on at the National Zoo, and I have an overwhelming desire to—well, discuss it with someone. Just the other evening, I had the strongest urge to go see Alberta Hunter at the Cookery, yet the prospect of *getting* there—hailing a cab and scaring up a ticket and positioning myself within shouting distance of a men's room, then somehow beating the rest of the crowd back out to the curb to scare up another cab—I don't know, it all seemed quite impossible to negotiate. Alone, I mean. Now, I can't abide sentimentality in the elderly, but sometimes it catches me by the throat, so I find that traveling back in time is a kind of antihistamine, clearing out all the passages and enabling me to breathe more clearly.

For instance, I can see that, during that summer of '52, Jackie and I both passed tests that could, from a certain angle, be described as chivalric. My reward was a clean record; hers was an invitation. Upon learning that she was visiting family in Newport over Labor Day weekend, Jack spontaneously (or so it seemed) invited her to slide on over to the adjoining Bay State at her convenience and join him on the campaign trail. "Poke your head in" was how he put it, and she was left to imagine what that meant. Was she to be introduced in any capacity? Granted pride of place? Would she be walking at his side or trailing a few steps behind? At this point, of course, she had only the most rudimentary understanding of the political process, but one afternoon, she descended to the *Times-Herald* photograph morgue and assembled from the detritus of the past five years a collage of political wives—studied them as she might a spy cipher. She determined that they all had in common the ability to sit utterly still, ankles touching and toes turned lightly out. They also shared the gift of radiating a fathomless peace. *I have made the right choice, and so must you.* Jackie actually practiced the look herself in her bedroom mirror and found to her surprise that her own heartbeat was dropping, second by second, as though she were lying down to hibernate. This, she thought, was how she needed to be for Jack.

To cover herself in the event of any conversations breaking out, she combed the *Times-Herald* front section and
rang up Jack's office for his position papers "Containing
Soviet Expansion" and "Pumping up the Massachusetts
Economy" (the latter of which she fell asleep to while reading on the train). But, not surprisingly, the element that most
consumed her was what to wear. She scissored up magazines and catalogs, squinted into shop windows, even asked
random women on the street where they'd gotten a belt.
("Lansburgh's, did you really? Oh, it's darling.") Her goal at
first was simply to avoid standing out among the Kennedy
sisters and, by extension, Kennedy voters (who were all jum-
bled together in her head), so she took Ethel as her initial
model. Ethel wouldn't wear velvet, that was too old. No
lace or orchids. Pearls, maybe, but graduated. Some kind of
jacket. A small red hat, possibly, pinned at a demure angle.
Sensible heels in case there was walking.

As the date approached, she developed a morbid fear of
getting a run or a snag or a roll in her stockings, so she
packed double the usual number, as well as a quantity of
facial tissue in case her lipstick smeared, and when she woke
that Sunday, she took the coldest possible bath before climbing into the hired car.

All this had been founded on the idea that she would be
making an *impression*, good or ill. Yet the barely pubescent
aide who greeted her in Swansea merely pointed her in the
direction of a charter bus. "You might want to hurry up,
ma'am. Driver doesn't wait for anybody." She squeezed into
a seat next to a plump, fervent Teamster wife and reached

for the nearest window, only to find the latch broken. In this fashion, she was ferried from Middleborough (League of Women Voters) to Somerset (Catholic Women's Club) to Mattapoisett (VFW potluck). Some sort of food was always waiting for them, always a little too long out of doors. Hamburgers and wizened hot dogs, corn still crunching on the cob, a platter of gray fried clams and, for the many drinkers, kegs of Ballantine IPA and Pabst.

Mr. Kennedy was nowhere to be seen, but Jackie did accidentally cross paths with Mrs. Kennedy, in her best Sunday hat, abstractly extending a gloved sparrow's hand to all comers, and, on a lark, Jackie presented herself to the flesh-pressing duo of Pat and Eunice, who had no choice but to smile back. As for Jack, he was simply the grinning apparition who appeared at the very last minute, gathering up the crowd's noise in the way that a dirigible gathers up helium. His effect was so global and yet so intimate that Jackie, at first sight, thrust an arm in his direction, only to find a sea of arms on every side. In the five minutes that had been carved from his schedule, he answered one or two of the crowd's lightly lobbed questions, told some locally oriented joke, begged them to give Massachusetts the leadership it deserved and then, with the faintest crease of apology on his face, went back into the wings, waving the whole way.

The first two or three times, the electricity of the experience was enough to keep Jackie's mouth lightly upturned in case a camera or his gaze was trained in her direction. By early afternoon, she had realized how absurd she was being. Sometime around two, she was herded into a high-school gymnasium in Brockton, empty of students but redolent of every basketball player and cheerleader who had ever exhaled there. Jackie sat in the back row of the bleachers as a local marching band worked its way through "El Capitan" and, in the downpour of humidity, felt her tiny red hat pitching and bobbing beneath her traitorously curling hair.

"Won't you please welcome . . . the next senator of Massachusetts!"

As quickly as the Kennedy masses formed that day, they reformed. Filed into the same bus, assumed the same seats (God help you if you tried to switch) and reemerged at the next whistle stop with the same air of wonder. In Quincy, an aide she had never seen before pointed her toward the front row, where she sat with a horde of unreconstructed Fitzgerald cousins and had the satisfaction of hearing one of them whisper: "She's a friend of the family." Her view of Jack's head there was obstructed and, in Boston, at best telescopic. She would later recall this as her first taste of fame's centrifugal effects, the way in which the unfamous are flung outward, but so gently they have no idea they're moving.

Yet, as she and the Fitzgeralds filed out shortly after, she felt a gloved hand tap her on the shoulder. "You're doing just fine, dear," said Mrs. Kennedy.

She was grateful and baffled in equal measure, for in truth she had been doing nothing—nothing at all—over and again.

The day's true epiphany came in Fall River, where the Kennedy staff had organized a tea party. This was the meet-and-greet that had become the key innovation of the campaign—in large part, I should say, because it targeted women, whom strategists had always presumed would vote the same way as their fathers or husbands. Mrs. Kennedy, answering to her own instincts, simply mailed out engraved invitations to all the available women in the area—Democrat or Republican, it didn't matter—and in startling numbers they came. Milliners, housewives, secretaries, high-school principals, all in their best hats and frocks, clutching their invitations to their bosoms lest anybody try to bar the door. They gratefully shook Mrs. Kennedy's hand. They sipped from her china, commented on her silver service, nibbled absently on the cookies. It took the candidate to magnetize them. Sauntering in an hour late—which was to say, right on time—he surveyed the ballroom and, with a twinkle whose warmth, whose *heat*, could be felt a hundred yards off, said, "Ladies, you're a sight for sore eyes."

There was a brief speech, but the ritual truly came into focus—cracked open, in effect, to reveal its nuclear core— with the reception line, into which the ladies of Fall River merged with no urging or instruction. One by one, they passed before the great man, took his hand, felt the soft splash of his smile, the whole concentrated force of him. Half of them wanted Jack for a son-in-law, the other half for a husband, but Jackie noticed it was the older women who were more likely to lose themselves in his presence and, for want of words, pounce. Watching it all from an enforced distance, Jackie grew steadily disenchanted, and it was just as she was finally turning away that she realized:

The whole spectacle depended on Jack being single.

Every woman in that ballroom had to go in there thinking she had some kind of chance, however remote, and had
to leave thinking that she and Jack had experienced, in their
two-second crossing, a flicker of understanding and that the
only way to keep that flicker alive was to pass it along, to
friends and family members, until they were all part of the
same lambent race of adherents, rushing to their precincts
on Election Day, voting Kennedy as if their lives and dreams
depended on it because they did. Show them Jack's girl, and
the flicker would have been snuffed out at first sight.

Dear God, she thought. *He'd be a fool to marry anyone.*

Yet, even as she reached that conclusion, contrary evidence rushed in. He'd *asked* her to come, hadn't he? Surely
he'd wanted to give her a glimpse of this life—the life she
might one day share—so that she could be sure it suited her.
Oh, it was true he hadn't come within twenty feet of her
the whole day, but that was a function of logistics, wasn't
it, not feeling? And hadn't Mrs. Kennedy cast an approving vote, and as the tea party was winding down, wasn't it
Ethel, just a couple of weeks shy of labor, who strolled over
and tendered her a not unfriendly nod and made some con-
spiratorial joke about Fall River ladies? No, hard as Jackie
looked, she couldn't find any evidence to suggest she didn't
have some role, however obscure.

Bobby arranged for a driver to take her to the Providence
airport, and she had just climbed into the passenger side
and closed the door after her when she saw a figure jogging
toward her. It was Jack. He motioned for her to roll down
her window, then, after cutting his eyes both ways, leaned
into the car.

"Thanks for coming."

"I was happy to."

"You're a good sport," he said, and kissed her.

Circumstances didn't allow for more than a peck. Decoding it, however, would be the work of days, because it tasted so different from earlier ones. Was it simply a good sport's reward? Or was it something more affirmative, more domestic? Painstakingly she rolled back the reel to the point just *before* he leaned into the car, the peculiar sheen in his eyes. He wasn't just saying goodbye, he was studying her. And, in that instant, it seemed to her, making a decision.

She thought now of all those besotted women guzzling Mrs. Kennedy's tea or swelling the ranks of campaign rallies, longing in the recesses of their hearts for the gift that Jack had so casually and (it seemed to her) conclusively bestowed on her. She had it in her to pity them. She had it in her, too, to relish the fact that she had, in her own way, been elected. "Just think," she told herself more than once. "He could have had anyone. Anyone at all."

TWENTY-FIVE

*A*ny hope of attending Jack's Election Night party was scotched when her editor insisted that she stay in Washington to report on a local Eisenhower event. But even as she was putting her story to bed, she was following the teletype machines for returns from Massachusetts, and when she saw that Jack had won by a margin of seventy thousand votes—roughly the same number as the women who had flocked to Mrs. Kennedy's tea parties—Jackie permitted herself three cigarettes in quick succession and a tumbler of the peach schnapps that she kept in her desk, *Front Page*–style, for special occasions. The next night, she called me in Baltimore, badgering for details. How many people were at the Bellevue? When did Lodge put in the call? What were the first words out of Jack's mouth?

I told her as much as I could remember. Coke bottles and martini glasses, TV sets on fruit boxes, an endless fugue of ringing telephones. Bobby, with a pencil tucked behind each ear, dashing from one precinct map to the next. An old guy in a green hat, stomping out ballpark-organ chords on a piano, and every half hour, a barbershop quartet, recruited from Brookline to croon the campaign theme song: *He's your kind of man/So do all that you can/And vote for Kennedy!*

"What did the sisters wear? Not those flared skirts with the VOTE FOR KENNEDY embroidery?"

"The same."

"Ethel, too?"

"She couldn't come. The doctors said it was too soon after the baby."

"As though that would stop her. I'm surprised she didn't get a dispensation from Archbishop Cushing. What about Mr. Kennedy?"

Ah, that was a subject all its own. After years of self-appointed exile, the patriarch chose that particular evening to stroll back into the light of the cameras. Who could blame him? All those months of strategizing, all that *outflow*. Checks sent to the right people, meaningful phone calls to Senator McCarthy and the *Boston Post*. The TV, the radio, the handbills, the phone banks. He'd shouldered it all in manful silence so that *now*, surrounded by the family he'd so rigorously molded, by the son he'd so monastically served, he might exult.

"By God!" he shouted. "We did it!"

AND WAS SHE part of that *we*? She had spent no more than twelve hours on the hustings, but she held out hope that, in some intangible way, she had buoyed the candidate. Like those political wives in the newspaper morgue, she had backed the right man. Someone who had risen from segregated origins to the most exclusive club of all. It filled her with a kind of hush, contemplating his whole arc, and watching hers bend toward it. "Senator Kennedy," she would whisper when nobody was in earshot. "Senator and *Mrs.* Kennedy."

She never knew if Jack had tried to reach her on Election Night—he wouldn't have found her if he'd tried—but he did track her down in the newsroom the following afternoon.

"I'll be expecting a little more deference from you," he said.

"Well, you're in luck, I've been practicing my salaam."

"You'll have to show it to me."

"I'll be pleased to."

"And how is your kowtow? Have you been practicing that, too?"

"With the greatest relish."

"If you could somehow combine the salaam *and* the kowtow . . ."

"I'm not sure that's even legal."

He was too busy to say much more. On Thanksgiving Day, she received a call not from Jack but from Jack's father, who hoped that she was enjoying her holiday at Merrywood.

"Family are so important, aren't they?" he said before handing the phone to his wife, who encouraged Jackie to go easy on the wine. "It's bad for the figure, dear."

Jack himself never got on the line, an omission that puzzled her, and in the silence that now ensued from his end, Jackie began to question the credo she'd carried out of Fall River. Perhaps he'd only kissed her because he didn't know what else to do.

Resolution came from an unexpected quarter. That very Sunday, Mrs. Auchincloss put down the morning paper and, in a voice as silky as her omelet, said, "Isn't it time we met this politico of yours? Oh, don't look so surprised, darling, a mother always knows what her daughter is up to, and if she doesn't, she asks the people who do. Now, let's see, I've been looking at the calendar, and I *think* we have the second Saturday in December open if he's available."

To Jackie's surprise, Jack said yes. He was greeted by swags of Christmas holly and fir and pine on the banisters and moldings, even an Auchincloss child in a Santa hat, yet the mood from the start was not festive but commercial. Mrs. Auchincloss installed Jack at her right and kept the wine flowing and the talk moving, repeating things as necessary for Hughdie and quizzing her guest as though he were just another young man on the rise. "Oh, that sounds fascinating, Mr. Kennedy. I can see you've given a lot of thought to the subject. Indochina, you say? What an interesting line of work you've stumbled into."

"Mummy," Jackie finally said. "He's not Mr. Kennedy, he's Senator Kennedy."

"Already? I thought senators don't get sworn in until January."

"That's true," Jack acknowledged.

"Oh, so I haven't got it wrong. What a relief."

"He's still not a mister," Jackie insisted.

"You're absolutely right, darling, I should be calling him Congressman. Or Senator-elect, how shall that be?"

And so it *would* be for the rest of lunch. Senator-*elect*, with a tiny lilt that suggested the people of Massachusetts might rise up any second and wrest the title back. Jack did not receive the favor of a postprandial stroll from his hostess, who brought the strict minimum of fuss to his leave-taking and waited no more than a second after his departure to announce in an enervated tone: "I thought he'd be someone to worry about. Now I see he'll be some other mother's problem. He'll be *many* other mothers' problem."

Jackie was more baffled than offended. The Senator-elect's effect on women was not to be disputed—she had seen it work on a revivalist scale. Why had it failed on her mother? Over the course of just a few hours, Janet Auchincloss had taken a leisurely circuit of the candidate, like a breeder surveying a yearling, and had reached the conclusion that he didn't have it in him for long distances. It was one thing, surely, for Jackie to doubt her own place in Jack's heart; it was another for someone to come to the same judgment independent of her. How quickly, it seemed, a prospect could come unraveled—as soon as someone pulled the thread. Maybe this was why she began calling me at home more often. Often enough, anyway, that Mother began

handing me the phone without a word, and Jackie would be
talking by the time I lifted the receiver to my ear.

"Tell me now. When your dad was courting your
mother . . ."

"You know I wasn't there."

"But there's lore."

"No, darling, we're Wasps."

"What I'm saying is there must have been some point
when your father . . . well, you know, laid *claim* to your
mother."

"Stop. Stop." My head fell back against the wing chair.
"Oh, my God."

"No, I mean some point when he *declared* himself, he
said . . . sorry, what's your mother's name?"

"Romaine."

"He'd say . . . really, it's Romaine?"

"Like the lettuce."

"He'd say, '*By gum, Romaine, it's . . . it's . . .*'" She swallowed hard, but she was already sputtering, and so was I,
and in the next few minutes, we came up with all the things
my father might have said under the grip of *amour*. "*Lettuce
make lettuces, Romaine,*" that line of wit. Thankfully,
Mother by then was out of earshot, so I felt no particular
irreverence, but I did grasp, at some deeply instinctual level,
what Jackie was after. A way into the man's heart. So I
wasn't surprised to hear her ask:

"Have you ever seen him tender? I mean, really tender."

I told her then that when Jack and I, still college boys, did
our grand tour of Europe, I came down with a bad virus in

Cannes. My temperature spiked to a hundred and three, and I lay tossing on a bare mattress in a run-down pension. Now, Jack had spent half his life in hospital beds, so he wasn't used to being on the other side, but when he saw I was in a bad way, he draped a wet handkerchief across my forehead and ran downstairs and, with his miserable French, scared up a bowl of beef broth and spooned it into my mouth. He piled on a stack of blankets and sat by me for hours, mopping my brow and telling me it would be all right. And the next morning, it was.

This seemed to satisfy Jackie for the time being, yet even when she'd rung off, I sat a while thinking about what it meant to be tender. In those days, of course, if you were a man, feelings were either to be reviled or drowned. You swallowed down pain, your fondest wishes, like Bromo-Seltzer, and sent it all back up again when nobody was looking.

I thought back to Choate, when upperclassmen, feeling a little lonely, might scribble messages to each other. On toilet paper so they might, in an emergency, be swallowed or flushed down. *Meet me by the stables. Meet me in the library lav.* Now, one June, purely as a joke, I sent Jack a toilet-paper letter. Wadded it up in one of his Oxfords while he was still sleeping. I didn't stick around to watch him read it, but later that evening, while we were changing for dinner, he looked at me and, in a starchy, affronted voice, said, "I'm not that kind of boy." Well, we had a good laugh about it because, of course, we understood it for the joke it was, and we valued our friendship too much to complicate it. And yet, looking back, I can see that I was seeking—well, there

isn't a better word than tenderness. From a boy who didn't
necessarily have that to give. At all times.

That's why, when Jack called me the day after New Year's
and asked me to come over for backgammon, I didn't think
it was my chance to *draw him out* on a particular subject for
the simple reason that, in 1953, men weren't to be drawn out.
The whole reason Jack played any game was not for the crev-
ices of confession it afforded but for the opportunity to stomp
you into the ground. It wasn't personal; he wanted to do that
with everybody and so never played anything—tennis, golf,
swimming to the nearest buoy—without betting on it. If, in
the course of playing, you tried to bring up an unrelated subject, he would accuse you of trying to distract him. So I was
surprised when, during the second game, he shook the dice
out of their cup and reached for his checkers and said:

"LeMoyne, I should like to consult with you."

"I charge."

"Apply it to whatever you're about to lose. It has to do
with Our Miss Bouvier. How would you describe her current state of mind?"

"Uh, a little confused."

"On my account, you mean."

"On your account."

"She's waiting on me."

"To . . ." The phrase came back in a second. "To declare
yourself." And when he showed no signs of understanding:
"Fish or cut bait. Shit or get off the pot."

"That's some metaphors you're mixing."

"It is."

"Seems to me I might be excused a little absentmindedness. Being a national figure, you know, it takes it out of a fella."

"Sure."

I said nothing more, waited. But whatever had inspired him to take up the subject fell away now in a brown study.

"You've created expectations," I said at last. "In light of that, I think it would be the kindest course to resolve them."

"Cut her loose, you mean?"

Startling, to have that be the first option out of his mouth.

"Or . . . give her what she wants," I suggested.

"And what's that?"

"You, God help her."

"Does anybody care what I want?"

I was about to retort but poured myself a glass of Scotch instead.

"I'm curious," I said. "If you could imagine your way into being a married man . . . ."

"This is getting sinister."

"What would it look like?"

"Not Dad and Mother, that's for sure."

"They're still together."

"That's a funny word for what they are."

"I won't dispute you, but they each have what they want from life. They have their freedom."

His eyes lit up, his face opened into a grin.

"In your usual doltish way, you've put your finger on it, LeMoyne. If I could be sure of being free, that would make all the difference in the world."

I studied him for a space. "By free, you mean . . . "

"The way Dad's free. I mean, she's so damned young, Lem. A girl like that's bound to bring expectations. Romeo and Juliet—oh, Christ, give me another example . . . "

"Darby and Joan."

"I have no idea what you're talking about. The point is she'll be under the spell of all these—lady authors who've never in their lives gotten laid and want to make sure nobody does."

"If you're talking about fidelity," I said, "you should remember that Jackie's father wasn't much for that either."

"All the more reason she'll want *me* to be. Right Old Dad's wrongs, rewrite the whole story, score it with angels' choirs. Oh, don't look like that. I've seen it happen."

"You can't really know what she wants unless you come out and ask her."

"Do you honestly think it's something a guy just can bring up? *Say, Jackie.* I may be cold-blooded, but I'm not French." He smiled then, a little shamefacedly, and advanced toward me. "What I require is an intermediary."

"Oh," I said. "Oh, no."

He told me then it would be nothing less than an act of Christian charity on my part to let her know how things stood, how they *would* stand, so that she could make the most informed possible decision about her own future.

"That's not what it sounds like," I remonstrated. "It sounds like you want me to end your engagement for you before you've even gotten engaged."

"That depends on how she reacts. If it's more than what she's signed up for, why, then she's better off bolting, isn't she?"

"What if she doesn't?"

"Then I'm in real trouble. The thing is, LeMoyne, I like her. I almost wish she didn't fit the bill as well as she does. I wish she weren't so damned smart, I wish she hadn't weathered my family so well. I wish I didn't want to get more acquainted with her neck, I wish I didn't want to sit and smell her for a whole afternoon."

"Chateau Krigler Twelve."

"That's not the smell I'm talking about. What I'm *getting* at, since you're too dense to follow, is I like her too much to do this to her without her knowing. And since you like her, *too*, I figure we can make common cause around Our Miss Bouvier. What do you say?" With just the tiniest cocking of his head, he added, "You'd be the best egg ever."

TWENTY-SIX

The plan was not long in forming. Jack would invite Jackie to the inaugural ball and encourage her to make a full evening of it by coming to the cocktail party he was throwing beforehand. I would be invited to the same party and would, at some point over highballs, draw Jackie aside for a conference. With so many guests about, she'd be unlikely to make a scene, and I could, as needed, sit with her or drive her home.

"Five to one says she's out," said Jack.

Of course, once Jackie recovered from the surprise of Jack asking her, she accepted the invitation in a rush of syllables, and only after she hung up did she remember that the *Times-Herald* had assigned her to cover the same ball for the next morning's paper. It became, then, a matter of reframing the task at hand. Society reporters were technically guests at the events they covered, nibbling on the hand that fed them. Wasn't a VIP pass better than slipping somebody a fiver just to get in the door?

"Imagine the eavesdropping a girl can do, Lem, when she looks like just another fool at the bacchanal. I won't even need to pull out a notebook, I'll just jot it all on cocktail napkins."

It's telling, I reckon, that she devoted less time to planning her dress than to scouting who would be there. Every night, she scoured the congressional photo directory, attaching names to faces. In those days, that was harder work than you might credit because Republicans and Democrats looked even more alike than they do in 1981. The gentleman from South Carolina was, in any detail that mattered, the gentleman from North Dakota. You could imagine them reaching for each other's briefcases, blundering into each other's houses, kissing the nearest wife. But Jackie was terrified at the idea of calling some senator by the wrong name or mistaking his wife for his mother. "Newport's one thing," she said. "I've known them all from birth. Washington's a whole other racket."

I reminded her then of the upside to being in such a public gathering. For the space of one evening, in the eyes of officialdom, she would be marked indisputably as Jack's.

"You're right," she said. "He can't palm me off as a stenographer. He has to take me by the arm, doesn't he?"

"And dance with you in plain view. Next day, you'll

be spread in every newspaper across every breakfast table. Between the grapefruit and the soft-boiled egg. 'Who's that girl with Kennedy?' 'Can she be as pretty as all that?' Oh, I just wish I could be there."

There was a longish pause on her end.

"Where are you going to be, Lem?"

I pointed out that I didn't rank quite as high as Jack and would be spending Inaugural Eve with the Maryland delegation ball. "Never mind," I said. "I'd just be the mastodon in the flashbulbs. Your editors would crop me out on first sight."

"Oh, but listen. Jack's throwing a cocktail party, and you have to be there."

"Well," I said. "If you want."

"Of course I do! Ethel will be there, for cripes sake, and one of the *actual* sisters, I can't remember which. It's too much family for a girl to face alone."

Something complicated was detonating in my chest as I promised her I would come. A sense of my own double-agentry, I guess. But on the appointed evening, I showed up at Jack's Georgetown row house in my black tie and tails, demanding to know where the pigs-in-blanket were and laughing harder than anyone at Billy Sutton's Nixon impression and kissing Ethel on both cheeks and asking her in my least filtered voice when she'd stop popping out babies. ("Never," she said, and meant it.) I sang along to the *South Pacific* LP, and when the host himself failed to appear— late, even to his own party—I started a chant among the guests. "*We want a senator/ Not a progenitor!*" The volume mounted to such an intensity that Jack pretty much had to come trooping down the stairs, still not quite dressed. It was left to me to tie his damn bow tie.

I brazened it out, in other words, but when Jackie arrived—later, even, than Jack—I faltered a little. She'd been on her feet since seven that morning, interviewing the guests in the reviewing stands. Strands of confetti had gathered at the back of her head, and she was still trying to scrape elephant dung off the bottom of her shoe, but she traveled to the nearest powder room and took off her traveling worsted suit and emerged ten minutes later a proper vision in gold-webbed Siamese silk with a deep-pleated three-quarter-length skirt.

I would have commended her for the world to hear, but somebody else was moving her way. Ethel's older brother, George Skakel Junior. Who, upon the untimely death of George Skakel Senior, in a plane crash, became president of Great Lakes Carbon until his own untimely death in a plane crash eleven years later. And who, up to the exact point of his incineration, was the vilest offshoot of the Kennedy tree I've ever encountered, and I've met every twig. This was the same George who, during his sister's wedding to Bobby, aimed a kick at my backside that sent me sprawling across the aisle of St. Mary's. He found the whole coup de theatre so amusing that, whenever he saw me afterward, he would *tell* it to me all over again as if I hadn't experienced it frame by frame.

It's a fact of life that, when you're a kid of a certain sensitivity, you encounter your Georges. They're handsome in a way that crumbles at the first breath of mortality, and even at fifteen, they're going to fat, a prospect that seems to fuel all the terror they visit on others. You think you'll leave them behind if you grow up fast enough but, against expectations, they follow you through your days. Into the foxholes, the ambulances, the lawns, the beach resorts. Adding jowls like trophies. Here, then, was George Skakel Junior, getting drunker on Glen Grant whiskey and (now that Jackie had given him the most lightly chilled of shoulders) scouting the room for prey.

"Hey, Lem, my wife's looking for a powder puff. Maybe you'll do?" "Hey, Lem, I heard you helped make Mamie's dress for her. No? You mean you kept it for yourself?" "Jesus, Lem, that's the highest goddamn voice I've ever heard on a man. Do you even hear yourself? No, seriously, if it goes any higher, only dogs will hear it." Always—always—I was the first to laugh because that was the signal that everybody else could, and their corporate sound was as much a relief to me as it was to them. *Nobody's harmed.*

As I recall, the only one *not* laughing was Jackie, who looked merely solemn, and I wonder if it was to escape her gaze that I finally slipped upstairs. All the way to Jack's bedroom, which, in those days, looked as if its occupant had been recently kidnapped. You'd find the underwear drawer still open and a shirt still on its hanger, waiting for an owner, and a food-spotted necktie dropped somewhere between the closet and the door, Jack himself long gone.

Yet, on the rare occasions I was left alone in his house, I found myself wandering toward this very room—possibly because it reminded me of our school days. I'd seat myself—just as I was doing now—on the edge of his bed and inhale in some half-voluntary way his scent, or maybe I just mean the scent of *us*, as we were then. Teenage boys, without a care for the future. And indeed, when Jackie came walking in that night, I started like a fourth-former caught smoking outside chapel.

"Would you mind company?" she asked.

"Of course not."

She gave the coverlet a once-over before lowering herself, with some reluctance, onto it.

"I'm sorry about that Skakel beast," she said.

"Oh, I only came here to rest. I've had a week."

"Me, too," she said, kicking off her shoes and giving her legs a stretch. Her eyes ranged from corner to corner, coolly recording each object. It occurred to me then this was the first time she'd been here.

"Cripes," she said. "He told me he had a valet."

"Oh, that poor guy has enough to do cleaning up the rest of the house. Jack drags mess wherever he goes. Do you know I once found the remains of a hamburger on his living-room mantel? Half-eaten, green with mold."

"And he never smelled it?"

"Nope."

"Well then. He won't know if we smoke in his room."

"He wouldn't know if we set it on fire."

I took out a pack of Luckys and a lighter, and Jackie fetched an ashtray from beneath a pile of old newspapers and set it between us and took three long drags.

"God, Lem, I feel ten years old and a hundred and everything in between. I keep telling myself it's not an inaugural ball, it's just another ghastly party."

"On a larger scale, that's all."

"And, really, it's so much better to be working it because I won't have time to ask what the hell I'm doing there."

"Listen," I said. "Can you help me out with something?"

"Sure."

"See, I have this dilemma, and the best way I can come at it is through metaphor."

"I adore metaphor."

"So let's say a friend of yours is floating down a river and—let's say there might—I mean, there *might* be a waterfall round the next bend."

"Ooh."

"Well, you'd feel the need to warn that friend, wouldn't you? Just in case?"

"Of course. And then speak to them about their unfortunate floating habit."

"Ha! Well, it's not the friend's fault, you see. The friend just sort of—fell *in* . . ."

"So not pushed."

"Nothing like that."

"Jumped in without knowing."

"More like that."

"Well, then of *course* you'd warn them." She studied me. "I'm wondering if all this is more of an analogy than a metaphor."

"You might be right."

"If that's the case, I'm betting the one on shore is you."

"That's correct."

"As to who's in the water . . . well, Jack's a much better swimmer than I am . . . in real life, I mean, so . . . I can't imagine him being swept away by anything."

"Me, neither."

"And I can't imagine you wanting to save George Skakel, so . . . I guess that just leaves me."

The dawning settled gradually over her.

"The only question left," she said, "is the nature of this waterfall."

"Well, you see, it's only a potential waterfall. Pertaining to—to Jack himself. Who, you know, being a longtime bachelor, has gotten into certain habits, which are not the habits a fellow gets *out* of necessarily."

"Lem, you're circling."

"Okay, so look at Mr. Kennedy. Married a good long time, fathered nine kids, done his duty by everyone, but once in a while, being a certain kind of fellow, he steps out. Nothing serious. Not an affair of the *heart*. It might be a hatcheck girl at Ciro's. A showgirl, that kind of thing." My voice was still light, but my hands, I noticed, were woven as tightly as two helixes. "Well, it's over before anyone knows it, and it's all very discreet, and if Mrs. Kennedy is any the wiser, she doesn't squawk because—well, I can't speak for her exactly, but she probably figures she's got what she wants out of life. Or she figures that's just how men are, the dogs."

I remember Jackie was still amused enough to ask:

"Is that how *you* are, Lem?"

"Oh, I don't mean me. I don't mean *all* men. The point is . . ."

She rested her cigarette in the ashtray's indentation, gave it a tap. A second tap. Then she did something rather discombobulating under the circumstances. She looked at me. And it was under that specific pressure . . . well, if I peer into Schrödinger's box, here again is the point where it all might have forked, if I had done what I'd been sent to do. Would she have doubled down? For exactly the reason Jack suggested, that she wanted to square accounts? Or would she have taken flight?

"The point is," I heard myself say, "Jack isn't *like* his father. He won't *be* that kind of man."

WHAT AMAZES ME, looking back, is that it was spoken with the same force as truth. Perhaps *more* force, because it seems to me now I was wishing it into being. And that's why, I think, my eyes were already drifting away from hers. Toward that ideal outcome.

"So you're saying he wouldn't be that kind of husband," said Jackie.

"No."

"Why not?"

"Because he cares for you, goose. More than he's ever cared for anyone, really."

"Then who needs to be saved?"

I blinked at her. "Who . . ."

"Your analogy."

"Oh, well, it turns out nobody. It's all fine. It was only a potential waterfall anyway."

"So the person in the water can stay there."

"Sure! If she wants." I reached out and gave her wrist a light squeeze. "Because there's someone on the shore. Making sure she'll be all right."

Now, for some reason, it was no longer a task to hold her gaze.

"I love you," she said. "I love you, Lem."

TWENTY-SEVEN

*B*ack when my friend Raul was coming over more often, I would sometimes find him peering at the framed photographs on my walls. I assumed at first he was just idly curious, but eventually, at some private cost to him, I learned that his family had come to America not long after the Bay of Pigs and that the Kennedy name had for him the effect of a lighthouse signal. It fascinated him, I think, to see the great man reduced to these segments, and once he had exhausted the photos, it was probably inevitable he should start digging into the cabinets and built-in drawers and the secretary. One morning, I found him sifting through a file folder of Jackie's *Times-Herald* columns, organized by date.

"Old newsprint is very fragile," I said. "Please do not paw."

He lifted one of the tannin pages to the light. "Papi, I believe you are the only man in the world who has kept these."

I was going to suggest that the news doesn't really die, but then, in a brusque voice, he asked, "Does she know you keep them?"

"You mean, have I told her? No, I keep them for me."

"When was the last time that you spoke with her?"

"Oh, I don't know."

He set the page back in the stack. "But you are friends and all."

"Well, of course. People get busy."

"Sometimes I wonder if you even know her."

He was kidding, of course. He'd seen the photos. Jackie and me in every setting, her cheek to my jowl. There's a picture I'm particularly fond of from those early years. The three of us sitting on some Washington, D.C. parapet, maybe the west side of the Capitol. It's summer, to judge from my cream suit, and the mood is summery, too. Jack has made some crack, and Jackie is recoiling right into *me*, for it's my arm that's curled protectively around her shoulder. Well, I would have to be the world's most spectacular forger to have inserted myself into that image, or indeed the countless other images where we were captured together. Take me out of those photographs, they no longer cohere.

Yet now, isn't it funny? Sometimes I will lift one of those same silver-framed pictures from its perch on the wall or the credenza, and some of Raul's skepticism must seep through because I pause in a wondering confusion. Was I really there?

I suppose, if I really wanted confirmation, I could simply pick up the phone. I still have the number but, for some reason, I've been less inclined to use it lately. A few years back, I did call her up to say Bobby Junior was in town and Chris Lawford, too, and wouldn't it be grand if she could bring over the kids. "Gosh," she said. "I'm not sure that works for us."

"Well, maybe next Friday? I've got a shipment of scrimshaw, and it's got John Junior's name all over it."

"Oh, you know, now's not a good time." There was only a touch more color to her voice when she added: "I'm just trying to keep them safe, Lem."

Which of us was the first to hang up? Did we promise to check in over the holidays? I don't recall feeling that a rupture had happened. More a puzzle that, having been severed into its component pieces, required only a little application to piece back together.

Jackie, I should say, had long since yanked her kids from the Hyannis bacchanal. She'd heard—the world had heard—the tales of expulsions, arrests, overdoses, Jeep crashes. And of all the Kennedy cousins, Bobby Junior and Chris were then on the wilder end of the gradient. It's why, I think, they liked to come and stay with me when they were in New York. They wanted at least one adult in their orbit who would suspend judgment and say, in so many words: *Have your fun. Come back alive.*

No, what troubled me about my last conversation with Jackie was the implication that her children were to be kept safe from *me*.

It's true that I haven't been averse to partaking of certain substances the boys brought home. You meet young men where they are, I've always maintained, or you don't meet them at all. If, from time to time, I've smoked a little weed, branched out to other, more adventurous things—I could ingest things far worse in a discotheque and throw it all up in the ten-minute cab ride home, whereas my experiments with cannabis, conducted in the true amateur spirit, have expanded my understanding of the world in ways I could never have suspected. In more open moments, I see the scales actually sloughing from my skin. Bobby Junior once told me I was the youngest old man he'd ever met, and I believe him.

Well, that was the last time Jackie and I spoke directly, though I still get a card every Christmas. I'm tempted to say I miss her, though I'm no longer sure what that means.

Perhaps it's me I miss—the prelapsarian Lem, the good time had by all. Was *I* having a good time? Without too much trouble, I can put hands on my invitation to the 1953 Pennsylvania inaugural ball—a ball I never attended. No great loss, I'm sure, but why? Was I still thinking about that conversation with Jackie? I can report that, immediately after, she marched downstairs and fastened herself to Jack's arm, whispered something for his ear alone. Over his face there stole the very nearly cerebral look he always made in response to an offer. He nodded, once, and followed Jackie back upstairs. To the room she and I had just vacated.

As for what happened at the ball, I assume they danced together, drew the eyes of everybody who counted, landed in more than one column. But the only evidence I had to go on the next morning was Jackie's reportage, which, lacking a byline, still rose in a pure way from the *Times-Herald's* pages. Reading them over my coffee, I imagined her slipping away to the nearest pay phone and murmuring her notes to the rewrite man. "No, *peau de soie.* S-o-i-e. That's right. And Mrs. Nixon's gown was peacock-blue t-u-l-l-e . . . and brocade, with a deep turquoise bouffant skirt. Mrs. Herbert Brownell Junior was a vision in striking fuchsia satin, with a cluster of velvet petals . . . yes, *petals* . . . appliquéd to the skirt. A-p-p-l . . ." Down the list she would have gone— from Mrs. John Foster Dulles to Mrs. John Sheldon Doud Eisenhower—and before running out of change, she'd have pointed out that chiffon was popular this year and that the overall mood was pastel.

The next morning, I was taking my breakfast in Jack's wainscoted dining room, mopping up the last bit of Margaret's French toast, when Jack himself wandered in, wearing an old Harvard sweatshirt, hair still bearing the imprint of last night's festivities. The first words out of his mouth were "Looks like I owe you one."

I looked up at him.

"So much more than one," I said. "I've been keeping a running tally, and it's one to the power of five or six."

He reached for his grapefruit section. "Jackie says you had the talk with her."

"Well, yes." I kept looking at him. "Did she say what the talk was?"

"She said you made everything clearer."

"That's the word she used."

"It's what we were aiming for, wasn't it?"

"Mm-hm."

With great precision, he loosened each grapefruit section from its membrane. "I hope you didn't have to get too clinical with her."

"No, it was all clean. Aboveboard."

"Well, whatever you said, she's all in now. I don't know if I should thank you, exactly, but let the record show you're not just an ugly brute, you're a pal. I'll even vouch for you with Saint Peter, though I don't think you'll make it there."

IN THE DAYS that followed, I was trailed by something unfamiliar: a sense that, in some almost Puritan kind of way, I had transgressed. Two or three times I found myself actually reaching toward a phone, in a rather urgent way, as if to alert somebody. But who? Jack was perfectly content with the state of affairs; Jackie was as happy as I'd seen her. Why should I propose undoing all that? To what end? I could neither answer nor quite excuse myself clear.

Later that week, she called me at home. So late at night that I was already in bed and Mother was fast asleep.

"Lem," she said. "Can I buy you lunch this Sunday?"

"Ohh." I dragged myself up to a seated position. "I'm awfully busy . . ."

"Lem, don't you see that the bright side of working for a paper that's about to die is that the expense accounts are always *the last things to go*. Mine needs to be spent before Mr. Hearst leaves us as carrion, and there's a darling little place out in Middleburg called the Red Fox Inn, where we won't bump into a soul we know."

Still I hesitated, until at last she said:

"Fine. I'll drive."

In the end, that was a greater sacrifice than I could allow her to make. As we motored into the Virginia countryside that Sunday, the roads thinned into ribbons, the fields rolled away in piles of stubble. The split-rail fences and unvarnished tobacco farms suggested we were crawling back through history, so that, by the time we pulled up to the Red Fox, its Georgian fieldstone exterior looked positively modern. As did the parchment tavern menu, with its tributes to mountain trout and Brunswick stew.

If Jackie had hoped for anonymity, she had miscalculated. We were barely seated at our table when a sun-ripened doyenne in tweed came trotting over. I learned later she was a friend of Janet Auchincloss's from the DAR. Judging by the way her eyes swelled at sight of me, she took me to be Jackie's suitor, and it required all the small talk in our arsenal to send her grudgingly back to her table, where she kept flicking gazes our way and whispering in the ear of her paralytic husband.

"Will she hear me?" wondered Jackie. "If I talk in this tone?"

"Not sure."

"So the words *nightmarish busybody* will never reach her."

I gave it ten seconds. "Not yet."

"Then let us carry on." She held her Scotch and soda in her hand, softly weighing it. "Have I told you much about my father?"

"Some."

"When he married Mummy, he was practically the same age Jack is now. I wish you could have seen him. So *dark*. There was a girl at Miss Porter's who came up to me on Parents' Day and asked me why I had to kiss that Negro in full view of everyone." She started to laugh, let it expire. "I'm sure Mummy thought she'd hit the jackpot. This exotic man with the exotic name. Boo-vee-*ay*. How's a girl with the last name of *Lee* supposed to stand up to that? Oh, she was warned, but she figured he'd settle down once he got the ring on his finger. The love of a good woman. He didn't make it a week. They were crossing the Atlantic for their honeymoon, and one night, he went to Doris Duke's berth and had himself a swell time. Came back with some cock-and-bull story about a poker game with the purser. Oh, she believed him the first time. Maybe. But there were too many other times, and after a while, he didn't even bother hiding. I should have hated him. Every time a row broke out, I should have taken Mummy's side, but I always came away thinking *she* was the unreasonable one. I remember once telling her if she were any kind of wife, he'd never—"

She broke off in a trance of incredulity.

"At ten, Lem. At *ten* I was saying these things. I suppose I thought if she'd just make—what do they call them, *allowances*—they'd stay together. That's what *I'd* do. Lem," she said, "do you ever get angry at your mother?"

"Well, no. I mean, not to be nakedly autobiographical, she's been through a bit, so I guess I don't want to be the last straw."

"Mummy's been through a bit, too, and I'm *still* angry at her every chance I get. I'm angry at her more than I'm *anything else* in life. It's like a diet or a prayer regimen. I go to sleep angry, I wake up angry, and what makes it worse is thinking how desperate she must have been at my age. Hanging on for dear life to this *man*. But that's what you've helped me to see, Lem, I don't have to be my mother, Jack doesn't have to be his father. We don't have to roll out the same mistakes or—screw Gloria Swanson in the doll room. We can *change*, can't we?" She leaned toward me. "*I* can change, too. I can be what the Kennedys need me to be."

"But, darling, you don't have to—"

"No, they've chosen me. God knows why, but they have, so I have to—I have to choose them *back* or none of this will work. There's only one catch, really."

"Yes?"

"Jack has to choose me, too."

"But he . . . he already . . ."

"No, I mean for good. For *good*, Lem. Can you help?"

TWENTY-EIGHT

*I*t's funny, when I look at some of her columns from that spring of '53, I can't help thinking she was her own best advocate. She was talking to him out loud, for everyone to hear. "Are wives a luxury or a necessity?" she wanted to know. "Can you give any reasons why a contented bachelor should marry?" And this shot across the bow on St. Patrick's Day: "The Irish author, Sean O'Faolain, claims the Irish are deficient in the art of love. Do you agree?"

How closely Jack was holding up his end I can't say, but they did go out to dinner on a regular basis, and for the first time ever, he agreed to be interviewed—on the subject of Senate pages. It was from Jack's own page that she learned how malnourished he was, and she began at once traveling to his office with an osier basket of lunches prepared by the Auchincloss cook. On weekends, if she could spare the time, she shopped for clothes, and, finding his complexion sallow, lured him away one afternoon to a touring carnival. Afterward, she showed me the pictures they snapped in the photo booth, not too different from the ones Jack and I took when we were lads applying for passports to Europe. The same stop-motion succession, each head angled toward the other in some changed way, each image related to and utterly distinct from the next. They stayed in the booth long after the camera had ceased snapping and came out disheveled and a little abraded.

Jackie was still looking for a way to be of use, and Ho Chi Minh provided it. As a newcomer angling for the Senate Foreign Relations Committee, Jack needed to get on top of the Indochina question, which was submerged in reams of French: a dozen or so books that covered everything from Asian colonialism to Algerian despotism. He would have remembered Jackie was a French literature major, but he couldn't have known she'd been studying the Indochina issue from her days in the Sorbonne. Nor could he have known that, having asked her to translate, she would spend so many hours each night squeezing those dry gourds for their secrets before carrying the translated pages next morning to Jack's office.

In April, he escorted her to Lee Bouvier's wedding. It was perhaps the couple's most public outing yet; it was also a carpet of landmines for Jackie, whose younger sister had developed the maddening habit of matching her every accomplishment. Debutante of the Year, French école, top-flight women's magazine. Now she had gone a step further. She'd beaten Jackie to the altar.

And had snagged not just some dime-a-dozen stockbroker but the adopted son of a wealthy publisher and (it was whispered) the natural son of British royalty. Even Mrs. Auchincloss was impressed. If Michael Canfield drank a little more than he ought and took more pills than were strictly good for him—if he would, before another seven years had elapsed, keel over dead on a transatlantic jet—at the time, he looked safe as houses. The only possible counterbalance Jackie could set on the scale was to hook her hand around the arm of a war hero and senator.

Only Jack, far from laying claim to her in the manner of a proper boyfriend, seemed to detach himself by the filmiest of degrees the moment they entered the church. Indeed, he proved such an object of desire that, during the after-reception, Jackie had to insert herself more than once between him and the guests, like a gal Friday dragging her boss to his next appointment. Once, he vanished from sight altogether, and although he was back again within ten minutes, behaving like one who had never left, she couldn't stop looking. Not at *him*, she realized, but his hair. Some hand had visited it. The obvious candidate was his own, but Jack guarded his mop the way trolls patrol bridges and, having once plunged his fingers through it, never touched it again. There was, moreover, a foreign layer of scent, in the jasmine family, pressed against his skin, waiting to be translated.

"Why do you keep staring at me?" he asked.

* * *

SHE BROUGHT IT up with me the next time I saw her, and I told her she was imagining things.

"Oh, I know," she said. "A man wouldn't just skip out on his date in the middle of a wedding and do that, would he? Men aren't that way, are they?"

She tried, but the scent memory wouldn't leave. Nor would the words of her mother, who, after the newly married couple had gone off in their hired Rolls-Royce, bent toward her daughter and said, "Your senator did well. Bachelors usually hate going to other men's weddings, but he was the calmest body in the room."

It was true. Jack had surveyed that vast matrimonial apparatus—the orchids, the trays of champagne, the golf-collared dress shirts, the jazz octet, the Washington and Lee a cappella group, the pearl-gray waistcoats, the gabardine going-away dress—with the serenity of one who would never be at its mercy.

At the newspaper, the Inquiring Camera Girl's questions began to take a darker tone. Perhaps she was still imagining that mysterious hand, combing Jack's hair. "Should engaged couples reveal their past?" she demanded to know. "If your spouse spoke another person's name in their sleep, what would you do?"

From there: "When did the romance go out of your marriage?" "What should a wife do if her husband is brought up in a prostitution case?" "Should a man ever tell his wife to shut up, in so many words?"

She knew he read her column because he always mentioned it when he called—the same with the translated pages she dutifully dropped off at his office—but how closely? As for the picnic baskets, they were now ending up in the steely grip of Mrs. Lincoln, who promised to hand them over as soon as the senator returned. From? The Senate floor, the Senate cloakroom—surprising perches for someone who'd missed as many votes as he had. Every so often, Mrs. Lincoln would simply declare him to be in transit—from where, to where, Jackie was never sure, and it surprised her to consider how many hours a public figure could spend out of plain view. Yet she knew him to be in the world; she read about it in the papers. He was lunching at the 1925 F Street Club. He was shaking hands at the Peruvian Embassy. He was rubbing shoulders with Perle Mesta, ambassadress to Luxembourg. One morning, Jackie gazed in fascination at a blind item from Drew Pearson: "Which handsomest of all pols has been voted 'Senate's Gay Young Bachelor' by the *Saturday Evening Post*? Our money's on a certain ambassador's son."

She bided her time until Wednesday, when they had a fish-fry supper at Duke Zeibert's, a half hour after it was supposed to have closed.

"Well, it's not my fault," he said, with a clouded face.

"I didn't say it was."

"What I mean is I didn't know they would use that headline."

"So they didn't run it by you first."

"Of course not. I would have told them."

"Told them what?" She heard the faint straining in her voice. "If they'd read that to you over the phone, how would you have corrected it?"

"I would have said, I'm not so young."

"And as to your being a bachelor."

"Well . . ." He drew up the question like sap. "I would have said that's only technically correct."

Only technically correct. If he'd shaken the entire English lexicon like an apple tree to see what fell out, he could have found no more wizened fruit. What, she wanted to know, did correctness have to do with a man's heart? And why couldn't she demand an answer of that heart in the exact moment he was withdrawing it? Instead, to her dismay, she withdrew, too, into stung silence, and felt herself becoming just one more extra on his life's soundstage. *Oh, Jack . . .*

That weekend, she invited me to a touring production of *The Fourposter*, a comedy whose subject was, by some cruel quirk, marriage. There must have been only so much she could take because, at the second intermission, she asked in the most direct possible way if we could go somewhere and get stinking. We adjourned to the bar at the New Willard and put away six Gibson cocktails between us.

"I know what you're going to say," she said, in a thickening voice.

"You do?"

"You're going to say—you're going to say Jack's not the sort to wear his feelings on his sleeve."

"Well, true."

"You're going to say just because he doesn't call you his girl doesn't mean you aren't."

"Also true."

"Here's the thing. Here's the *thing*, Lem. If he doesn't call you his girl, how can you possibly know if you are?"

"Well, you go about it in a different way. You ask yourself a certain set of questions."

"Okay."

"To begin with, is he dating anybody else?"

The scent-memory of jasmine must have rushed in, for a fierce crease bisected her forehead.

"I'll take that as a no," I sped on. "Does he call you regularly?"

"Enough."

"How often?"

"Four . . . five times? A week?"

"That's a lot."

"Is it? Yes," she said, with a sudden rush of certainty. "That's a lot."

"Is he—oh, very well, you don't have to answer, but is he physically affectionate with you?"

"Is he . . ." Her head dropped an inch. "Yes."

"Here's the real question. Do you make him laugh?"

"Laugh?"

"Yes."

"I sometimes make him laugh."

"I mean, really laugh? Catch him off guard. Double him over, even."

She thought.

"This has happened," she said.

"Well then. He's yours."

Although that made no sense because I had made Jack do the same thing, on numerous occasions. Then I heard her ask what it even meant to be *his* and heard myself answer, more brutally than I intended:

"Is it a ring you're after?"

"Don't be vulgar, Lem, I'm talking about . . ." Her eyes went quiet. "I don't know what I'm talking about. Do you know what I'm talking about?"

By now I was a little too far gone to suggest I didn't.

"You want to be loved," I suggested.

"There's that. Do you know what I've decided, Lem? If he moves on, it won't kill me. The only way I will be killed is if he *doesn't*, and only if I can't find a way to free myself and—"

"You should leave," I said.

Her eyelashes made a slow downward sweep.

"How leave? He's not even mine to leave."

"I don't mean leave *him*, goose. I mean *leave*. In the— the *intransitive* sense of the word. Or . . ." I was feeling the Gibsons. "If you need a direct object, leave the *city*. The state. The country, if you can manage. Catch the first rocket to the moon."

"I spy, with my little eye, a girl running away."

"Tell her she's running *toward*. Tell her the farther she roams, the more he will tug back."

"You sound awfully sure."

"I am."

"How can you be?"

"Because that's what *she* used to do."

TWENTY-NINE

*W*henever I speak of Rose Kennedy in private or public, I make a point of enumerating her virtues, not the least of which has been her kindness to me through the years. Indeed, there have been times, I'm touched to report, when she has introduced me to family friends as her fifth son, with just the barest brush of quotation marks. We've always got on, and it's because I know her as I do that I still enjoy watching America try to figure her out. Watching her image migrate over the past four decades from mother of champions to Mother of Sorrows—or, if you like, Mary at the manger to Mary at the cross. Neither extreme captures the hard, indestructible seed around which she is wrapped. Biographers have made hay with the index-card file she kept

for each of her children, the notes she taped to their walls
or pinned to their pillows, the mandatory calisthenics at
dawn—that whole arsenal of muscular Christianity. They
imagine her unblinking, ever on the spot. But in fact, for
as long as I've known her, she was gone as often as here.
Gone sometimes even when she was here. In Jack's six years
at Choate, she visited precisely once, and that was for Joe
Junior's graduation. Never again did she darken our door,
not when Jack was on the verge of being expelled, not when
he lay for days in the infirmary, mysteriously wasting. No,
you can't understand Mrs. Kennedy until you understand
that she was a chief executive officer who, in exchange for
keeping the family stock high, was rewarded with lengthy
annual leave. The place was always Paris, where, depending
on the day or hour, she could be found in the front row of
a fashion house or on her knees at Saint-Germain-des-Prés.

She might be gone for weeks, and Kennedy family lore
has preserved the moment when little Jack snarled, "Gee,
you're a great mother to go away and leave your children
alone." Yet, as I burrow back toward that boy, it seems to
me he must have assumed he was the reason. If he'd been
neater, more orderly; if he'd tucked in his shirt or picked up
his clothes, declined to pick fights with Joe Junior—maybe
then she would have stayed. Mrs. Kennedy's school of par-
enting was premised on two suspended possibilities. She
would one day approve of you, and she would never. It was
how you kept children in line in those days.

And we never do outgrow our child-selves, do we? Jack,
as long as I knew him, hated to be abandoned. There were

evenings he'd make me take the next morning's train back to Baltimore because he didn't want to stare down midnight alone. And if, God forbid, you left him in *anger* (which is how Mrs. Kennedy often did), he'd be beside himself until you came back. "Come on, LeMoyne, when'd your skin get so thin? You know what a blockhead I am."

I was never above profiting from this, even if it was just to get him to cover a round of drinks, but, in those days, Jackie was new enough to his psyche that she couldn't quite see what she had to gain from ceding the field. What tipped it for her was an out-of-the-blue summons from her editor.

Would she care to cover the royal coronation in London?

THE YOUNG AMERICANS currently salivating over Lady Di's upcoming wedding could never understand, I think, what a big fucking deal Princess Elizabeth was. Monarch to a quarter of the world, handsome enough to captivate the remaining three quarters or give their fantasies room to run. You couldn't travel from one end of Manhattan to the other in those days without finding Lilibet's face in a window or on a ceremonial plate. Tea towels, lunch boxes. Americans begged their friends of friends, their second cousins of maiden aunts, for the tiniest spot on the Westminster parade route. Even Mr. Kennedy, with his mountains of capital, couldn't rout up a single invitation, and here was Jackie, granted the golden triad of travel, room and board.

"Lem," she said. "I know you told me to *leave*, but this seems extreme."

"It's the Northern Hemisphere, isn't it? Here's the thing to remember. When you tell Jack, he won't raise an eyebrow. He'll tell you how fortunate you are, what a fascinating experience it'll be. He'll share anecdotes from his dad's embassy days. The tame ones. If I know him, he'll give you a list of book titles to buy while you're there. He'll promise to repay you, but keep all the receipts."

She called back two nights later.

"God, Lem, you're a prophet. It was just like you said, right down to *I'll pay you back*. Here's what I'm wondering, though. If he's playing it so cool, how will I know it's even bothering him that I'm gone?"

"You'll know when *he* does. First will come the telegram, then the transatlantic call. Be sure to keep the phone close to your bed, and have all the fun you can manage, darling!"

In the last Inquiring Camera Girl column she filed before she left, she asked: "Does absence make the heart grow fonder?" It was, I think, the one question she posed during that brief career of hers that was directed strictly at herself.

I'VE KEPT THE articles she filed in an acid-free cardboard box at the back of the Amish pie safe. The pages are separated by alkaline-buffered tissue, and I wash and dry my hands before touching them. When I scan the headlines—"Crowds of Americans Fill 'Bright and Pretty' London"—I feel I'm staring at another moment in Jackie's history when it might have gone either way. There was the night, for instance, she was covering Perle Mesta's clambake and watching Lauren Bacall, scarlet-nailed in a white-lace dress, dance with

Omar Bradley and then the Marquess of Milford Haven until Humphrey Bogart, gangster-lean in white tie and tails, inserted himself. Imagine now that, having dressed herself with such professional care, having gauged her assets against all rivals, she impulsively casts aside her reporter's notebook and, like a nearsighted ingénue, stands blinking before a new romantic destiny. Dukes and earls rush in. A North Sea oil tycoon, the foreign minister of a Central American dictator. She bats her raw, enormous eyes, the more seductive for being so unused to glare. She considers her options and departs from that great gold-and-white ballroom on the arm of—

Or else she leaves with nobody but imbibes the spirit of Dorothy Parker and casts an agate eye across the room, *every* room, the whole ball of Windsor wax. She notes where the portrait of Lord Castlereagh has gathered a pelt of dust. Where the Mayfair dance floor has shrunk down to the size of a human fist. The peculiarly overwhelming smell of roast oxen at a time when meat rationing is still in force. The drenched cockatoo finery of the Queen of Tonga, who declines to raise her carriage roof during the processional rain because how else will she be seen? One apercu is piled on the next, and a humorist is born, specializing in short sharp shocks.

I suppose what I'm saying is that, over the course of that week in London, Jackie might have wandered down any number of avenues, toward any number of contingent destinies. A fashion model, or the private muse of an Ealing Studios cinematographer. A gaily dressed sidewalk artist along the Pall Mall.

Then I pause to consider how things really work. I recall how, four days after Jackie sailed, the Emerson Drug operator put through a particularly urgent call from Palm Beach.

"Lem," said Mr. Kennedy. "The girl appears to have bolted."

I sat up straighter in my swivel chair.

"It's just for a short time, sir."

"That still makes her gone."

"Well, it was rather a—a plum assignment, as I'm sure you appreciate. I don't think anyone could have asked her to—"

"You keep bringing up her career, Lem."

"Only because it's something *she* brings up. As in taking it seriously."

"So you're telling me this is a *professional* move on her part? It's not about punishing Jack?"

"Well, I—"

"Oh, don't get me wrong, Jack deserves everything he's getting and more. Here's this girl waiting on him hand and foot—brown-bag lunches, for Christ's sake—and he can't be bothered to seal the deal."

"With all due respect, sir, it sounds like he may not want the deal."

"You think I did? A man seals the deal, then works around if need be. Listen, Lem?"

"Yes, sir."

"If she gets in touch with you, I need you to tell her to hold on."

"Hold on."

"That's all you have to say. Hold on."

"For how long, sir?"

"If I could tell you that, I'd be cornering the stock market. I can only guarantee that it will be a finite amount of time."

"Uh-huh."

"All she has to do is hold on and leave the rest to me."

"I'll share that, sir."

"Tell her I know how to deal with recalcitrant boys. I've been doing it all my life."

I never had to deliver that message because Jackie never got in touch with me. That's not true, there was a postcard, arriving in the dilatory way that postcards do, as if it had been dozing on some faraway beach. I've saved it, of course. It's a snapshot of Westminster Abbey at twilight with a message scrawled on the other side: *Dearest L, The royal family won't let me get any closer! Wish you were here. Xoxo J.*

By the time I'd received it, Princess Elizabeth had long since been crowned, and in every other respect, fate had done its work. A day after my conversation with Mr. Kennedy, Jack wired Jackie a telegram. *Articles great, but you're missed.* It was as emotive as he'd yet allowed himself to be, and though she didn't respond, I'm guessing she carried the words around, took them out every so often to examine them. Sending a wire was the easiest thing in the world, she knew that, and indeed, no wire came the next day, so it was the purest kind of surprise when, on the night of June the second, his highly expensive telephone call came flying, Lindbergh-like, across the Atlantic.

Even in June, the flat that she'd rented had a benthic chill, and she might have let her flatmate pick up the phone, only Aileen was soaking her feet in hot water, so with great reluctance Jackie threw off her blankets and took quick mincing steps to the phone. The voice came charging through the static, not even stopping to identify itself.

"So how's about it?"

"Jack?"

"How's about it?"

"How's about what?"

Whatever head of steam had got him to this point subsided, and the silence was so thick she began to wonder if she'd imagined the whole thing.

"Are you still there?" she asked.

"You know, they're awfully fond of you."

"Who?"

"The family."

"They are?"

"Why, sure. As am I."

"Well, that's nice."

Another pause, nearly as long as the last.

"So what do you think?" he asked.

"About what?"

"About this being something—more on the permanent side of things."

From her periphery, she could see Aileen craning her head around the lavatory door. She could hear the light tympanum-like dripping of water on the tile floor.

"Is that what you want?" she asked.

"Sure," he said. "Why not?" And then after a pause: "Don't you think?"

It was here, at the very brink, that she flinched. Although, looking back, she could say it was more a case of splintering. There in her ear was Jack. There at the edge of her vision was Aileen, dripping. There, rising up through the column of her bare legs, was the sulfurous London cold. There, a mile or two away, a newly minted queen. Each audience brought its own demand, and each was buzzing in some separate lobe of her brain, and what should have been overwhelming, short-circuiting, was merely a party. A minute later, she was setting the phone back in its cradle, and Aileen was stepping apologetically toward her.

"Is everything all right, Jackie?"

"Oh. Sure."

"I know it's none of my business but—was it someone close to you?"

Someone . . .

"Jackie, is there anything I can do? Would you rather I leave you alone?"

Only now did she grasp the problem. She didn't look like she was at a party.

"Is it your father?" Aileen was asking. "I'm so sorry . . ."

"No! No. No, it's not. I mean, it's fine. I mean . . ." A tiny giggle shook free. "You can come to the wedding if you like."

"The . . ." Aileen's frown cut deeper. "You mean that was *him*?"

Jackie nodded.

"And he was . . . ?"

Jackie nodded.

"And you said yes?"

She was about to nod a third time, but the question instantly recomposed itself.

"I must have," she muttered. "Didn't I?"

"Well, I didn't *hear*, darling, I was trying not to pry."

They spent the next five minutes trying to piece together the one-minute conversation that Jackie had just had.

"Start at the end, darling. What was the last thing he said?"

"He said . . . um . . . I think it was 'I'll see you when you get back.'"

"Those were his final words?"

"I think so . . ."

"Not *I love you* or . . ."

"Oh, cripes, no."

"Well," said Aileen, rallying. "*See you when you get back* is even better. That means things are moving forward. If you'd said no, there'd be no seeing him again, would there?"

"I suppose not. But what if I didn't say anything at all?"

"All right, think hard. Did he mention a date? Because if they don't give you a date . . ."

Closing her eyes, Jackie reached back through the fog bank and extracted from it the word . . .

"September!"

"Oh, that's soon. What about a place?"

Another extraction.

"Newport!"

"Well now, there you are. September in Newport. A girl couldn't ask for better."

"No," said Jackie, faintly.

"And best of all, it no longer matters what you said or forgot to say to him. The train is moving, and you're *on* it."

Again, Jackie's face must have failed to impart that particular sentiment because Aileen stared back at her.

"Darling, are you quite sure you're happy about this?"

"Of course I am."

"You do know there are a million girls out there who'd be thrilled to be in your shoes."

"I know. I'd be thrilled to be me, too."

And then laughed at putting herself in the conditional tense.

Through all the months of suspension, she had assumed it would only take a few choice words to right herself. Now the words had come—however clumsily—and she was no more in balance. Why had he even called? Was it simply, as Lem predicted, a matter of her being absent? Or was there just a moment in every bachelor's life when he runs out of time and space? Flying back across the Atlantic, she imagined him a famished, half-feral animal, pulling hard at his lead and realizing after a sorrowful interval that it has reached its full length. Turning then and, with an air of defeat, saying: "Why not? Don't you think?"

THIRTY

*S*he had this much in the way of security: an engagement ring from Van Cleef & Arpels.

Art Deco in styling, with a 2.84-carat square-cut emerald,
a 2.88-carat matching diamond, and tapered baguette-dia-
mond accents. It was Mr. Kennedy who bought it for a price
that hovered, the columnists suggested, around a cool million. Jackie wouldn't necessarily have blanched at the sum
or the fact that her future father-in-law had chosen the ring.
(Jack hadn't the slightest interest in jewelry.) She was even
ready to accept Mr. Kennedy's suggestion, warmly put forth,
that she should have it photographed for mass consumption,
but that was more than Mrs. Auchincloss could abide.

"Tell that corned-beef parvenu my daughter is not a professional model."

The message, watered down, was delivered to Jack, who brought it in even briefer form to the old man.

"Well," said Mr. Kennedy, "if that's how they feel."

Jackie was surprised by how quickly he backed down, but from my current vantage point, I can see the old man was just husbanding his energies for the battle that really mattered.

In those days, if you'd been asked to pick a winner between the Auchinclosses and the Kennedys, you'd have fallen back on categories: Wasp assurance vs. immigrant pluck; clipped vowels vs. broad. What you might not have allowed for was the value of research. Long before Jack had lobbed his marriage proposal across the Atlantic, Mr. Kennedy, with an instinct as natural as breathing, had launched an inquiry into the Auchincloss brokerage. He learned that investments were tanking, that venture capitalists were looking elsewhere, that a founding partner lay near death and that none of the other partners had the cash to buy up his shares.

"No offense," Mr. Kennedy once told me, "but the worst thing about you Wasps isn't that you lack liquidity, it's that you think it's beneath you. The less goddamn cash you've got, the more you look down on the shanty clowns who do."

And when you get right down to it, he thought, what's a more cash-based enterprise than a wedding? Now, if Mr. Kennedy had still been the Wall Street corsair of the 1920s, he'd have heaved toward the Auchinclosses at midday and swarmed their forecastle by sundown. In this case, he bided his time until the exact weekend they invited him to Newport. Jackie would later speak of the chill she felt watching him step off his private plane with that adolescent, carnivorous grin. *Oh, Mummy*, she thought.

Not even the shingled twenty-eight-room splendor of Hammersmith Farm was safe from Mr. Kennedy's scrutiny. He cast an eye over every bowed brick, every rotting window, ran a silent tally of servants and rodents and fed everything straight into his mind's abacus. It would gird him for what lay ahead and, in particular, for Mrs. Auchincloss. Who, in case I haven't made it clear, was no more on board with a Kennedy son-in-law than she'd been six months before and was, as Jackie well knew, prepared to do everything within her to power to block it—without giving the impression of doing anything.

It was delicate as balancing acts go, but Mrs. Auchincloss had been practicing her whole life, and although she was—no, *because* she was only a little further off the boat than the Kennedys, she was all the more at pains to discourage fellow climbers. It's why she invited her guests to lunch at Bailey's Beach Club, an establishment that, on normal days—and how remote those days seem to me now—would have barred Kennedys and indeed all Roman Catholics at the door. Jack himself was nearly turned away for wearing shorts and a rumpled Oxford, and it took all of Mrs. Auchincloss's persuasion to get him a place at the table.

"Standards," she explained with a light shrug.

The oysters Rockefeller and lobster Newburg and crab imperial were ordered, and Mrs. Auchincloss, calmly but tenaciously, plied herself against the Kennedy she thought might soonest give way.

"Dear Mrs. Kennedy," she began. "I'm so sorry we couldn't have you up earlier. Our calendar's been absurdly swamped, and I just couldn't find anyone to say no to. There was bridge with Paul and Bunny Mellon, there was champagne with the Vanderbilts . . ."

On and on it went. Name dropping, we might now call it, but in Mrs. Auchincloss's world, it was simply diary. If, by chance, she had crossed paths with dear friends and neighbors, why pretend it didn't happen at the Breakers or the Southampton Bathing Corporation? If somebody had said the *funniest thing* the last time he was at this very club, why act as if it weren't Pierre du Pont?

"Oh, dear," she said at last. "Listen to me prattle. Mrs. Kennedy, won't you tell me how things are in your neck of the world? So very charming, your Hyannisport. How I love driving *through*."

It was the moment to which she'd been building all along. Rose Kennedy was about to *sing*, and the entire listening world was about to hear.

Now, through the years, I've heard many unkind words used to describe Mrs. Kennedy's voice: caw, croak, screech, cackle. I myself have been less struck by its timbre than its perseverance. Pull the string and the string pulling itself.

"Oh, boy, those are some scrumptious-looking oysters, but I hope nobody thinks *I'm* going to eat 'em! No sirree, I've got to starve myself to the bone if I'm going to fit in my gown come September. It's Balmain, of course, I saw it last spring, and I said to myself, I said, I don't know if any of my children are getting married any time soon, but *just in case*."

"How prescient of you."

"'Be prepared' is my motto. Like the Boy Scouts. Oh, and speaking of *prepared*, when we were flying over here, I got to thinking about the music for the ceremony. Being a classically trained pianist, I've a great many ideas. For organ, you can't top Mrs. Maloney . . ."

"Ah."

". . . and there's an Irish tenor from Boston who sings the most beautiful 'Ave Maria' you ever heard. It's Schubert or else it's Gounod. You'll *weep*."

"I'm sure I shall."

"Now, for the reception, I think Meyer Davis's orchestra would be grand, don't you? Nobody gets 'em up on their feet like he does. Naturally, he's booked years in advance, but we've got an in with a certain gentleman named Morton *Downey*, if that rings any bells. And Jiminy Christmas, I don't even know where to start on the guest list! Our phone's been ringing off the hook. *'Please, Mrs. Kennedy, can I get an invite?'* Times like these I forget how many Fitzgeralds came over on the boat."

"Nobody was counting, perhaps."

"And a good thing! What I tell these freeloaders is you've got to stand in line, don't you, behind *all* one hundred U.S. senators and their wives and every member of the Massachusetts Democratic party who ever existed. Just cuz you voted four times in one day in the dear old North End doesn't give you privileges, do you hear?"

Mrs. Auchincloss let her eyes shudder to an ecstatic close. She was no longer listening to the words but the *music*, and she knew her daughter was listening, too, and, more important, *understanding* that, if this marriage were to go forward, these would be the woodland notes filling her ears.

"Now, as to flowers, I hope you won't accuse me of disgracing my name, but I say *no to roses*! It's too late in the year, and the hothouse sort are perfectly *déclassé*, don't you agree? Mums would be the obvious choice, but I still have a soft spot for carnations, I don't care who knows it, and I think it would be terrific fun if we could arrange them all to spell something."

"*Spell* something . . ."

"Well, sure!"

"I'm beside myself with suspense to know what."

"Oh, I don't know, maybe a big *J*. Or *two J*s, wouldn't that be darling?"

Once again, Janet Auchincloss closed her eyes. Once again, the telepathic message flashed between her and her daughter.

Your future.

"Oh, I don't mean in the church, of course. Archbishop Cushing wouldn't stand for *that*. No, I was thinking somewhere outside—in the parking lot, maybe. You know, it would almost be an act of charity for all those photographers. Give 'em something to snap while they're standing around!"

Mrs. Auchincloss's eyes blinked open. Hughdie gave his hearing aid a slight twist.

"Photographers?" he said.

"Why, yes," said Mrs. Kennedy.

"In the plural," he said.

"Oh, sure."

"Isn't that excessive?"

It was the first sign that Mrs. Auchincloss had underestimated her opposition, for in the next instant, almost by prearrangement, Mrs. Kennedy fell as silent as clay, and Mr. Kennedy, interlacing his fingers, leaned forward.

"I, uh, I suppose you all appreciate that your daughter is marrying a public figure."

"Define *appreciate*," said Mrs. Auchincloss.

"What I mean is these particular nuptials will have news value quite outside our small little circle. Hey, America's not going to let its number-one bachelor get dragged to the altar without getting a look at the girl who drug him there. So photographers, of course."

"The *still* kind," suggested Hughdie.

"To begin with. But, of course, we couldn't keep away the newsreels, not if we tried, and Jesus, Mary and Joseph, the television."

There were no television sets in all of Hammersmith Farm, not even for the groundskeepers.

"I mean, you can't keep *them* away," said Mr. Kennedy. "They damn well *find* you, I don't care who you are. And of course, we should be prepared for a fair number of spectators."

"In the church?" asked Hughdie.

"No, right outside."

"What number is a fair number?"

"I dunno, a thousand? Two at most."

"At what will they be spectating?"

"Uh, *your* daughter and our son."

"For what purpose?"

"They're *fans*, Hugh. If I may use the common parlance."

"I didn't suppose Jackie had fans."

"She does now."

"And they're allowed just to show up like that?"

Silence gathered over the white linen.

"Say now," said Mr. Kennedy, leaning farther in. "I'm glad we're having this conversation because you should know what's about to descend."

"Or what's not," said Mrs. Auchincloss.

"The wear on the lawn," suggested Hughdie.

With a flap of his hand, Mr. Kennedy said, "Seed it again next spring."

"Disturbance to the livestock."

"Give 'em earmuffs."

More silence, as Mrs. Auchincloss took the tiniest draft from her martini. Like any good combatant, she was recalibrating. She had come in with the hope of scotching the whole business before luncheon was over, and she was wary even of imagining how the wedding would play, for that would give it too much the imprint of a real thing. Now, having been forced to picture Hammersmith cows with muffs, she began to wonder if the real thing might do the trick after all.

"Tell me, Mr. Kennedy. Just how many guests are you envisioning at this putative affair?"

"Well, I sure don't blame you for asking. My feeling is that if we're very strict about the guest list, we can cap it at a thousand."

"A thousand? That seems better suited to an MGM backlot."

"Maybe so."

"We could enroll everyone in the Screen Actors Guild."

"Ha! I could arrange that."

"Of course, the expense of hosting all these *extras* would be perfectly exorbitant."

"I don't know about that. I've been running the numbers through my head, and I think you could bring it home for half a million."

Hughdie's mouth didn't quite form itself around the number, but his soul did. "Gad," he whispered, a retreat that spurred his wife in the next breath to charge forward. To declare, in effect, the line past which the Auchincloss family would not cross.

"I'm afraid that we couldn't possibly countenance such a grotesque spectacle."

Nobody spoke for a second or two. Then Mr. Kennedy unexpectedly flashed the same smile he had flashed coming off his plane.

"Well now," he said. "I like me a woman who speaks her mind. No, I do! And I completely understand your position. In fact, I even anticipated it. It's why I was going to propose two weddings."

Mrs. Auchincloss's head drew back at most a half inch. "Two?"

"Why, sure. Your intimate and tasteful ceremony here and then a more robust *spectacle*, as you call it, on the Cape."

"What, simultaneously?"

"Ha! I don't see how we can manage that, do you? It takes an hour and a half by car and that's without the late-summer traffic. Longer by ferry. No, I figure you could have your discreet little society event in the afternoon, and we could have ours in the evening. Or vice versa if you like."

A cold awareness dawned in Mrs. Auchincloss's eyes.

"Only yours will have all the cameras."

"Well, yes. For the reasons just discussed."

"And that's how the world—*your* world, Mr. Kennedy—will see my daughter. Without her mother at her side."

"Well, you'd certainly be welcome to come. I just wouldn't want you to feel like—you know, *extras*."

Mrs. Auchincloss had come in believing that the Kennedys needed Newport and its Wasp respectability. In this she was not entirely mistaken; where she erred was in thinking that Newport could thereby extract concessions. In this she was the victim of her own class prejudices, which was a weakness only because she herself was blind to it and Mr. Kennedy was not. Had, in fact, sniffed it out from the start. No wonder he was smiling.

There was no use enlisting her husband. Mrs. Auchincloss's only remaining recourse was to fall back on the person who'd been sitting silently at her side.

"When it comes down to it," she declared in a halting voice, "I only want what my daughter wants."

The move was as risky as it was unexpected. She had not

rehearsed it with Jackie in advance and didn't know where
her daughter stood on any of these questions. She had merely
assumed that Jackie, being the byproduct of an upbringing
more or less like her own, would imbibe, in the manner of
breast milk, some of the same assumptions, would cringe
at the idea of Mrs. Maloney and carnation *J*s and madding
crowds and would demand—insist on—a level of decorum
fitting her station and, failing that, turn tail.

And Jackie wasn't immune to any of these considerations.
But what her mother failed to account for was that Jackie—
in those pre-paparazzi days—wasn't immune to the prospect of cameras, either. Or *fans*, no matter how mysteriously
they arrived. Her response, then, was not to ally herself with
either side but to drift rather far out to sea—so far that it
was hard now to see what lay directly around her. Was the
choice simply one wedding versus two? Hammersmith versus Hyannisport? Was there some larger concern eluding
her? In her confusion, she turned not to her mother but to
Jack, who had been just as silent as she through the whole
conversation and who now sat slumped in his chair, as if the
whole conversation had been drawing out his blood, milliliter by milliliter. She heard herself say, in a pale echo of her
mother:

"I only want what Jack wants."

A glint of irritation sparked from his eyes, and with a
grating sigh, he sat up and said, "Seems to me one ceremony
would be plenty. It's all the Queen got."

"In that case," announced Mrs. Auchincloss, "it shall be
here. As tradition dictates."

There was a pause. Then, from across the table, Mr. Kennedy let loose with a roar of laughter. Snatched the white linen napkin from his lap and waved it like a flag and shot his arms toward the ceiling.

"I surrender!" he cried.

Jackie would remember later that Mrs. Auchincloss was the only one at the table who abstained from the general laughter. She was too busy studying Mr. Kennedy, for she knew that surrender was its opposite. At last, with a soft exhalation, he took off his specs and gave each of his eyes a tender rub.

"Say now," he said. "Since we're all agreed where this wedding is going to be, I was wondering if I could ask you folks the tiniest of favors? What I mean is, it would be tiny to *you*, but to me and Mrs. Kennedy, it would . . ." He paused to gather himself. "The thing is I'm starting to think of you two as—as *family* if that doesn't—I mean, does that embarrass you? Are you sure? Well, feeling the way I do, I find I can't abide the thought of you shouldering the cost of this wedding. No, no, I understand it's tradition, and I know you're people of deep pride who want to do right by your ancestors."

"Just so," said Hughdie faintly.

"But, gosh darn it, my boy Jack there, he may not be my firstborn but he's—he's the one who's *left*." Mr. Kennedy laid his hand with great care across his wife's wrist. "And I'll tell you something else. His brother Joe, if he were alive right now, would want us to give Jack the best by-God send-off we could muster. And that's why I'm asking—as a *father*

I'm asking—that you let me fund the whole kit and caboo-dle. No, no, I insist! Soup to nuts, it's—" He paused, looked away. "It's the least we could do for Joe's memory."

Outside of the opera house, Wasps in those days weren't accustomed to such emotional appeals, so the awkwardness must have been extreme. Jackie herself felt it and, ducking her head away, found her gaze again landing on Jack, who, strangely, seemed the least embarrassed person in the room, had even the ghost of a smile on his lips.

"Of course," Mr. Kennedy quickly added, "if you *want* to cover all the costs—I mean, if it would mean that much—I'd be the last one to deny you the privilege. God knows you've *earned* it, haven't you, Hugh?"

"Oh, well, that's—"

"I mean, when I think of all that Standard Oil has done for this nation. Does any American believe we could have won two wars without petroleum? No. Stood up to Joe Stalin without petroleum? No, I tell you. A thousand times no."

"Oh, that's very kind of you to—"

"And even though Standard Oil has long since been div-vied up and scattered to the winds, and even though the remaining cash reserves can't be anywhere near what they once were, a grateful nation still remembers your family's service, Hugh. And as one of that nation, I ask that you now let me pay you this tribute. Won't you please?"

Hughdie cast a single fearful glance at his wife, put a hand to his button-down collar.

"If it would mean that much to you."

"It would."

"Well then, I shan't be the one to stand in your way."

As soon as the words were out, Hughdie's shoulders subsided, and acrid relief steamed from every pore. He had heard the bullet whistle past his ear and was still, by some miracle, alive.

It was left to his wife to scope the shot's true trajectory. In a single nervy thrust, Mr. Kennedy had secured himself both Newport and the wedding itself. From that moment forth, he would have autonomy over every detail: organist and bandleader, canapés and china pattern. The carnation formations. Every photographer in the land would descend in a Mongol horde, and whatever protest the Auchinclosses might lodge would be muted by their new status as bed-and-breakfast proprietors, compensated for the use of their grounds and their tactful silence.

In the space of a few seconds, and before a crowd of largely uncomprehending witnesses, Mrs. Auchincloss had been routed. Worse still, she could lodge no protest, for if there were a greater sin than raising one's voice in Bailey's Beach Club, it had yet to be discovered. Jackie told me later that her mother reminded her then of a falcon around which invisible bars have sprouted—bars of gilt wire, against which the bird beats its wings in vain, for they have been there all along. It was a moving enough sight that Jackie, in a spirit of true pity, leaned toward her mother and whispered:

"It's time to give up, Mummy. This is what I want."

THIRTY-ONE

*I*t would be natural, I guess, to presume that, as her wedding date approached, Jackie's nerves were stretched to their breaking point. America was watching! The world's largest swarm of worker bees had gathered in some hive in Brooklyn just to tat the lace for her gown! To that I say: Jackie in those days was at the loosest kind of ends.

Mr. Kennedy was calling every last shot, right down to that gown, and she was no more in charge of her own nuptials than a rani. From time to time, the latest guest list would come fluttering down, and she would gaze in a bemused sort of way at the names. The Trumans. The Luces. Herbert Hoover, J. Edgar Hoover. MacArthur, McCarthy. Speaker Martin. Ed Sullivan. Irving Berlin. Hearst and Mrs. Hearst and the de facto Mrs. Hearst. Who knew how many of them would actually show up? But to Jackie, the very proliferation of names left them canceling each other out, and the possibility that she might have to greet or be greeted by them struck her as fantastically remote.

Her wedding, in short, seemed to have relatively little to do with her—a conclusion that I believe she found oddly liberating. Especially now that she was out of a job. Her editor had been fired while she was in London, and once the news of her engagement leaked, the top brass assumed that any girl who'd gone and lassoed a Kennedy had more important things on her mind than interviewing sweaty proletarians. I think they were wrong. I believe that Inquiring Camera Girl was how she came to terms with her world. I still keep, hermetically sealed, her final column, published on June the fourth. "What is your candid opinion of marriage?" she wanted to know.

It can be a hard transition, I expect, from news gatherer to news object. As a journalist, Jackie had cultivated a certain professional anonymity, instinctually hiding herself behind the barricade of a Leica. Now she had wandered into the unmarked landscape where your camera, as if possessed, turns on *you* and the man on the street is more intrigued by *your* opinion than his, and the girl at Miss Porter's who once wrote you off as fatally callow sends you a bouquet of orchids with the inscription, BELLE DAME SANS MERCI, and the Kalorama hostesses who never thought or knew to include you now insist their garden parties would wither and die and be swallowed by the earth without the solar power of your face.

Invited up to the Cape for the last weekend of June, she found to her surprise an entire photo crew from *Life* magazine waiting. The results are ripely hilarious (for, of course, I've kept the issue). Jackie running with a football, Jackie playing softball—she hated both sports—and, in maybe the most startling juxtaposition, sitting barelegged between Jean and Eunice, the three of them chattering away like the swim team at a Poconos camp. If you consider what fascinates people about *today's* Jackie—the sense, I mean, of a deeply guarded personality blossoming under the pressure of a camera lens into something deeply suggestive—that mystery is nowhere to be found here. The Jackie of twenty-three is all in. Her smile crackles, her hair flies away with every cross-breeze. In one photo, she leans back on the veranda rail, leg extended like a chorine's, her face perfectly framed in the shadow of her straw hat, and the Atlantic nothing more than a black-and-white scrim at her back. *Crowing*, by the looks of it, and which of us shall blame her? In the words of *Life*, she'd gone and nabbed "the handsomest young member of the U.S. Senate."

But what I come back to is the magazine's cover photo: Jack and Jackie "alone together" on the *Honey Fitz*. She's holding on for dear life to something—the boat's mast, probably. Her hair is blowing straight toward the sky, and her face is refulgent with joy. I linger on this image because it seems to me that whatever reservations she was feeling that summer, they weren't about him.

Then you look at Jack. Knees drawn to his chest, eyes cutting rather sheepishly her way, hair unusually matted (somebody must have forced headwear on him) and the smile a little matted, too. A deliberated set of enamel. "Senator Kennedy Goes A-Courting" is how the sans-serif headline reads, but who's courting and who's being courted? Did he taste, via that premeditated photo shoot, some of the camera-ready charisma that his fiancée would impart to a nation and a world? Did she, as a result, leave feeling more squarely positioned in his heart? Or, conversely, did she grasp even more the imbalance built into loving him?

By the time that issue of *Life* hit the newsstands, he was back in the hospital. A recurrence of the old wartime malaria, it was put out. We had long since been banned from speaking the disease's actual name, not even to his fiancée, who kept reasonably planning trips to Jack's bedside, with chocolates and cold compresses and lullabies. One by one, the family telephoned her, begging her to keep her distance. Jack needed his rest, that's what Mr. Kennedy said, and what would be less restful than a pretty lady in the room? Mrs. Kennedy said that a boy wanted to be strong for his girl. Even Ethel got into the act. "Jackie," she said, "it's tiresome. Trust me."

This was the most revealing response of all for it implied that Jack's hospital stays were so chronic by now as to be banal, and indeed, to those of us who'd known him all our lives, even last rites were a little déjà vu. No one was more bored by the whole fire drill than he was, and nothing would have filled him with greater horror than Jackie swooping in with her silent-movie eyes. By way of forestalling that moment, Jack took the unusual step of calling her regularly from Georgetown Hospital. "No, dear, I'm just waiting it

out. Thank God for *books*," he quickly added. "They're all
the company a boy needs." The voice was still vigorous, the
manner ironic. By the sound of him, he wasn't ill at all.

Yet there was something about being so conspicuously
kept away that kindled in her an opposing reaction. She was
certain now that a mystery lay harbored inside Georgetown
Hospital, and she would begin by going at its softest point.

"Lem," she said, "I've been meaning to send Jack some
flowers, but I don't know which room he's in."

"Oh, just leave them at the front desk."

"I don't dare! Someone might walk off with them."

So, with a room number in hand, she showed up one
Sunday afternoon, bearing an actual bouquet—marigolds
and snapdragons—and ascending the rear staircase to better conceal herself. She actually trembled a little, reaching
for the door. What if the whole clan were there? As it turned
out, there was only Jack and Mrs. Lincoln, in quiet conference. At sight of her, they were utterly silent. Then, in
answer to an invisible signal, Mrs. Lincoln packed up her
manila file folders and trooped out.

"I'll have to speak to someone about the security," said
Jack.

"You really should."

Most of the room's surfaces were occupied by other bou-
quets, in various states of decay, so she left her own flowers,
still in their wrapping, on the bedside table, then retreated
to the chair furthest from the bed, a modular number with a
brown-leather cushion that seemed to sigh beneath her.

"I know I disobeyed orders," she said.

"That's okay."

"I won't stay long."

"That's fine."

In the silence that followed, she absorbed, in a half seeing way, the pistachio green walls, the tartan curtains drawn across the casement windows, the TV set on a tripod in the corner—before settling at last on the blue chevrons of Jack's hospital gown.

"You look fine," she said.

"Fit as a fiddle."

"Do you—"

"What?"

"Need anything? A soda. There's a machine downstairs."

"No, I'm fine."

"How about . . ."

A *snack*, she was going to say, but then her eyes snagged on the peanut-butter-and-jelly sandwich, largely uneaten, resting on a tray at the end of the bed. She remembered then, with a peculiar sharpness, all the dinner plates he had pushed away during their times together. ("Late lunch.") All the stairs he'd had to brace himself for, like Hillary climbing Everest. The way his collar kept drawing away from his neck, the strange ocher tones that bled through his Palm Beach tan.

"It isn't malaria," she said.

He made a quiet study of his fingernails.

"It's no worse," he said.

"Are you sure?"

"Course."

"Then you can tell me what it is."

She would later try to parse his pause. It wasn't a case of his being unwilling or unready, more a matter of setting the right tone. For the only way he could explain it to her was to rejigger it as an existential joke, delivered in Brooklynese.

"See, when a guy's adrenal glands ain't workin' right, it's a terrible thing. The ticker don't always beat like it should, so he faints like a fairground tent in a high wind. The immune system don't always show up for work so he catches whatever germ's hitching a ride in his general direction. The gut gets screwed up in knots, so he can't eat like he's s'posed to. All a gentleman can ask in those specific circumstances is to figure out what he's got so they can get it under control, like."

"And is it?" she asked.

With that, the true Jack voice returned.

"Is it what?"

"Under control."

"Mostly."

"How?"

"Cortisone injections. Back of the thigh, twice a day."

"Who does it?"

"Me."

"Does it hurt?

"Only like hell."

"Can other people do it?"

"I'd rather they not."

With a feeling of embarrassment—as if she'd found somebody's cast-aside dentures—she stared at the exact point where the intravenous tube entered his arm.

"Sometimes the cortisone doesn't work," she said.

"Well, yes."

"And you end up here."

"Wherever they've got a bed. Not too long ago, I got to know the Tokyo general hospital quite well. Even picked up a little Japanese. Yes, ma'am," he said, with an uprush, "you throw in my bum back, and I'm a regular piece of human flotsam in multiple hemispheres. The good news is I catch up on my reading."

Now for the first time she noticed the books. Not on his side table, where you'd expect them, but rising up from the floor in a hardback plinth. *All the company a boy needs.*

"Why do you tell people it's malaria?" she asked.

His head seemed to tilt toward the question.

"Dad thinks, if they knew, it would be the end of things."

"Politically."

"Well, there's no cure, you see. And nobody's going to vote for a dead man."

It was all the more appalling for being delivered with the full Kennedy grin.

"So it's something you could die from," she said.

"That's not out of the realm."

"And it could happen any time."

"I guess that's so."

"And didn't you think I should know?"

The question seemed to catch them both off guard, for they fell still before it.

"I guess I figured I'd lose your vote, too," he said.

"For something that's not your fault?"

"Oh," he answered easily. "I've got plenty of faults, too. You needn't worry about those."

Digging her heels into the floor, she dragged her chair closer—closer—until it was almost touching his bed.

"Were you afraid, if you told me, that I'd want to leave? Or were you afraid I'd want to stay?"

Now, for the first time since she arrived, he looked genuinely discomposed.

"Can we just leave it as I'm glad you're here now? Because I am," he said. "I desperately am."

She smiled a little, gently pushed the arm lamp away to take the glare out of her eyes.

"You know," he said, "you can get out of this whole marriage business now."

"Why would I?"

"Because you'd have to get used to this kind of thing. And maybe the other side of the thing."

The other side. She tried in that moment—tried hard—to imagine herself as a widow, in black crepe and veil, jet jewelry, wailing over an open grave, but the figure she conjured didn't have any face at all, let alone hers.

"Next time you're here," she said, "I'll wear my naughty-nurse costume."

"Ooh." A signal light flared from his eyes. "You look plenty naughty now. If I could . . ."

He reached a hand in her direction, but she was already rising from her chair and intercepting it.

"Will you tell them?" she asked.

"Tell who? You know, this isn't an infectious kind of disease, we could still—"

"Tell your family."

"You could nurse me back to health right here and now."

"I know," she said, and waited for his eyes to track back with hers. "But you need to tell them."

"What?"

"That you told *me* and it didn't break me and I didn't turn tail or get the vapors or whatever they thought might happen."

He regarded her for a moment.

"I'll tell them."

THIRTY-TWO

*S*he left that hospital, then, with the feeling of having passed another chivalric test—a sense bolstered by Mr. Kennedy, who called her that night to commend her for "cheering up Jack to no end." Indeed, so buoyant would his spirits prove that, as soon he was cleared from the hospital, he cast his eyes across the sea. It was the height of summer, and if you were a man who'd escaped another brush with the Reaper—at any rate, if you were Jack—the best way to celebrate was to charter a yacht in the South of France and sun yourself, sans fiancée, in Cap d'Antibes.

The official explanation was that he was consulting with the French government on Vietnam policy, but Jack's folks didn't bother keeping up that pretense. Mr. Kennedy assured

Jackie it would just be a little bachelor party. Mrs. Kennedy said it was something a bridegroom needed to get out of his system. Mrs. Auchincloss could not be so sanguine, and indeed the impotence to which she'd been reduced by the wedding planning only intensified the clench of her voice.

"Darling, I'm in such a quandary. What sort of man goes away by himself two weeks before his wedding? Oh, I remember! Your father."

Jackie turned away, but there was no escaping her mother's croon.

"What a sorority we shall be!"

As luck would have it, Black Jack Bouvier was currently in the South of France himself. He had checked himself into another sanatorium—or somebody had done it for him. Through the intermediary of his son-in-law, Michael Canfield (who was either in the same facility or prowling just outside), he assured Jackie that he was drying out faster than Oklahoma and would be ready to squeeze himself into his best evening coat and escort her down the aisle.

If she'd had her father in the same room, she'd have asked how a man could come to a certain kind of understanding in a hospital room and then act as if the understanding had never happened. She'd have asked if a conventional marriage was really the kind of straitjacket a real man couldn't wriggle out of fast enough. Wasn't there something to be said for the man who came home every night, ready to engage in ritual displays of affection, however tedious? Was there not, in fact, a peculiar loneliness that lay just outside those rituals?

Remembering all the scholarly articles she'd translated on the subject of Indochina, she wondered why Jack hadn't at least thought to bring her along to France as interpreter. I didn't have the heart to tell her that interpretation wasn't the issue, nor did I have the stomach to pretend that all would be wholesome. Yes, Mr. Kennedy would be going along as chaperone, but the third man in the party was Torby McDonald, Jack's old college roommate, who had graduated from being Harvard's star halfback to Jack's offensive line, clearing obstructions. So I made the same noises as the Kennedys. *Just a few days. He'll come back right as rain, raring to go.*

But, at the same time, I figured she would crave some diversion of her own, so I suggested a place neither of us had been to. In those days, the Marshall Hall amusement park was a despondent piece of southern Maryland real estate sitting directly across the Potomac from Mount Vernon. Formerly the property of slave owners, it had transformed itself first into a picnic ground, then a gambling venue. It was, I recall, the only place outside of Nevada where you could legally play the slots. The proprietors must have concluded that if a man was prepared to gamble away his family's milk money, his family should be distracted while it was happening, so there rose up Potemkin-faced storefronts dressed in the accents of backlot Westerns. There was a cotton candy depot, a haunted house called Laff in the Dark, a whirligig named The Scrambler, and a roller coaster, traveling no higher than a hundred and fifty feet, billed as the "Thrill of a Lifetime."

Jackie was as enthusiastic about the idea as I was, and so we drove down 210 with light hearts. I spoke of Mother and her dying dogwood, which could not be saved even by nightly infusions of gin, and Jackie spoke in no particular order of her horse and her tennis game and her future mother-in-law, whose speech patterns she had already uncannily mastered.

The heat came for us as soon as we got out of the car. To anyone who's grown up north of Mason-Dixon in air-conditioned wombs, it can be hard to explain how our generation answered summer's challenge—the great pains we took both to retain and surrender dignity. A man like me, for example, didn't put on a hat and a jacket and tie in the trough of August because he was an ass but because, with the world's blessing, he was concealing the disturbance below— the riot in steerage. You *walked* with the heat in those days, you swam in it, it claimed you from toe to crown, and you consoled yourself in knowing that everyone around you was perpetuating the same lie. If a gentleman tipped his hat to a lady, he clapped it back on his sodden head in the same motion. If a lady drew a fan from her reticule, she took the greatest possible care not to show her primal urgency. Even so, there was something about Marshall Hall Park in late July that was unusually exposed to the elements. Within an hour of walking its half dozen saloon streets, Jackie and I were gasping for relief, and the only drink on hand was Pepsi, which, after the third cup, came streaming back through our pores in a phosphoric mist.

Jackie, at least, had put on the sleeveless top from her *Life* spread and—in an amusing repudiation of her current coutured self—a pair of dungaree shorts that might have been swiped from an Appalachian maiden. Her example must have liberated me because, before another hour had passed, I stripped off my white jacket and bow tie and tossed them into the car. We did another tour of the haunted house just to get into the shade, then the carousel, then the bingo parlor (shade). We made a shared dinner of licorice sticks and cotton candy (or, rather, I ate them and Jackie looked as if she might). It was well past seven before we climbed onto the Ferris wheel. We'd saved it for last because she'd never been on one and, though she professed to be bored by them, the truth was she was a little scared. It's funny to think that a girl who rode horses at breakneck speed, scorning every hurdle and water jump, would pale before this particular test, but to distract her, I bought a box of Cracker Jack. "Every time you get nervous," I said, "you just bite into one." The first time we sailed over the apogee, she grabbed my arm with one hand and the caramel corn with the other. After half a dozen circuits, she began chomping down as though both our lives depended on it. On our final revolution, the wheel took a sudden lunge toward earth, then rebounded toward heaven, then resolved at last into an unstable rocking, like a caravel in a storm-harrowed ocean. In the next instant, Jackie tossed me the box and put the back of her hand to her mouth. Not, as I first assumed, to contain her nausea but to stop the cry that was budding forth.

We waited for some time, our digits entwined, before a courtly voice called up. "Ladies and gentlemen, we appear to have lost power. We will let you know when the situation alters."

"Yes," I called down. "Let us know."

How instantly the space around us expanded. Sky to earth, east to west.

"Well," I said, "you can't die in a Ferris wheel, your mother wouldn't allow it."

"It's true, she'd kill me."

And still the rocking wouldn't quite resolve, and I wasn't sure how exactly I was going to brazen this out until there came the most unexpected of offerings. A clear and pure stream sluicing down to my right. Soda-pop was my first thought before the metallic notes blossomed forth. Somebody—and we never did establish if it was male or female, young or old—was *relieving* just above us. The wages of Pepsi. Jackie, bless her, began to laugh, which gave me the same license.

"Talk about something," I said. "Anything."

She cast her eyes across the river. "It's my birthday on Tuesday."

"Oh," I said. "Sorry."

"Why?"

"I should have remembered."

"I don't remember yours."

"But I've had more. So they become less remarkable. The good news is you should be down by Tuesday."

"That is my hope."

"You're almost twenty-four," I said. "How does that almost feel?"

"Do you know I think it's the first birthday where I've felt—oh, what? That I'm moving *away* from instead of toward."

"Away from what?"

She paused to puzzle it out. "What I might have been, I guess. I sometimes think about what Berenson told me."

All this time I'd known her, and I had to wait until we were stranded on a Ferris wheel to learn she'd met the great critic Bernard Berenson. Who, back when I was a young art history major, was my sun, my moon. It's not too much to say I was going to *be* Berenson—tell the world exactly what it should be seeing.

"Oh," said Jackie, "he was a perfectly charming man. We met him at his villa in Florence, and he told me you should only marry someone who will constantly stimulate you, and you him. Don't waste your time with people who are—what was his—people who are life-*diminishing*. You had to live for your art."

"It helps if you live in Florence."

"Oh, no," she answered, with a pulse of urgency. "You can do it anywhere."

That's when she told me about coming down from the Alps into Grenoble. All of twenty years old, and hurling herself at France in the pitch of summer, and finding, like an apparition, a flat scorching plain and above it a vast enfolding hot blue sky. Rows of poplars on the edge of every field to protect the crops from the mistral, and short spiky palm trees with blazing red flowers growing at their feet.

"I couldn't imagine anything more beautiful, Lem. I remember thinking, *What if I stopped right here? Never left?* Oh, I don't know how I would have managed it. Knocked on some farmer's door, I guess, and begged for lodging—in the barn, maybe. I wouldn't have had any useful skills to offer, but maybe I could have peeled potatoes or weeded the onion patch or something. I think I would have done anything they threw at me if I just could sit every day at the same time and watch the same sky, the same trees. Isn't that ridiculous? I mean, do you really see me as a milkmaid? The dirndl and lace cap?"

"Someone has to do it."

"Thank God it wasn't me."

Her head, through some axis of weariness, declined toward my shoulder. It was strange, I remember, to feel in the midst of that humid evening air the more particular humidity of another body.

"I'm not making a mistake, am I, Lem?"

"How do you mean?"

"Getting married."

"Of course not."

"Berenson would be so angry. I won't be living for art, I'll be living for a man."

"Oh," I said, "there's an art to that, too. Ask any wife. Besides, you're marrying the finest man I know."

IT'S FUNNY. UNTIL that moment, I'd never described Jack that way. Why should I have done so now? If you'd asked me to anatomize it, I might have mumbled something about a rich, dilettantish young man, able to live exactly as he liked, making the extraordinary decision to live in a way that mattered. To be of *value* to people who weren't rich and didn't winter in Florida and who struggled even to put food on the table. Seen from that slant, power for him was just a tool for sharpening his value to a particular point.

Or was I really just thinking of his value in my own life? When we first met, I had several inches and three dozen pounds on him, yet, from our earliest days, he was my defender. From the fascistic enforcers of the sixth form. From the hated housemaster who backed me up one night against our fireplace and shook me until I cried. "You should get your hands off him," I remember Jack snarling. Nobody ever believes loud people can detect undertones, but I can't tell you how many times I overheard someone encouraging Jack to, in so many words, get rid of the court jester and hearing him respond—or not respond at all, with equal eloquence—that we were a package deal. And in his world, a deal was a deal.

None of this was I able to articulate to Jackie atop that Ferris wheel, but maybe some part leaked through because she gave my hand a light squeeze and murmured, "What a good friend you are."

And then added:

"But, you know, fine men don't always make fine husbands."

"This one will," I said. "You can trust me."

"He just needs to get it out of his system, is that it?"

I looked at her, then looked across the river toward Mount Vernon, which stood in the clotting dusk like a doll's house of white Palladian matchsticks with a red-shingle play-roof.

"Do you think they're looking back at us?" she asked.

"Who?"

"The Mount Vernon ladies. They're very, very tiny, and they're staring back at us through lorgnettes. They want to know who are those curious aerial creatures."

"Who fly up but never come down."

"Precisely." She curled her hand around my arm and leaned into me.

We sat in silence for a while. Now and then, a harassed electrician's voice would call up some reassurance—a new circuit was being assembled—it was only a matter of time—and I wanted to call back and ask what was time and what was space. We had entered that strange hour of evening when light and night merge, and the usual coordinates are scrambled and the old distances are elided. Mount Vernon was about as close as my wingtip, and the ground, for all I knew, was a thousand feet away. In a daze, I reached into the Cracker Jack box that was resting in Jackie's lap and came away with a tiny plastic satchel. Nothing more than the trinket that came with every box. A second later, the wrapping was peeled away and the prize was resting in my hand. A gold-tin ring with a vermilion mock gem. I can't say even now what possessed me, but in the next moment, I was slipping it onto Jackie's finger. With what I would now call a feeling of presentiment for I was in no way surprised to see how easily it cleared the hurdle of the second knuckle and nestled without a trace of embarrassment against Mr. Kennedy's million-dollar ring.

"It fits," she said.

"Of course it does."

It was then, on the purest of whims, that I twisted toward her—the chair rocking from the surprise of it—and took her hand in mine.

"Jackie . . ."

"Yes?"

"If things don't work out with you and Jack . . ."

"Yes."

". . . might I be your backup husband?"

Looking back, I see how many contingencies lay embedded just *there*. She might have flushed with embarrassment or contrived the tinniest of laughs. She might have chided me, begged me not to talk nonsense. In a spirit of charity, she might have ignored me altogether. Instead, there rose from her face a grin of such resplendence that I felt—well, apprehended.

"I would be honored, Lem."

The sun had long since set and the hour was approaching nine when the Ferris wheel at last shuddered to life and began descending in asthmatic segments. Just seconds before we landed, Jackie slipped the ring from her finger and rested it with a quiet emphasis in my palm and whispered, "I love you, Lem."

THIRTY-THREE

*J*ack reemerged from the Mediterranean a week later,
shaggy-haired and browned—and in no way ready to
address himself to the hard logistics of his own wedding. Like
his fiancée, he had long since ceded control to Mr. Kennedy, and
he cared less about what his best man Bobby would be saying
than what kind of cigars would be available for the reception.
So when he invited me over to his Georgetown row house the
Sunday before, I was under no illusion we'd be trying on morning coats. Margaret had, in a helpless way, thrown together
some leftover baked ham with leftover baked beans and a bowl
of salted pumpkin seeds. By way of compensation, there was a
full pitcher of Bloody Marys, salad included. Today, I suppose,
they'd call the whole enterprise brunch, but back then, it was a

Catholic boy tumbling out of bed too late for Mass. Jack didn't bother to dress but threw on a monogrammed silk robin's-egg blue bathrobe that he didn't trouble to cinch the whole way. We played a few rounds of backgammon—I lost three dollars and seventy-five cents—and then Jack reached, in an arduous sort of way, for the last slice of ham.

"The condemned man's last meal," I was moved to say.

"Monday, Tuesday, Wed—no, I've got a few more."

"Poor you. A beautiful girl forever at your beck and call. The saints weep."

"Why bring in the saints? Some things are just unwelcome. When regarded in a different light."

That's how I regarded him now.

"How exactly did the light alter?" I asked. "Between now and two weeks ago? Please don't tell me some girl dragged you to the nearest *justice de paix*."

"I was neither drugged nor dragged."

"Then what happened?"

"Gunilla."

I ran the syllables along my tongue in order to trust them. *Goo-NILL-a.*

"She sounds like a wasting disease," I said.

"She kind of is."

"Does she have a last name?"

"Von Post."

"Kraut?"

"Swede."

I took the celery stick from my Bloody Mary, gave it a contemplative draw.

"She wouldn't be your first," I pointed out.

"She's different."

"A *sweeter* Swede."

"If you like."

I returned the celery to the glass.

"Jack, whatever went on, and I'm sure as hell not going to ask, but it's past tense, as we both know. It's practically past perfect."

He didn't answer at first. Just stared into the nearest pocket of space as if it were a washroom mirror.

"You won't believe me when I tell you, Lem, but I swear to God it was so fucking *chaste*. A few dances, a goodnight kiss, whiffs of perfume. Now I go to bed smelling her, I wake up smelling her. I've written her a letter every day since I got back, and if I'm not careful, I'll cry out her name on my wedding night."

Now, in operas like *Don Giovanni*, the seducer's libido doesn't require much in the way of analysis: He wants what he wants. The psychological variability comes from the seduced. Does she rashly agree to be his eternally? Or does she, like Gunilla von Hoozie, leave herself unclaimed, through either timidity or foresight, making herself eternally more desirable?

"Well, never mind," said Jack with a light trailing-off. "Torby says we should just arrange a congressional junket to Sweden for next summer."

"A junket."

"Hell, yeah. It's one of the perks of the job."

"But what would its purpose be?"

"Didn't I just tell you? I can spell her name for you if you like."

I stared at him. "You know this wedding can't exactly be canceled."

"No one is more aware of that than I."

"And you know, next summer, you'll be a married man."

"I'm aware of that, too."

"I'm just submitting my remarks for the record."

"Whose record? Just what's climbed up your ass, LeMoyne?"

"*She* has. Jackie."

"Why?"

"Because she loves you."

Already half ashamed of my words as they dribbled out. For all I knew, Gunilla loved him, too. People had been loving him his whole life. It was the least expensive of commodities.

"Well now," said Jack. "I wish I could figure out why you're bringing her into this when it has nothing to do with her."

"No?"

"Jesus, Lem, you're the one who explained to her how this would go. Were you not listening to your own message?"

And whatever high ground I might have fancied myself to hold now crumbled away.

"I was listening," I said.

"Then what's the problem here?"

"You asked me to be her friend."

"Not to the exclusion of your other friends. You know, I'm not used to feeling judgment from you, Lem."

"That's not what I—"

"You used to be the kind of guy someone could confide in without getting this whole *She loves you* business. I used to count on you for that, Lem. It was one of your specialties. I mean, do you ever see me judging you?"

"For—I mean, what would you have to—?"

"Oh, how you spend your nights, *where* you spend them. Why you don't settle down and have kids. I don't even *ask* you those questions, Lem, because I don't want to know. It's like I've always said"—and only here did the anger reach, with a kind of relief, toward platitude—"Friendship matters as much as the friend. And maybe more." He frowned down at the table, gave the belt of his robe a light tweeze. "I guess I thought you felt the same way."

Adrenaline, like dry ice along my jaw. And, confusingly, a certain blankness, as though I were being erased.

"You *could* have asked me," I said. "If you'd wanted to."

"I don't."

If anything, I think he was having a harder time of it in that moment than me—he always hated being cross with people—so whatever anger was still simmering in him, he swallowed it down with the rest of his Bloody Mary. Out came the smile, with all its restorative properties.

"Listen now, Lem. You know how highly I think of you. How highly we *all* . . ."

He paused, and there rose to my mind the single conclusion that he was firing me.

The air around us seemed to bend and break beneath all that would follow—the gold watch, the certificate of appreciation—IN TRIBUTE TO YOUR YEARS OF SERVICE—the lightest of shoves out the door. For want of anything else to look at, I studied his feet at the exact point where they emerged from the slippers. The seconds piled on.

"Hell," I said, "did I even want you to get married in the first place? No. So, Christ, don't do anything differently because of me. Or *do* if you . . ." At last, I raised my palms to the ceiling. "I'm plumb out of advice."

He stood for a while staring out the Italianate window.

"Lem, all I want is your remains smeared across the backgammon board. I could use another drink, though, couldn't you?"

WE DID DRINK, and he did beat me at backgammon—it was a relief, really—and the terms we parted on were as friendly as ever, but the ghost of the argument followed me back to Baltimore. It was the first time I had ever been accused of having a specialty in our relationship, and I began canvassing our history to see where I had been caught practicing it. It was then I remembered a Sunday morning back in '49— well before Miss Bouvier had entered the scene. Jack and I had stayed up rather late the night before, and he'd suggested that, instead of rushing to catch the last train to Baltimore, I should just stay over in the guest room. I don't think I'd slept more than three or four hours before he was shaking me awake again. "Lem," he said. "A favor is required."

I sat up in bed, groped for my glasses. Morning had just shown its face, and in the moiré pattern of light and shadow, the only things I could see as clear as day were the lines around

Jack's mouth. He was saying something about a female who'd
come knocking and who'd been told he wasn't home but who'd
barged in anyway and who was down in the foyer and there
was no budging her and there was no use calling the police . . .

"Wait a minute," I said, rubbing the feeling into my skin.
"Who is this *who*?"

"I dunno, some girl who works for Smathers."

No surprise there: Jack and the gentleman from Florida
hunted in a pack.

"What's her name?"

"Lem, I don't know her name. Jesus, can you make her
go away?"

I reached for last night's shirt and trousers. "I should just
say you're not here?"

"It needs more than that, Lem. You need to disabuse her
of coming again. You need to advise her of the unfortunate
consequences that should ensue were she to come again. Do
you think you can handle all that?"

Now, over the years I'd seen many of Jack's girls to
the door. Steered them down the steps, hailed them cabs,
wished them bon voyage and bonne chance. It had always
been an amiable ritual. This was the first time one of them
had declined to be steered, and as I came down the stairs in
my rumpled shirt and trousers and stockinged feet, I found
myself stepping with exaggerated care.

She was seated on a velvet love seat, her knees pressed
together, her hands in her lap. A fairer type than Jack usually
went for, with a profligate fall of auburn hair and a complexion of lactic purity—the kind of face they used to put on bags

of flour or boxes of pancake mix. The only discordant notes came from her eyes, pale green and retracting as I approached.

"Good morning," I said, pausing to sweep the last tile of sleep from my brain. "I'm sorry to say Congressman Kennedy is indisposed right now. Is there something I might help you with?"

The ridges of wariness fell away. She regarded me with a clean line.

"I don't think you can."

"Maybe I can take a message," I suggested.

"I don't think so."

"Let me assure you anything you say would be held in strictest privacy, Miss . . ."

No name was forthcoming, and indeed, the prospect of giving her name seemed to drive her back into watchful silence.

"I think I might have come down with something," she said at last.

Now, as a Wasp, I am fluent in all manner of euphemisms, but here I was stumped. She could have caught a cold, she could be carrying triplets or the plague. "Have you seen a doctor?" I ventured.

"Not yet."

"Do you need the name of one?"

"No."

"Is there . . ." I gave a quick scratch to the back of my head. "Is there something you'd like the Congressman to do? In particular?"

Again the pale eyes retreated.

"I'm not pregnant," she said, in an even voice.

"Well, that's a relief."

"What I've got, there are drugs now."

"Of course," I said, blood massing in my throat.

"I don't know how I'm going to square it."

"With whom?"

"God, I guess."

I should say she was in no way dressed for church. It was all government-girl navy. She looked as if she were heading straight back to Congressman Smathers's office to book constituent visits and Capitol tours.

"I could point you to a priest," I suggested.

"No, I just wanted the Congressman to know. I don't know why I came," she said, with a vehemence that surprised even her and left her standing palely in the foyer. "I won't come again."

So, in the end, I had only to stagger out of bed and exchange a few words, and mission accomplished. Jack waited a minute or two, then sauntered downstairs with his hands in the front pockets of his bathrobe. "Christ," he said, "don't you hate it when they become a bore?"

Well four years had since elapsed, and now, traveling back to Baltimore, I wondered for the first time what had become of that girl. I couldn't imagine her hurling herself from the Fourteenth Street Bridge—the congressional staffers I knew in those days were terrestrial. Perhaps she'd found some nice Chamber of Commerce lobbyist and was already on her way to having four unthinkingly healthy children. But as I thought back on her, sitting alone in that foyer, I realized I'd never said a single reproachful word to Jack—I suppose for the very reason he was now suggesting. Friends accept each other as is, with no returns. So why, I wondered, should Jackie have any different standing than that girl whose name I never learned?

It was late when I got back home, but I still found myself reaching for my phone with the full intention of calling her. And here, another road not taken. What if I *had* called? What if I had told her everything that was lying heavy on my heart? Would she have listened? Would anything have changed? Or would I simply have lost them both?

THIRTY-FOUR

*I*n the week leading up to the wedding, the only question that lingered in my mind was a selfish one: How, in light of our quarrel, would Jack receive me when I got there? Mr. Kennedy had dictated a letter to the groomsmen, asking us to arrive in Newport four days in advance and make a real saturnalia of it, but for work reasons, I couldn't get there until Saturday, which meant I got to miss the ushers' dinner and an awful lot of touch football games on Bailey's Beach. None of this was a hardship. No, the big challenge was stumbling into the rehearsal dinner, where Jack, at first sight of me, broke out into that palomino grin.

"You old bastard," he said.

And with that I knew all was well. I was as welcome as I'd ever been.

As for the wedding itself . . . well, I know I gave a toast or two, but I can't for the life of me recall what I said, nor what anyone else said. The words vanished right into whichever champagne flute they emerged from. When I want to really remember that particular event, I have to consult my photo album. That's where I find the crowds gathered from earliest morning, straining against police cordons for the most evanescent glimpses of bride and bridegroom. I see Jackie's gown, the ivory silk taffeta off-the-shoulder number with the fitted bodice that she hated and the fifty yards of faille flounces she also hated. I see Bobby, the best man, and Lee Bouvier Canfield, the matron of honor, and Archbishop Cushing, twinkly and hawk-nosed as a Donegal priest.

I see, from a myriad of angles, some portion of the eight hundred church guests. Family, friends, governors, members of Congress, Newport summer-colony veterans, all cramming into the canyonlike, incense-clouded confines of St. Mary's Church. I see the annunciatory stripes of sun piercing the Austrian stained glass just as the bride and groom kneel at the altar—a Hollywood effect that you could have sworn Mr. Kennedy paid for, like the four-foot-tall, five-tier wedding cake from Plourde's Bakery.

I see the reception guests at Hammersmith Farm, sitting under canopies and parasols and gazing off, between swigs of champagne, at a distant arrangement of Auchincloss cows so platonic it could have been painted by Constable or Poussin. On the menu were creamed chicken and pineapple salad in a pineapple half shell and ice scream sculpted like roses. When the whole event drew to a close, the guests flung rice and rose-petal confetti at the newly married couple as they piled into the convertible that would take them to the private plane that would take them to Acapulco.

I know it's a cliché to speak of a bride's radiance as she slips into the waiting car and rolls up the window and disappears into the sunset. But when I stare at those old photographs, what I'm most struck by is that Jackie has been in the public eye for a good eight hours and has dragged that infernally heavy dress halfway across Rhode Island and has shaken hands with thousands of well wishers. She might have been excused for looking a little done in, yet she's as fresh as a sunset, and her face is the same unposed, unguarded, undissimulated canvas that stared out from that *Life* cover. I ache a little, looking at that Jackie, pondering the survivability of hope. The girl who gets into that car still believes she is a princess.

WELL, THAT'S SILLY, of course. Nobody is really a princess; no wedding is really an idyll. Isn't that why we go to them in the first place? To see if the best man throws up in the baptismal font or the maiden aunt gets handsy with the organist? Or if a thunderstorm, defying all predictions, shunts a column of rainwater straight at the bride's tiara? Every wedding carries within it the seeds of its own destruction, so when I say that this wedding came off, I mean, of course, just barely.

The most foreseeable problem was Black Jack Bouvier. As I mentioned, he had dried himself out in anticipation. Lost some weight, bought a custom cutaway that fit him, relatives said, like a suit of light. But whatever resolve he

carried from his latest sanatorium didn't carry him all the
way to church. That morning, in the slow-melting shadows
of his Viking Hotel room, he began once more to drink.

Relations were dispatched to fetch him. One of them,
arriving just before ten, found Black Jack still up to the task:
gait slow but steady, speech thick but coherent. The problem was his son-in-law and drinking companion, Michael
Canfield, who had been at work for some hours, plying
Black Jack with champagne and highballs—the kind of
room-service fount that every recovering drinker dreads and
longs for. As Black Jack's relations struggled to get him into
his garters and dress shirt, Michael kept pouring, and Black
Jack began to reel. Half an hour later, Janet Auchincloss
phoned to tell them that, if her ex-husband were to show his
face at church in his current condition, he would be barred
at the door—a humiliation broadcast to the world by every
waiting news outlet.

She was more than happy to carry the news to her daughter. "Darling, it's for the best. We can't have him stumbling
down the aisle, can we? Not when Hughdie's perfectly willing to step up. Now, don't worry, we'll tell the reporters he
has the flu, there won't be a whiff of scandal. I mean, it's not
the first time we've covered for him, is it?"

Jackie saw it another way. She knew that the rancor her
mother felt toward her father was as unquenchable as the
Maccabean lantern, and she knew without being told that
Janet Auchincloss had sent Michael Canfield to that hotel
room with a specific mission and, in so doing, had claimed
her crowning revenge. Later that morning, a photographer

would capture Jackie walking toward St. Mary's on her stepfather's arm. Hughdie is glancing rather anxiously in her direction, but Jackie is looking straight ahead toward the brownstone lancet arches with an expression of coldest fury. Murder in her soul.

A CODA OF sorts. When the service had concluded, and I was ushering out my rows of guests, I paused to gaze upon a gentleman in the back row. Unusually swarthy by Newport standards, with an Indian-head-penny profile that looked both strange and suddenly familiar. Black Jack Bouvier. He made it to the church after all.

SO, YES, THINGS go awry at a wedding because they must, and it's the wedding itself that contains it all. An Episcopalian rector once told me that, back in the sixties, a progressive couple convinced him to open his nave for an entirely free-form wedding. No liturgy, no hymns, no exchange of vows or rings, certainly no homily. The bride and the bridegroom would gather with friends and family and do whatever the spirit moved them to do. Within an hour, fights were breaking out, glasses were hurled, scandals were dragged from the closet, uncles and aunts were weighing in with words and fists, and the two people who were supposed to be uniting their destinies were sitting exhausted in opposite corners of the church, like prizefighters waiting for their cutmen.

What I take this to mean is that the wedding ritual channels love's turbulence into love's performance, and it's the performance that saves us, and this is precisely why wedding receptions, lacking the same liturgical scaffolding, are so much more open to disaster. I speak from experience. On September 12, 1953, I walked into the reception at Hammersmith Farm and came out a different man.

Not too long ago, I looked at some old home-movie footage of the event, sat through the usual lurches and swish pans until the camera swung its way toward me and then stared at myself, as if from the bottom of an aquarium. Good-time Lem, grinning to beat the band. The same amiable creature may be found in the photo album, lounging with Jack and the other groomsmen against a split-rail fence. Yet, when I consult my own memory of that day, all I remember is despair dragging at my heels. A psychologist to whom I later (briefly, unwisely) consigned myself told me that my symptoms that day were those of a panic attack. I will admit that I perspired a lot and reached for my inhaler more times than I'd done in the previous month, but, based on my own experience, it was closer to a bad acid trip. Without benefit of hallucinogens, I was able to lift the skin off everything, and the news wasn't good. I had outstayed my welcome. I wasn't just losing my best friend, I was losing the safe passage he'd afforded me all these years, the passport to the enchanted realm that was never really mine. All of it gone! The news came from the lawyer-novelist in the pale linen suit and tortoise-shell spectacles, from the plump singing-group alumnus in the rumpled pink shirt and plaid bow tie, the fashion editor in the salmon dress and dark veiled hat, the sunburnt girl in the sleeveless, backless dress straightening her boyfriend's fresh-pressed necktie. Every arm was waving me farewell. Even six-year-old Jamie Auchincloss, in his short black velvet trousers—with every arc of his lace jabot and cuffs, he was showing me the door.

So perhaps it was to forestall that leave-taking that I drank more than my usual amount. Lunged at every champagne tray, tapped my wineglass at every passing waiter. Even Eunice was moved to say, "Easy there, big guy." I had the sense of wanting to erase myself before anybody else could, but as the hours wore on, I remained stubbornly there, and because I was, in fact, growing less and less competent, I couldn't defend myself from the truly proximate perils like—well, like Ethel's brother, George Skakel Junior, who showed up as jowly and belligerent as ever and who tugged on the sleeve of my morning coat whenever I wandered too close.

"Hey, Lem. I thought you'd be in the bridal party."

"Ha."

"Lem, do you remember when I kicked you in the can?"

"Yes, I do."

"Wasn't that a freakin' riot when I kicked you in the can?"

I paid him no more mind than you would a midge. Indeed, I had ceased to think of him at all until, traveling back from the gents to my table, I felt my legs give way before me. I went down hard and lay there, all one hundred and ninety-three pounds, in the late-summer grass of Hammersmith, drawing up the chlorophyll of each blade. From the square of sky just above me came the Chicago bray of George Skakel.

"Gotcha!"

I rolled over. My glasses had fallen off, and between me and the sky there lay interposed a ring of bleary faces, *Kennedy* faces, laughing with such alarming synchronicity that I had to assume they were all puppets. Puppet George was the most convulsed, but Puppet Ethel wasn't too far behind, and there were Puppet Pat and Puppet Jean, too, and even little Puppet Jamie Auchincloss, in his page's costume, flapping his puppet mouth. Something there is, I guess, about a big fella toppled in the grass that strikes at the funny bone, but as I stared up into their half-human orifices, I thought: *My God, how they hate me. Every last one of them, down to the cellar of his soul.*

Somebody must have helped me to my feet. Somebody must have, I don't know, tried to brush the grass stains from my coat or asked if I was all right. It's possible. But the message I took away was bare as could be: *Your hour is nigh.* And rather than resign myself, I decided at some barely articulated level that the solution was to keep moving. They couldn't expel me if they couldn't catch me, so I staggered from table to table, pausing only to wave at the faces I recognized (before they could recognize me). How grateful was I for the protective cover of Meyer Davis and his orchestra, the fortress of big-band sound they erected between me and the rest of the party. I couldn't exactly hide myself behind the pavilion columns, but I could at least anchor myself to one of them. The introductory chords rang out, and onto the dance floor came Jackie, her train gathered into a bustle, and, dragging behind, Jack, his discomfiture more attractive for being only slightly concealed. They danced, I remember, to "I Married an Angel," and I was sufficiently lulled that I could even croon the words to myself.

Jackie, of course, had come up through the exacting dance school of cotillions, and Jack (though he would never have confessed this) had long ago taken lessons at Arthur Murray, so neither of them was exactly a slouch, but of course, their pictorial effect was what carried. It was as if the two best-looking people in the room had, against all odds, found each other and were preparing to go off and create a new human race. You would have had to be an intimate to know that Jack's spine had been imploding from the moment he walked into St. Mary's and that Jackie was still seething about her father and that two people who scarcely knew each other were being forever yoked, with who knew what calamities to come. All that mattered was the tempo, which was medium-slow.

From there the band segued into another Rodgers and Hart tune, "I'll Tell the Man in the Street." Jack, with grim resolve, pivoted toward Mrs. Auchincloss, and Jackie whirled in the direction of Ambassador Kennedy, who danced, it must be said, more suavely than his son and at a closer proximity. When the song was done, though, he rested his hands in a paternal way on her shoulders and, with a smile nearly as wide as the tent, said, "Welcome to the family."

I was close enough to hear. Close enough, too, to see how Jackie actually paled before those words. I have to think, in that moment, it was all coming together for her. This *was* her family, *her* destiny, and whatever alternative paths she might once have entertained were now officially sealed off. As if in acknowledgement of that, she nodded—once or twice, at nobody in particular—then began traveling in a dazed and stately procession toward the back of the tent.

Escaping.

That was the first thought that crossed my mind, perhaps because her face was the exact external correlative of how I felt. And so, without a word, I tottered after her, losing her briefly and then finding her again, a vision of unravished stillness, in the area just behind the fourth trumpet. She turned back to me then, crackling with the shock of being discovered, and I saw her stillness for the lie it was. A disturbance, large and general, had overtaken her.

"Jackie," I said.

Did she even recognize me? Did she know that I had come to save her?

"Jackie," I said, sinking to one knee. "Darling."

I reached into my pocket. Not knowing even what I was reaching for and realizing, as my hand closed around it, that I'd been carrying it, like a rabbit's foot, ever since that night on the Ferris wheel. Without another thought, I slid it onto her finger and marveled again at how it glided without obstruction past the first and second knuckle and rested with a purr against the gold ring that Jack had deposited there hours earlier.

"It still fits," I murmured.

Her eyes widened. Then the fingers of her right hand began to claw softly at the fingers of her left, and the ring went flying in a parabolic arc that subsided somewhere in the sod of Hammersmith Farm. At once I began to grope for it and heard the voice, small but peremptory, cutting toward us.

"*Jackie.*"

It was Bobby. Doing what he always did: correcting a situation.

"Is everything all right?" he wanted to know.

I kept groping through the grass.

"Lem's helping me find something," said Jackie.

And still I kept groping, a perfect madman in a morning coat. I heard her say:

"Please don't bother, Lem. It's not important."

THIRTY-FIVE

*W*as it important? I wonder now. And what exactly did I have in mind for Jackie and me? Was there a particular route picked out?

Surely in the back of my mind there lay imprinted that flat blazing Grenoble plain, at the foot of the Alps. Rows of poplars, short spiky palm trees with blazing red flowers—all preserved for me as clearly as if I'd seen them myself—and if Jackie had lifted me to my feet in that moment and said, "Yes, let's go," well, I don't think anybody alive could have stopped us.

What would we have done for money? I'm sure Jackie could have charmed us into some hostel or pension, and from there, we would have done the necessary scrounging. Under these conditions, I might have discovered much earlier my talent for flipping houses. Yes, I think I could have developed quite a good line turning barns into *chambres d'hotes*. My French would have remained clumsy, but my clients would have known what I was talking about and, without admitting it, would have appreciated my American penchant for deadlines. As for Jackie, well, I imagine her becoming a writer for real. The French correspondent for a string of prestigious U.S. publications. She would take lovers with my blessing; I would do the same. The thought of marrying would never cross our minds. Mr. Kennedy's engagement ring would have long since been returned by parcel post or else deposited in the back of a secretary drawer.

That's a lot of alternative reality to construct from a single crossing. All I can say is that, in the way of recalled time, those ten seconds grow endlessly elastic. Jackie's face alone—for I had a clear view—seemed to toggle through every response. Confusion, that goes without saying. Surprise, we grant that. A note or two of horror because somebody—somebody besides her—was making an unscripted spectacle at her wedding. But I can't ignore the possibility of a tiny spark of fellow feeling, for we were both outsiders to this clan and would always be.

Did I honestly think she'd say yes? Throw up her bouquet and chase after me into the clear blue sky of a Newport afternoon? Perhaps I only hoped, and that's a different bird.

I think of all she would have missed by jumping with me into the nearest cab. Her whole epoch of glory on the world stage. Her two beautiful children—who would wish them unmade? Not me. That's why I cling instead to the alongside life, where new laws take hold, and she and I gather each evening at six at an old farmhouse in the Quartier Saint-Laurent, a little back in the hills to escape the tourists, not too far from the old Gallo-Roman walls. We have a clear view of both the Isère and the Alps, which never shed their white scalps even at the height of summer. We sit under the plane tree, nibbling on walnuts and slathering our baguette slices with Saint-Marcellin cheese and persimmon. One of us—me, I'm thinking—has become a cook and has prepared *raviole du Dauphiné*. We talk of Mitterrand and *le parti socialiste*, of Thatcher and Reagan and Sakharov and Bobby Sands—and Tom Selleck and the two pandas struggling to get knocked up at the National Zoo. Nothing we say solves anything. At the end of the evening, we go to our separate bedrooms with a book and a chaste kiss and a cordial of Chartreuse. The cathedral bells wake us every morning, always a little earlier than we're expecting.

The reality was something different. Soon after her honeymoon, Jackie learned that her new husband, far from settling into married life, had simply resumed campaigning. His new national stature required him to travel from Montana to California to Missouri to Texas, wherever there was a stump speech to be made or a donor to be squeezed. His weekends belonged strictly to others, and if, by some miracle, she kept him at home more than two nights in a row, one or both of those nights was given over to a political function.

Even there, she couldn't feel him to be entirely hers. On more than one occasion, she saw him funnel his last reserves of energy toward a young woman who couldn't quite believe her luck. A caterer, a Russian translator: the more insignificant she was in the Washington scheme, the more his interest was piqued. Once, in the middle of a Rock Creek salon, he slipped

away—just as he'd done at Lee's wedding—and reemerged as
before with a whisper of foreign scent. Two months later, it
happened again; again, a month later. Worse than the unsched-
uled absences, she found, were the looks that the other wives
directed at her while she was waiting for him to come back.
Everyone, it seemed, had heard the rumors of assignations at
the Mayflower Hotel, of girls streaming into the Carroll Arms.
Jack was always "in transit" now, and it wasn't always in the
direction of home.

Still, whenever I saw her, she put on a bright face. "Oh, I
know," she told me. "He's not a typical husband, but I'm not
a typical wife, either. The two of us would have been so lonely
with the normal kind."

Yet she *was* lonely, in those days—like so many other congressional spouses I've come across—and it was all the more
pronounced for that she was rattling around in a new home,
a white-brick Georgian pile called Hickory Hill, where her
only company were servants, whom she didn't yet grasp how
to manage though she'd grown up entirely around them. She
read voraciously, took a course in American history at the
Georgetown School of Foreign Service, but history was the
last thing Jack wanted to talk about when he came staggering home from his travels, his spinal column so wracked
there was nothing to do but put him to bed.

Wouldn't it be nice, she thought, *to have a child? A child
would solve everything.*

But that was hard going. She had a miscarriage. The next
year, she got pregnant again. An actual bump was showing
during the '56 Democratic convention, where Jack lost the

vice-presidential nomination but still managed to emerge as his party's heir apparent. His self-awarded consolation prize was to disappear once more to the Mediterranean with (once more) Torby McDonald, as well as his brother Teddy and, come to think of it, George Smathers. Jackie by then was a month away from delivery, but fathers in those days weren't required to stand by for every pang of labor, and she kissed him goodbye with the usual mingling of melancholy and respite. She would be all right. She would spend the last few weeks of her confinement at Hammersmith Farm. Her mother would see to everything.

A week before the delivery date, Mrs. Auchincloss called me at work.

"Where is he?" she demanded to know.

"Sorry?"

"The bastard my daughter married."

"Oh, he's . . . somewhere off Capri, isn't he? Elba . . . ?"

"I know all that. The point is he's not here."

"No."

"And it's stillborn."

That word lodged somewhere inside the phone receiver.

"I can't . . . you said . . . "

"The baby is stillborn."

"Oh, my God. I'm so sorry."

"Not half as sorry as he'll be."

"Well," I said, instinctively covering, "perhaps he doesn't know. It's awfully hard to reach people when they're—"

"Oh, he knows. His blessed Bobby told him, but the Senator doesn't think there's any reason to come back. What's done is done, he says. That's a direct quote."

Even as I was trolling for another cover, Mrs. Auchincloss came rounding back.

"She wants to see you."

NEWPORT HOSPITAL HADN'T bothered moving her out of the maternity ward—perhaps she hadn't wanted to—but she had a private room, at least, a little wonderland of pastel blankets and floral prints, with a high casement window that gave onto the east lawn. When I walked in, she was dozing against the raised headboard, and I was debating whether to wake her when her eyes fluttered open.

"Oh," she said. "Hello."

"Hello."

Gradually reorienting, she gazed about the room, gazed at her feet, her hands, me.

"It was good of you to come," she said.

"Of course, darling. I'm so very sorry."

"Oh, you're a dear, thanks. I was just going to . . . what was I . . ."

She waved a hand in front of her eyes, as though she were cleaning a glass.

"Her name," she said at last. "It was going to be Arabella."

"That's lovely."

"I hadn't really told anyone. Not even Jack."

"Well, I'm sure he'd—"

"Oh, and Bobby spoke to the priest. The Church . . . oh, she's—she's *baptized by intent*."

"Ah."

"So she'll be fine."

Being a cradle Episcopalian, I was slow getting there. Arabella's parents had *intended* to baptize her, so Arabella's soul could vault straight from limbo to heaven. It was in times like these I recalled how hard the old faith gripped.

"Have you talked to him?" she asked.

"Not since he left."

And with that the message that had been balled up in me since leaving Baltimore came unballed.

"Darling, I hope you won't believe anything you've read in the columns."

She regarded me with the deepest placidity. "What have I read in the columns?"

"Oh, that he's—I'm not even going to dignify it."

"'Floating Mediterranean love nest.'"

I sat up a little straighter. "That's one."

"Mummy keeps me up to date."

"Of course it's all untrue."

"Of course."

I peered a little harder into those vacant eyes, which were looking less vacant by the second.

"If you want my opinion," I said.

"Yes?"

"I have to believe he's grieving just as hard as you are right now."

"How do you know?"

"Because I've seen it. With Kick, Joe Junior. When he's hit hard like this, he doesn't gnash his teeth or pull his hair, he gets *quiet*. He turns inward. But, of course, that doesn't mean he doesn't feel it, dreadfully."

"Why can't he feel it here?"

I tucked one finger into my shirt collar, then another.

"Jackie, there's something that helps me sometimes in thinking about Jack. Now, I would never tell him this to his face, but I happen to think he's a great man, and the world asks a lot of its great men. When I think about that convention, for instance, what he was able to do. I mean, a lot of people can lose a shot at the vice presidency, but how many can rise above that and still come out *ahead*? I watched it on TV, like everyone else, and I was still in awe. The willpower, the nerve it took to accomplish that."

"What are you saying, Lem?"

"Just that when one finds a man who's capable of such things—as you and I both have—one cuts him allowances, that's all. One gives him his *rein* because this is somebody above the common, and all the old rules, they don't necessarily apply."

Rules. I suppose I was thinking in that moment of all the times he'd referred to me out loud as the walking ape man or *Pithecanthropus erectus* or needled me for my bad breath or my bad lungs or my poor eyesight. Narrated my circumstances, like a Grimm brother, for the surrounding guests. "Ladies and gentlemen, there was a boy named Lem, and his mother always sewed his name into his socks so they wouldn't get lost, and to this day, she sews his name into his socks. So they will never be lost. Show us your socks, Lem."

That kind of thing. But, as I was making the case to Jackie, I noticed two circles seeping through her hospital

smock, exactly where her nipples were, and slowly enlarg-
ing. Not blood, as I first thought, but milk.

I turned my gaze toward the casement windows. Imagined
I had never even set foot in this room, but her voice stole
after me.

"You really do love him, don't you, Lem? I wish he loved
us half as much."

She reached then for my hand. Gripped it with surprising
force between both of hers.

"Lem, do you remember that scenario you once sketched
out for me? I believe I was floating toward a waterfall."

"Yes."

"Only it didn't matter because there was someone on
the shore who was watching out for me the whole time and
making sure nothing happened. Do you remember, Lem?"

"Yes."

"There was a lesson, and it was hiding there the whole
time. *Nobody's* watching, Lem. Nobody at all."

"Dear one," I said, and leaned in with an intensity that
was matched by her recoil. Thus, we beheld each other.

I don't think it's too much to say that, in that moment,
I was face-to-face with a new Jackie, forged from the ruins
of the old one. Everyone who has lived in America in the
years intervening has seen that face. Under a pillbox hat, at
a state funeral, on a Mediterranean island, at a gala, in the
glare of some paparazzo. I passed it just the other day in the
East Village and recognized it as something wounded into
impermeability. I wish I could feel some pride of ownership,
but mostly I just feel it staring back at me.

I DON'T MEAN to suggest a rupture. For as long as Jack and Jackie lived together, I was welcome in their home, wherever that was. How many of their pals had his very own weekend guest room at the White House? I remember Jackie once saying to a Secret Service official that Mr. Billings had been her houseguest for as long as she could remember and she couldn't see that changing anytime soon. I smiled at that and smiled, too, when I overheard her describing me to Arthur Schlesinger as "that cozy funny fellow." Because, of course, that's all I'd ever aspired to be.

Whenever I saw her, there was good cheer, good humor, a fund of anecdote, everything that would make a man feel welcome. There was also the memory of what was lost. Never again would she be *my* Jackie.

The curious thing is that Jack would never again be my Jack. Not exactly. What I mean is that, after our pre-wedding conversation, he became a little less forthcoming with me—certainly about his girls. I like to think that, with his customary prescience, he gave me the out I didn't know I'd need. Whenever one of those biographers asks me some prurient question along the lines of Marilyn this, Judith that, I can truthfully say I know nothing about it. But it may be that he just no longer trusted me with such privileged information and that, in defending Jackie, I lost him and that, in defending Jack, I lost her, and that I'm still not clear what that leaves me with.

THIRTY-SIX

My friend Raul once asked me why I had so many framed photographs of the Kennedys. "You have more pictures of them than your own people," he said.

Well, he has a kind of Cuban fixation on birth families, so I had to explain to him that the Kennedys were "my people" quite as much as if I was born to them.

"And Mrs. Onassis?" he asked. (For he insists on calling her that.) "Is she your people, too?"

"I certainly think of her that way."

"And does she have many photographs of you in her apartment?"

"I have no way of knowing."

"Oh, why is that?"

And when I failed to answer, he suggested it was because I was never invited over.

Which led to another flare-up, and days went by, and then he showed up out of the clear blue sky with a propitiatory gift. A framed photograph of him! Taken some time around his collegiate days when his hair was still becomingly floppy. I was so touched by the gesture that I put it on the Pembroke side table, next to Kick Kennedy. I began then to think of his various kindnesses through the years: the postcards he sends from right across town, the phone calls for no reason, just the way he laughs at my jokes sometimes. He even enjoys buying me ties, though I haven't worn one in years.

I thought, too, with great affection of the rumpled figure he always presents when he comes over. Bermuda shorts and flip-flops in nearly all weather, a T-shirt that hangs off his welling belly. The whiskers he doesn't bother to shave. The way he plants his feet so unthinkingly on my ottoman. There's something so domestic about him in these moments—as if he's always been here.

And why shouldn't he? Always be here, I mean. I began to think that the arrival of his photograph was one of those moments when an alongside life pulses briefly into view, waiting to be either grasped or abandoned. And honestly, how many more such crossings will I have? My doctors have been coy about an expiration date, but let's say it holds off another year. That could translate to dozens more opportunities to see Raul's hairy toes on my ottoman. Which, all things weighed in the balance, could be a worse way to finish out the whole business.

Well, I kept my counsel until the next time he came over. We chatted and drank some rather nice bourbon and watched the Mandrell sisters, a country trio who sing harmony and play a great many instruments. I can't explain my affection for them—I mostly loathe their music—but I think it has something to do with their indomitable cheer. Raul, as usual, put up with my latest enthusiasm and had a great deal of fun decoding the Mandrells' Presbyterian white blouses and black-leather skirts. The evening was passing along in a perfectly relaxed spirit, and it was then I said, with all the insouciance I could muster:

"You know, you could always keep some clothes here."

He didn't appear to hear at first. Then he slowly leaned his head my way.

"Why would I do this?"

"In case you ever decided to stay over. A toothbrush, even. I wouldn't be offended."

He was silent for a good time.

"I don't believe Ross would be pleased with this," he said.

How grateful I was in that moment for the Mandrell sisters. They gave me somewhere to look.

"Ross," I said. "I don't believe we've ever met."

I could feel him studying me.

"Would this have made a difference to you? Meeting Ross?"

I reached for my glass, tightened the cord of my bathrobe. "I suppose he's younger."

"Why?"

"That's how it works, isn't it? Younger people find other younger people."

"Is that how it worked for you?"

"Oh," I said, with a flap of my hand. "Don't go by me."

"Why not?"

"Because I took the road less traveled by, I guess."

It's funny, I used to have a sort of speech lined up for these occasions. Yes, I would say, I could have done the obvious thing, the *majority* thing—settled down with someone, had a family even—but what could have been a more rewarding life than being Jack Kennedy's best friend? No, sir, if that were the only destiny I was to be granted, I couldn't have asked for more. The words were all lined up, but for some reason, they wouldn't come out. I said:

"Maybe you should get back to your Ross. He's probably wondering where you are."

"He knows."

"And he approves?"

"It is not his to approve or not."

"Well," I said. "Seems to me if—if you feel strongly about somebody—you ought to want to keep that person around."

"Ah, you are a love monopolist, Lem."

Now, I certainly never introduced the word *love* or the word *monopoly*, but I admit that I'm curiously traditional on some questions. You can take the boy out of Pittsburgh, I reminded him, but not the Pittsburgh out of the boy, at least not the whole way.

"Papi, shall I explain my relationship with Ross? In terms that have nothing to do with geography?"

"If you must."

"No matter what we do with our evenings, he wants to wake up in the morning with *me*. No, I mean, *to* me."

"I fail to see the distinction."

"Suppose I was to stay with you tonight. Tomorrow morning, I tell you this from experience, you would awaken in a state of deepest confusion. You would not be able to say, reliably, who I am or who you are."

"I take pills to help me sleep. There's no crime."

"The point is you are the kind of man who needs to wake up alone."

THE VERDICT HAD been gathering the whole time without my knowledge. Without my consent. And what, after all, does it say about a man's character? I'm here to tell you that Jack Kennedy would have been the happiest fellow on earth if he could have woken up alone every morning. Can you honestly imagine him lying face-to-face with a girl? Watching her slumber? Waiting for her eyes to tremble into sentience? Of course not. Two adults had entered into a transaction. You might call that brutish, I call it knowing your nature. Knowing it well enough never to promise anything that lies outside it. Only now, having uttered the credo, do I realize that I have been Jack's student. And that the pulse of that other life—the possibility of being someone other—was just something an old man tells himself.

IT ENDED WELL, all in all. No lachrymose goodbyes. Raul still has hopes for my soul and still has improving literature he's longing for me to read and, all in all, he enjoyed his gambol with the Mandrell sisters, and he enjoyed me, too, though he won't always admit it, and he says he looks forward to the next round of pop-culture flotsam I float his way and to whatever else follows.

"Lem," he said. "You are a continuing education."

So we parted on the same terms as we'd met. Silly me, trying to queer that arrangement. If I play my cards right, if I don't fly off at the first offense, his hairy toes will be found on my ottoman for as long as we both choose. I call that a victory.

Still, the frowny part of Raul's soul must have lingered because, the other day, I decided to take down all the framed photographs from my west-facing living-room wall. It was strictly an experiment in design, but all the same I found myself apologizing out loud to the people in each picture. "So sorry, Mr. Kennedy," for here was a snapshot from his 1963 birthday party (when he was mostly paralyzed). "Not to worry, Kick," for there we were, the two of us, goofing for the camera at Palm Beach, Christmas 1940. And look! Me and Bobby on a diving trip off the Bahamas. Me and Bobby Junior with Masai warriors in Kenya.

As for Jack, well, I gave up apologizing to him, for he was in most of the photographs. Clapping an arm around me at Hyannisport. Feeding the pigeons in St. Mark's Square. Here was his Choate yearbook photo: "To Lem. A neat guy and a swell gent. You're aces with me. Best luck now and always, you horse's arse."

I handled each photo with the greatest care, blowing away its harvest of dust and finding the most stable pile on which to set it. Then I stood back for I don't know how long, trying to see what was there. You'd think that a wall without art would look merely blank, but what you get instead is a checkerboard of lighter shapes against a darker background—the part of the wall you haven't seen rising up from what you've always seen. Look long enough, and the lighter sections seem to acquire a dimension; you can imagine crawling through them to somewhere else.

THINKING ABOUT HER as much as I've been doing, I shouldn't be surprised that she should invade my dreams. Just last night, she was jogging around the Central Park Reservoir. I suddenly remembered that I had something to tell her, a phone message of some kind, and I started to run after her. This being a dream, I wasn't my usual short-winded self, but she still outpaced me with no trouble, so I decided to wait until she circled back around. At once, she changed direction, and no matter where I stationed myself, she was always on the far side of the reservoir, gliding away, and whatever I was planning to tell her was already seeping out of me in pearls of sweat.

I woke expecting the usual descent of melancholy but found myself, on the contrary, seized with action. Wouldn't it be grand to take the dog to the park? It's just a couple of blocks, for Chrissakes, and you can't find a better time than April, and Ptolly always gets such an atavistic bounce in his step when he sees a whole forest rising before him.

It's a drier park than I'm used to. The drought, I guess, has stopped the fountains, and the lake is as low as I've seen it, but saints be praised, there are still rowboats, scarred with graffiti, trucking across the algal water. I once preferred the stillness of the Conservatory Garden, but today I rather like the mob that gathers here of a Friday morning. The mimes building their usual fruitless walls and the joggers in their high-cut nylon shorts and the power walkers in striped knee-high athletic socks, swinging their hips in perfect, ludicrous rhythm. A little boy in overalls pushing a Tonka truck straight into the nearest obstruction and a steel-drum band and a Mister Softee truck and a cat resting like a tsarina in a bicycle basket.

Ptolly slumbers by my ankle. Noon furrows over us and, from the swirl of figures, one grabs my eye. A girl, sixteen maybe, on roller skates. She has a cut-off T-shirt that reads COOL CHICK, and she's spinning in contemplative circles to the music that's being fed to her through her boom box, which rests on her shoulder like a newborn calf. She smiles, mostly to herself, and then, with the same secret air, makes room for another figure. Willowy and purposeful and queerly languorous as she strolls toward me. The oversized sunglasses are nowhere to be seen; the Secret Service, neither. She has nowhere else to be.

"I had the funniest dream about you," I say as she takes the patch of bench next to mine and curls her hand around my arm.

"I know," she says.

ACKNOWLEDGMENTS

Jackie & Me is, without apology, a fictional work and an exercise in alternative history. My affection for Lem Billings compels me to add that he was never, to my knowledge, arrested for solicitation; this was merely a typical experience for many thousands of gay men of his generation. Any reader looking for a definitive nonfictional take on his life should consult David Pitts's *Jack and Lem*.

My research was greatly aided by Abby Yochelson, Maureen Shea, Mark Allen, and the mother-daughter team of Robin Clarke and Alden O'Brien. I am grateful to David Walter, whose *Princeton Alumni Weekly* article, "Best Friend," first introduced me to Lem Billings, and to the Seeley G. Mudd Manuscript Library for preserving Lem's senior thesis on Tintoretto.

Thanks to Dan Conaway, and thanks to my Algonquin team, prominently Michael McKenzie and my ever-abiding editor Betsy Gleick. And thanks to Don.